THE DOOR BEHIND US

John C. Houser

Dreamspinner Press

Published by
Dreamspinner Press
5032 Capital Circle SW
Ste 2, PMB# 279
Tallahassee, FL 32305-7886
USA
http://www.dreamspinnerpress.com/

The Door Behind Us
© 2013 by John C. Houser.

Cover Art
© 2013 by Paul Richmond.
http://www.paulrichmondstudio.com
Cover content is for illustrative purposes only and any person depicted on the cover is a model.

ISBN: 978-1-62798-074-6
Digital ISBN: 978-1-62798-075-3

Printed in the United States of America
First Edition
October 2013

For Mom.
Sorry you didn't get to read this one.
I think you would have liked it.

CHAPTER I

1965

THE YOUNG man still had a dressing over one ear and a crust of blood inside one nostril. The doctor paged through the chart. Notations recorded progress as good as could be expected for such a recent amputee. "Mind if I look?" He pulled back the sheet and noted the wound drained normally. "How'd he rest last night?"

The resident pulled at his narrow tie. "Poorly. He was yelling and thrashing around. That's why I asked for you to look in."

"Hmm. Has he been given anything to help him sleep?"

"No, he even tried to refuse the morphine."

"That's interesting." He watched the steady rise and fall of the muscular chest. "He's a sergeant. Was he a squad leader? Do you know what happened to him?"

The resident shook his head, yawning. "Nope. He hasn't said much."

"Does he know about the leg?"

"We told him there was too much nerve damage."

"The nightmares started before the surgery?"

"Before." The resident yawned again. "From the first night he was here."

"There's not much I can do for him until he wakes up. You'll have me paged?"

CHAPTER 2

1919

FRANK CAME into the barn sniffing the air like the scent might tell him whether the place was dangerous.

"About time you got here. Saw the note, I take it? Any questions?" Charlie watched the boy take in the stone barn, from hayloft to the three-legged stool where he sat. "Questions?" he prompted the boy a second time.

Cocking his head as if sorting through a stack of mental index cards, the boy eventually picked a pair of questions. "What happened to me? Why can't I remember?"

"You received a head injury, maybe from a shell explosion. That's what the quacks at the hospital told us. But that doesn't answer your question, does it? Why don't you remember anything? I don't know. Here, grab a bucket. I expect your hands remember how to milk a cow, even if your head don't." Charlie watched the boy's hand creep upward to touch his head. "Queenie knows you, even if you don't know her."

Frank picked up a bucket hesitantly.

Charlie nodded at a Jersey cow that stamped impatiently at her stanchion. "She's waiting."

What was it like for the boy to discover who he was every morning from a note tacked to the door of the privy? If the boy had any feelings about it, he never told Charlie.

THE BOY discovered the note after waking in an unfamiliar room. Pale light filtered through a dusty window at the end of a tunnellike dormer. Feeling exposed even under a woolen blanket, he slid to the floor and rolled part way underneath the bed. More comfortable with the solid frame looming over him, he stayed for a time, staring upward. As the light strengthened, he let his gaze follow the lines of wood grain in the window frame. The builder of this house had cut matching pieces for the verticals, their patterns mirrored on either side of the window.

Eventually he rose and struggled out of the tangled bedclothes. A small writing desk, cluttered with loose sheets of writing paper, a fountain pen, and an inkpot, was tucked into the dormer. A stack of unopened envelopes lay next to the writing supplies. The first was postmarked in July of 1918, and the last in October of the same year. *Why didn't this fellow, Francis Huddleston, open his mail?*

Gut fluttering like an anxious bird, he peered under the bed for a chamber pot. Finding none, he rushed down to the second floor looking for a toilet or the way to the privy. Steps led down toward either end of the house. The set in the back were coarse and painted rather than finished, a servant's stair. He knew the term, even if he didn't know where he'd learned it. Down again, he found a large kitchen and heavy door framed in pantry shelves. He ran out into the yard. A well-worn path led to a small, clapboard structure with high windows. A minute later, as he tried not to breathe the acrid stink, he noticed a ruled sheet of writing paper tacked to the door in front of him. GOOD MORNING was blocked out in square letters.

GOOD MORNING

> *Your name is Francis "Frank" Huddleston. You are a soldier, returned from the war in Europe. The white-haired man milking the cows in the barn is your grandfather, Charlie Clark. He will welcome your help with the chores. When you return from the barn, the gray-haired woman in the kitchen will give you breakfast. She is your grandmother, Edith "Eddy" Clark.*

Charlie continued to milk his own cow and watched as Frank began to squeeze a stream of milk from Queenie's teats, the familiar act calming the boy. Soon the milk squirted steadily, and Frank fell into a kind of trance, his movements automatic, until a diminishing stream and restless stamp from Queenie signaled time to change to a new pair of teats. Shifting to a new set, he rested his head against Queenie's side and continued mechanically.

Charlie finished first and went to stand behind the boy. When Frank was done, he placed his hands on his knees and looked around. Charlie held his breath and watched Frank's face. But there was only a tightening around Frank's mouth and a narrowed gaze. Charlie sighed and placed a hand on Frank's shoulder. "It's all right, boy. I'm your grandfather, Charlie Clark. You're Frank Huddleston, come home from the war with a head injury. That's why you don't know me. Let's go in and meet your grandmother. She'll give us something to eat. Are you hungry? Don't forget your bucket."

EDDY'S SPOTTED hands twisted in her lap as she spoke. "Charlie isn't a young man anymore. You're a great worker, Frank, but it's the forgetting. With one of us staying with you all the time to answer your questions, we can't...."

Frank fidgeted in his chair and let his gaze wander over the worn fixtures and scarred wood of the kitchen. He wondered if they would ask him to leave, the strangers who had fed him for months, judging from the thick wad of notes in his hand. Would their faces ever be familiar?

"... so Charlie and I, we've posted a notice at the Grange Hall. We hope to have someone here by the harvest."

Frank became aware the room had fallen silent—except for the tap dripping in the sink and the birds calling outside. Eddy and Charlie. They watched him closely as if they expected something, as if they were unsure of his response. He didn't know why. Eddy's careful announcement seemed to have little to do with him.

"Will you hire someone I knew... before?"

"No, Frank. You were with your parents in Philadelphia before the war. Nobody around here knows you." Charlie looked away. His voice took on a rote quality. "They thought you might be more comfortable here with us while you recovered."

"Will the new person stay with me or work with you?"

Charlie rubbed fingers across his forehead like he was trying to erase the wrinkles there, but Eddy answered in firm tones. "We have to be careful with our money, Frank. It may be cheaper to hire somebody to keep an eye on you and to help you remember when you have one of your spells. Charlie will work around the house."

Frank fingered his notes again. "So... you want me to keep feeding the horses and milking the cows?"

"Yes, you'll do that and other work as well."

"Now, Eddy." Charlie's voice was gentle. "The boy's still recovering. I'm not dead yet."

"He's strong as a bull, Charlie."

"I don't mind doing more, if that's what you want." Frank shifted from face to face until he focused on the sharp furrows at the side of Eddy's mouth. "Just tell me what you want."

"That's what the new man will do," Eddy said, looking at Charlie.

Charlie's gaze dropped to his callused hands.

CHAPTER 3

JERSEY'S LEGS flew from under him and he landed on his back, air driven from his lungs. He rolled and saw Andy and the sergeant run from cover at the edge of the clearing to get the shooter, who was sprawled among the Germans. Their bayonets rose and fell in unison. Time slowed and Jersey watched, helpless, as little puffs of dust formed a line across Andy's khaki uniform. His best friend's mouth opened, and his body jerked up and back, before settling in an awkward heap. Jersey's diaphragm loosened, and he gasped, flooding his nose and mouth with the smells of blood and gunpowder.

JERSEY WOKE panting, his sheets damp with sweat. He trembled for a moment before reaching for his crutches. He would not sleep again tonight. He put on his robe and banged through the kitchen, torn between his need for company and his desire not to trouble his parents. What was the point of waking them? He never spoke of his dreams. They knew he did not sleep, but he told them it was the phantom pain from his missing leg. His leg *did* hurt, but not so much as he let them believe.

He maneuvered through the back door onto the porch, where the air was cooler, and tried to clear the stink from his nose. Eventually, his trembling slowed to an occasional twitch at the hoot of an owl or the rustle of the corn. He settled into the porch swing to watch and wait.

"I SAW a notice at the Grange Hall today might interest you." Jersey's mama's voice was light. Her hands moved deftly from cutting board to pot. "They're looking for someone to help out at the Clark farm. You know, other side of Taperville." She paused, clearly waiting for him to protest.

Jersey sighed and gave her what she expected. "Mama, you know I can't do that kind of work no more."

"You could do this. *Supervisory only, no heavy work required*," she recited like a schoolgirl at a spelling bee.

"If I'm supervising, who's doing the work? Old man Clark? He don't need supervision."

"No, it's his grandson, come back from the war like you. Kirsten Wehr told me he's big as an ox."

The image flashed into Jersey's mind as sharp as a photograph: Andy lying in a heap, one leg bent under him in a position that no living man could tolerate. Jersey shook his head and put his trembling hands under the table where his mama wouldn't see them. "What's he need me for?"

"Well now, I asked that question, and Kirstin said that he's a little funny since he came home." She picked up speed, even as Jersey tried to slow down his skittish thoughts. "She saw him twice at the Farmers' Market in Taperville. The first time, she said he seemed a little distracted maybe, but he was friendly enough when Mr. Clark introduced her. So when they met again, she gave him a big hello—she's like that with any hunk o' meat, ever since she was a girl, don't matter she's been married twenty-five years. Anyway, she was real friendly, and he acted like he'd never laid eyes on her. She was coming to a boil from the slight when Mrs. Clark came over and apologized for him. Said he'd had a little trouble with his memory since he got hit on the head during the war. He was a doughboy too. That's why they need someone to keep an eye on him."

Jersey laughed at her disordered sentences. "Why can't old Charlie keep an eye on him?"

"That's what I said! Kirstin thinks it's because Mrs. Clark—everyone calls her Eddy—wants Charlie under her thumb, you know since he had that spell and fell off the hay wagon last summer. She's worried about him getting too old to work the farm."

"Hmm." *This job ain't for me, even if the doughboy's had his noggin clocked.* The last thing he wanted was to spend his days in the company of another soldier.

"So will you go talk to Mr. Clark?"

"I dunno, Mama. I was thinking about asking if they had work for a man like me in Mr. Ford's factory. They say he's holding jobs for veterans."

His mother's hands came to a sudden halt on the cutting board. "Oh, son," she whispered. "We just got you back. I know you can't mope around here forever, but Detroit? That's so far away."

Damnation. He wasn't the only one in the congregation who was too easy to bring down. "I'll think about it."

JERSEY STARTLED awake at the thump of his father's feet hitting the floor of the second floor bedroom. He was wrapped in a blanket on the porch swing, his good leg propped in front of him. Shivering, he tracked his father's footsteps as he dressed and came down the stairs. As the steps neared, he tried for a carefree expression.

His father pushed open the screen door and leaned out. "What are you going to do when it gets cold outside, Jerry?"

"I told you!" said Jersey, hoping his father couldn't hear his thumping heart. "I go by Jersey now, Papa."

His father stepped onto the porch and took a pipe and pouch out of his pockets.

"What's wrong with Jerry? We've called you that all your life."

"Turns out Jerry wasn't such a great name for a soldier, least ways on our side. To the Brits, jerry's another name for a piss pot. To our boys, he's the enemy. Piss pot or German, it weren't no good either way."

Jersey's father digested this for a moment while he struck a match and sucked on his pipe. When it was drawing satisfactorily, he put a foot on the porch rail. "All right, but why Jersey?"

"I dunno, Papa. It was just something the boys started to call me—which was better than *Jerry*."

His father's foot dropped from the rail. "No need to get sharp, son. I was only curious. If you want us to call you Jersey, we'll call you Jersey."

"Hell, Papa, I dunno why I'm so short fused."

"Leg hurting?"

Jersey shifted his weight on the swing where he'd spent most of the night. "Not too bad. Want some company? I should maybe practice standing around; you never know when I might need to supervise somebody."

"Your mama'll be glad."

"Let's not get all giddy. I haven't got the job yet."

"Hmm." His father tapped out his pipe. "We better get to the milking."

THIS IS a bad idea. Bracing his crutches against the wind, Jersey watched dark clouds approach from the southwest. He felt like a clown on stilts, with his flapping pants calling attention to his missing leg. In his brief answer to Jersey's inquiry about the job, Mr. Clark had said he would stop at the south side of the Farmers' Market after Mrs. Clark finished her shopping. Jersey hoped they would get here soon. The *Taperville Current* predicted a storm for the afternoon. He no longer found storms exciting. Truth be told, they were a little too exciting. Distant thunder had nearly convinced him it was time to give up the ill-conceived meeting when an open Model T clattered around the corner and rolled to a halt.

"Mr. Rohn?" A white-haired man of about sixty-five wearing a straw boater gestured from the front seat. "We'd best be on our way, if we're to get to the farm before it lets loose."

Next to him, a firm-lipped, ascetic woman of a similar age sat with her hands folded in her lap. She did not speak, but nodded briefly while examining Jersey through hard eyes.

Jersey hesitated.

"Come on, boy! It'll be pouring by midday or I'll be a monkey's uncle. Get in."

Jersey lurched into motion. He threw his crutches in first, then took hold of the side of the car and jumped one-footed onto the running board, spun, and more or less fell backward into the rear seat. He was still getting himself sorted out when the car jerked into motion.

The ride to the Clark farm was grim. The Clarks weren't inclined to talk, and it was all Jersey could do to keep his seat as the car bounced down the gravel road. They followed Clear Creek to the north, then turned east and uphill toward a low ridge. They came down from the top through a copse of hickory. Between the trees, Jersey saw a narrow valley of alternating gold and green. On the right, a stone barn nestled into the hillside, while to the left, a clapboard farmhouse, surrounded by a covered porch, overlooked the fields. Beyond the house, extending uphill, a close-cropped pasture scattered with lichen-covered rocks held cows and horses, their jaws moving steadily, their tails flicking occasionally to keep off the flies.

His father's patch seemed plain in comparison. Jersey shook his head at the disloyalty of the thought. Mr. Clark stopped the car in a gravel patch next to the barn and shut off the ignition. The engine clattered to a halt, and Jersey felt a sudden rush of damp air.

The rain struck with a clap of thunder that seemed to explode inside Jersey's head. The storm's artillery undid him. For a few minutes, he could only close his eyes and hang on like an amateur rodeo rider as his wayward body bucked and shuddered. When he came to himself, he was soaked, shaking violently, and to his shame, slung like a sack of feed over a broad shoulder. The man carrying him—surely not Mr. Clark—crossed the yard at a good clip, jumped up the steps to the porch, and set Jersey down on a wicker love seat. Before he could compose any remark appropriate to the circumstance, his rescuer disappeared into the house, only to reappear a minute later with a coarse woolen blanket. He proceeded to rub Jersey down as impersonally as you would a horse after a brisk ride—all without saying a word.

"Feeling better?" Jersey heard from behind. "Quite a spell you had. I've heard about shell shock, but I can't say I ever thought I'd see a case flopping around like a fish in the back of my automobile." The silent young man giving Jersey the rubdown was replaced by Mr. Clark, his straw boater dripping. "Don't fret. You just sit there as long as you need. Mrs. Clark is getting coffee. We'll talk when you're ready."

It occurred to Jersey, if he had a gun, he'd shoot himself. But Andy's laughing voice answered that thought. *No point trying, chum. You're shaking too hard to aim.*

TEN MINUTES later, the rain was letting up. A mug sat on a stool next to the wicker love seat, although he didn't remember anyone putting it there. The young man who had carried him from the car sat next to him, his expression curious, but detached, as if he were examining a set of animal tracks instead of a person. He was blond, gray-eyed, and big in the shoulders. He had a pale complexion and apple cheeks of the kind that would flush when he was excited or embarrassed. Blond stubble trailed up his jaw line. Jersey knew he stared like a toddler. He ought to say something or look away. "Uh… I'm Jersey, Jersey Rohn. I guess you must be Frank."

"Francis, but they call me Frank." The young man fingered a lump of something that filled his shirt pocket. "I like Frank. I don't remember Francis."

"Huh." Jersey considered thanking the guy for the ride from the car, but decided not to mention it. "Nice spread."

Frank nodded slowly.

The guy's silence was disconcerting. "Yep, my name's Jersey, like the cow. It's a tradition in my family started by my great-grandfather who couldn't get married until he had the money to buy a cow. The story goes he was so happy at achieving that goal—and getting himself a wife to boot—that he named my grandfather Jersey, when he arrived nine months later."

Frank's expression did not change, nor did he respond. Jersey found himself talking again. "Actually, I made that story up. My real name is Gerald. Couldn't never stand it. Everyone called me Jerry when I was growing up, but that didn't sound so good after the war got going. So when our unit was moved to Camp Dix—New Jersey—for training, I started talking like one of the natives. Just as a joke, you know, because they sounded so queer to me. But the boys thought it was funny and started calling me Jersey."

Frank pulled the wad of notes from his pocket and examined them. "I was a soldier too. Eddy told me."

Jersey had difficulty thinking of Mr. and Mrs. Clark as Charlie and Eddy. "Did you train at Camp Custer?"

"I don't remember."

"It don't matter."

Frank stared at Jersey's empty pant leg, which Jersey's mama had pinned up for him before he left the house. "Your leg is missing."

Jersey wasn't used to people letting on they'd noticed the leg. Most people thought it impolite to be caught staring. Sometimes they wouldn't look at him at all. Too much of that had him feeling like a ghost at his own funeral.

Frank just seemed curious. "May I see?"

Jersey heard whispers from the house behind. *Ain't no way I'm getting this job.*

"May I see it?" Frank repeated.

Jersey hesitated. He found the garish scar embarrassing, but Frank seemed so guileless he went ahead and unpinned his pant leg. "Suit yourself." The red-and-white scar tissue had repelled his mama when she saw it, but Frank examined the stump like he might a specimen in a jar. He reached out as if to touch it, his hand stopping short.

"You boys getting to know one another?" Mr. Clark spoke through the screen door. Jersey hastily covered his stump and repinned his trouser leg.

"Yes, sir." Jersey and Frank spoke almost in unison.

"Well, then. If you're feeling better now, Mrs. Clark and I would like to speak with you, Mr. Rohn."

Here it comes. It was just as well. It would be embarrassing enough seeing Mr. and Mrs. Clark around Taperville. Oddly, he didn't feel that way about Frank. He started to get up.

"No, stay there," said Mr. Clark. "Frank, would you mind taking Jersey's cup into the kitchen?"

But Frank left Jersey's cup where it was. He seemed to be working up to something, his face twisting. He stood, but didn't leave the porch as Mr. and Mrs. Clark came out. There was an awkward pause, then Mrs. Clark's mouth settled into a firm line, and she looked at Mr. Clark. Mr. Clark sighed, not meeting her eyes. "Mr. Rohn, we're sorry that you had to come all the way out here for nothing, but Mrs. Clark and I have decided that it would be best—"

"I want him to stay." Frank's voice was firm. "I want him to stay and help me."

CHAPTER 4

MR. AND Mrs. Clark were apparently so shocked to hear Frank express a clear statement of preference that it left them unable to muster arguments against the notion. Mrs. Clark clearly wanted to. The skin drew taut across her face. Frank gave his grandparents little chance to argue, stating that he wanted a soldier who could tell him about the war. There weren't any others applying for the position.

It came as a shock, after lunch, when Frank didn't remember Jersey. Mrs. Clark had dispatched Charlie to the Grange Hall in Taperville to deliver a note for Jersey's parents. Jersey reclined on the love seat, wishing he'd thought to bring the Sunday paper from town. Mrs. Clark asked Frank to help put away the lunch dishes. When they finished, Jersey heard Mrs. Clark suggest to Frank that he sit on the porch for a spell. Frank stepped onto the porch, saw Jersey, and stopped.

"Looks like the rain's clearing," said Jersey.

The pale, clear skin of Frank's face flushed, and he smiled uncertainly. "I'm sorry, are you here to meet...."

Jersey remembered his mama's story about Mrs. Wehr meeting Frank at the market. Pushing aside a feeling like he'd been abandoned at the altar, he forced a smile. "Frank, it's okay. My name is Jersey. Your Grandpa and Grandma have hired me to help you work the farm. Sit a spell. We can get to know one another."

Later, he wondered whether Mrs. Clark had deliberately engineered Frank's confusion by keeping Jersey out of sight just long enough for Frank to forget.

THE NEXT day, as Jersey sat on the Clarks' porch, his father's wagon rattled into view through the hickory trees. Jersey grabbed his crutches and swung himself into the yard.

"Whoa." His father halted the wagon in front of the house. "Hi, son. Your trunk's in the back. Your mama sends a big hello and congratulations on the job."

In his note, Jersey had only said he'd gotten the job. He'd not mentioned his fit of nerves.

"I'll get that." Frank's deep voice came from just behind Jersey's right shoulder.

Jersey flinched and nearly lost his balance. "Damn it, Frank, you oughtn't to startle a person like that."

Jersey's father patted his coat for his tobacco pouch. "I don't expect Mrs. Clark will like hearing you swear, son."

Mr. Clark came around the corner of the barn and shook hands with Jersey's father. "You must be Gerald Rohn. I'm Charlie Clark. You're welcome to stay for dinner if you've a mind to."

"Kind of you to ask, Mr. Clark, but I've work to get back to." Jersey's father hesitated and took a draw from his pipe. "Your grandson was in France, I take it."

Behind Jersey, Frank's footsteps halted. "Yes, he was." Mr. Clark didn't elaborate.

Jersey's father nodded at the boys. "That's good, then."

Mr. Clark gave Jersey's father a long look before nodding back. "Frank! Get a move on," he yelled, not turning his head. "Get that trunk off the wagon. Mr. Rohn wants to be on his way." He turned to the barn. "I'll get some water for your team."

Jersey watched Frank maneuver the heavy trunk off the back of the wagon and onto the porch as if it were a child's toy. The muscles of Frank's blue-veined, pale arms seemed independently alive as they bunched and released. Jersey reminded himself not to stare. These people had enough reason to think him touched.

After Mr. Clark returned with a couple of buckets for the team and they'd drunk their fill, his father turned the wagon around in the yard. "Take care of yourself, son. Come visit when you can. Your mama will be missing you."

Jersey nodded, a lump in his throat.

His father flicked the reins. "Let's go, boys."

Mrs. Clark came out onto the porch. She nodded at Jersey. "You'll sleep in the spare room, door off the mudroom. Probably just as well with those crutches."

"I've got chores," Mr. Clark said, picking up the buckets. "Eddy'll get you settled." He headed back to the barn.

"I'll show you where it is," Mrs. Clark said. "Frank, please bring Mr. Rohn's trunk." Once Frank settled the trunk at the foot of the small bed that dominated the spare room, Mrs. Clark left, saying something about bread to bake.

Frank leaned against the doorframe. Jersey looked around the room. It wasn't much, but it was clean, and it had its own window. Best of all, he could get out to the porch without disturbing Mr. and Mrs. Clark. Thinking he ought to hang his good suit in the wardrobe, he threw his crutches on the bed and lowered himself onto his knee so he could open the trunk.

"I'd offer you a seat, but I ain't got one," he joked, wondering if he was going to have an audience all afternoon.

Frank straightened. "If I had wood, I could make you one."

Jersey felt his face warm. "I didn't mean it that way. Nobody need put himself out for me."

"I'd like making something for you. I don't remember much, but I know about tools."

Frank's directness made Jersey uncomfortable. *That's about the longest thing I've heard you say yet, sunshine.* "Were you a cabinet maker before the war?"

Frank grimaced. "I don't know. I lived somewhere else, I think. I don't remember."

"What happened to your parents?"

Frank's apple cheeks darkened, and his gaze dropped.

Jersey unclasped the lid and opened the trunk. His uniform was right on top with his medals pinned to the blouse. "Christ, Mama!" he muttered under his breath.

"Frank is fortunate the Creator has provided him a place to live and a family to care for him," said Mrs. Clark, stepping around Frank. She dropped a set of towels on the bed, her eyes on the trunk. Jersey hurriedly shifted the uniform to the bottom of the pile. He didn't know what to make of Mrs. Clark. Didn't she want Frank to know about his parents?

"You were a corporal," Frank noted.

Mrs. Clark sniffed and left the room.

"Yeah, I flew right up the ranks. I thought you couldn't recall the war."

"I can't, but I still know things." Frank pointed at the stack of clothes that hid Jersey's uniform. "I know what those badges mean." He hesitated, his hand drifting to the top of his head. "They told you I have trouble remembering things?"

"Yeah."

"I just want you to know that if I forget... if I forget who you are, it's not because I don't like you. I leave notes for myself." He took the wad of loose paper out of his pocket. "I want to put down your name, but...." He shrugged, red-cheeked.

Jersey pulled himself up to sit on the bed. "If I tell stories, you ain't gonna remember 'em the next day?"

"Not unless you tell them slowly enough I can write them down." Frank held up his pencil.

This is going to be peculiar. Jersey reached for his crutches. "My name is Jersey. J-e-r-s-e-y. I was in the infantry."

THEY FELL into a pattern in those first weeks. At dawn or shortly after, Frank would find a note in the privy or on the kitchen table. The note would direct him to find Jersey on the porch. After introductions, Frank would carry Jersey's stool into the barn, where Jersey would balance precariously and direct Frank in the morning chores. Frank did not speak much, nor did he require much in the way of supervision, so Jersey mostly told stories. If he was in a silly mood, he might even sing a little.

Frank might not know his own name, but he knew the daily work of the farm: milking the cows, mucking out the horse stalls, pitching fresh hay from the loft, feeding the chickens. The physical work calmed him—at least until he reached a break between jobs, when, often as not, Jersey had to remind him who and where he was.

Jersey found telling stories therapeutic. But he hadn't realized until he met Frank how he tended to build characters and settings over time and from one story to the next. He constructed a realm that Frank, despite his polite attention, could only visit green with every new day.

"MY MAMA, y'know, she picks at me 'cause she says I talk too much but don't say nothing. She wants me to tell her about the war, because she's got this fool idea that talking about it is gonna do me some good—make me less nervous or something. She read this story in the *Current* about a doctor up in Scotland who's had some luck treating people with shell shock. They called it battle fatigue, but it's the same damn thing. I keep telling her I'm not like the fellows she reads about. Loud noises make me nervous is all. Talk, she says. Like I'm gonna tell her about Lieutenant Heiser getting his head sliced clean off by a machine gun. When she gets ragging on me particular hard, I think about telling her 'bout that—just to shut her up."

"Don't do it."

Jersey, in his own world, was startled by Frank's reply, and by his vehemence. He looked up to find Frank had stopped tossing fresh hay from the loft and was jabbing randomly at a fresh bale.

"She won't like it."

"Okay, Frank," he said, tossing off a ragged salute. "I won't."

ONE DAY, he told Frank about Andy. "My best buddy was this Polack kid from Detroit, named Andrei Malinowski. We met at Camp Custer and went through training together. Andy signed up because he heard the Russians were fighting back home in Poland and he wanted to help his kin. Kid didn't realize that the Russians were on our side. I liked him anyway, because he was big and strong and made me laugh. He had a way of saying things that made 'em funny. Some other lout could say the same damn thing and it wouldn't be funny at all."

SOME WEEKS after Jersey came to live at the Clark farm, they were in the barn when Jersey stopped to catch his breath after a soliloquy on French military uniforms before and after they discovered that red pants made great targets for German snipers.

Frank had been silently mucking out horse stalls while Jersey talked. "How did you lose your leg?"

Jersey was stunned. *This is new.* Frank rarely asked questions. When he did, it was generally something like, "Who are you?" Jersey had told the story of his injury before, more than once, as if telling the story again and again could make it less real, make it into a fairy tale involving some person from the distant past. He would not have talked about it if Frank had shown any sign he was listening. "You usually don't remember I lost my leg 'til I stand up."

"Yes, I forget a lot. But I want to hear how you lost your leg."

Frank had never before asked for a specific story, but an audience request was not to be denied, no matter how addled the storyteller. Frank wouldn't remember anyway. Jersey took a breath. "I lost my leg because I was stupid, that's all. Stupid."

He stopped, surprised at his own heat, then continued. "We were cleaning out a patch of woods for the third time in a week—I think it was the same patch—when we came across a nest of Germans. It got hot for a spell—there was a machine gun cutting us down like wheat to a scythe. We were losing boys until the sergeant threw a bomb into the middle of 'em. After that, we thought they was all done for, so the sergeant ordered us forward. We were still taking sniper fire, so we couldn't clear the bodies, even our own. I had to scramble over 'em to get forward. When I stepped on one of the Germans, I heard him grunt. I should have given him my bayonet right then, but I kept going. After I passed him by, damn if he didn't rise up and shoot me in the back of the knee." He paused and rubbed his stump. "I might've kept the leg, but I got gangrene and the doctors decided to take it off."

Frank leaned on his shovel. "Do you remember when they removed it?"

"Up to a point." Jersey looked out through the barn door at the faint outline of the low hills marching off into the distance. "Do you know what the doctor who took it off said to me? He said they needed to do it just to be safe. Just to be safe! I lost respect for him after that. I think the ones near the front got so used to seeing men with missing parts, they didn't think twice about sawing off another. Well, *I* thought twice about it."

"I don't think I could get used to something like that."

"No? In my experience, a body can get used to 'bout anything—if they got to."

CHAPTER 5

1965

HE WAS nearly ready to head home when the doctor realized he still had not received a page from the resident. He followed the yellow painted line through halls to Post-Op. Stepping into the room, he noted there were still no cards, flowers, or other signs of visitors in the drab green room. The sergeant had been back in the States for what, three days? Where was his family? Were they unable or unwilling to come? The damn war was tearing a lot of families apart.

The young man moved his head from side to side and mumbled something. The doctor leaned close to make out the words. It was garbled and seemed to include some Vietnamese. The sergeant had been in-country for a while, then. He looked at his watch. He'd be late for dinner if he stayed much longer, but a few minutes wouldn't hurt. He pulled a chair over to the bed and adjusted the angle so he could rest his leg straight out in front of him.

Christ, he's young. That's more down than stubble. He doesn't look much older than I was when I lost mine. The sergeant cried out incoherently and thrashed about, threatening to pull out his IV and drainage tubes. The doctor stood and put a hand on the boy's forehead. "Shh, shh. It's okay. You're all right now." He brushed the boy's hair back. "You're all right." The boy opened his eyes suddenly, revealing soft brown irises. He stopped thrashing. "There. That's better. You were having a bad dream, Sergeant Dunn."

The sergeant opened his mouth to speak but produced a dry croak.

"Wait." The doctor poured the boy a glass of water from the pitcher on the bed stand and held it while he drank. "Better?" He sat down again and stretched out his leg.

"You're not the surgeon or the other guy."

"Nope. Dr. Geary asked me to stop in. I'm a psychiatrist. I help out folks like you, now an' agin."

"What do you mean, folks like me? I'm not crazy."

"Nobody thinks you're crazy. Dr. Geary was concerned because you weren't sleeping."

"Fucking dream."

"Not exactly, I don't think," the doctor said mildly.

The young man's eyes widened slightly. "None of your business."

The doctor smiled. "Maybe not. Sometimes people find it helpful to talk."

"You wouldn't understand."

"You might be surprised." The doctor stood. "Sorry, I'm getting a crick in my neck from twisting like this. The leg only bends so far." He unbuttoned his shirt, reached inside, and shrugged out of the harness. Then he bent down and rolled up his pant leg, unbuckled a strap, grasped his leg just above the knee, and slowly worked it off. He placed the leg carefully on the floor, then hopped around to face the young man, and sat down again in the chair—this time facing the sergeant directly.

"That's better. I can see you without breaking my neck."

The young man's breathing was loud. "I haven't anything to say to you."

"Okay, I'll just rest for a while. It's been a long day." Whistling, the doctor rolled his pant leg up and removed the knit sock that covered his stump. White scar tissue decorated the narrow, pink stump. He massaged the stump, giving out a soft groan of pleasure.

"That's disgusting. You should do that in private."

"It's private enough here. It's after visiting hours."

"I don't want to see this."

"Why not? Yours looks pretty similar—a little fresher." The doctor watched the sergeant carefully. "Or haven't you checked yours out yet?"

CHAPTER 6

1919

FRANK WOKE from a daydream. He was mucking out the barn. He smelled manure and watched hay dust drift in the shaft of sunlight from the open shutters in the hayloft. The light touched a young man perched on a three-legged stool just inside the barn door. Frank recognized the source of the voice that had haunted him for weeks. It was as if he were seeing the man for the first time. The man—boy really—balanced on uneven thighs, one muscled, the other bone thin and ending in a stump.

Catching Frank's stare, he tilted his head, his wide mouth wavering uncertainly between a smile and a grimace.

Frank thought the boy's eyes were gray until he moved and the sun transformed them to sea green. He laughed at the trick, and the boy's smile steadied and widened. The boy had been with him, had been talking to him for days. The words were gone, but they hung in the air with the dust.

"How did you lose your leg?"

WHEN HE finished the story, Jersey grabbed his crutches and stood. "Let's go back to the house. I'd like you to meet your grandma and grandpa. He stopped. "You wouldn't happen to recall their names?"

Frank hesitated, a boy poised to dive from a riverbank. But he shook his head and looked past Jersey, out into the morning light. "Is this their farm?"

"Yeah. You been living here since you came back from Europe, near as I can tell."

"When did you come, Jersey? You've been talking to me… forever."

"You've known my name all of ten minutes and I've been talking to you forever?"

"I'm sorry. I didn't mean—"

Jersey saw Frank flush and he wanted to kick himself. "No, I've a mouth like the backside of a horse. You've been ill, and I'm sassing you."

"How long have I been ill?"

"I'm told you came back from Europe in June. It's September now."

"Four months."

"I dunno when you got clocked or how long you were in the hospital."

"I don't remember that." Frank's mouth kept twitching as though he wanted to smile. "Or anything, really, before the sound of your voice."

Mr. and Mrs. Clark were ready to mount a parade when Jersey took them aside after breakfast and told them that Frank had remembered his name and recalled some of their time together. He tried to gloss over the part about having to tell Frank their names, but Charlie caught on and asked, "Do you think he'll remember us tomorrow?" as though Jersey were an expert on broken heads.

"I reckon something might stick. We got to see."

JERSEY CHOKED on gunpowder and blood.

The room was dark and hot; his curtains might have been fashioned of tin, so little air moved through them. When his shaking subsided to the point where he could maneuver, he rose, prepared to go out onto the porch and await the dawn. But he heard a muffled yelp as he passed the stairs and swung into the kitchen instead. He moved slowly, trying not to knock his crutches on the table or chairs. Thrashing sounds followed another yelp. He hesitated, unsure whether to wake Mr. Clark or try the stairs, and heard a yell and more thumps.

Frank tumbled down the stairs in his pajamas. Wild-eyed, he stared past Jersey without recognition.

"Whoa, Frank, what's the—"

Frank punched him in the face. The blow knocked Jersey off balance, and he stumbled over a chair. He went down, hit his head on the table, and landed painfully on one of his crutches.

Frank bashed open the screen door and ran out.

The coppery taste in Jersey's mouth told him his nose was bleeding.

"Hell and damnation! What happened in here?" Mr. Clark came in from the dining room in bare feet, britches, and a nightshirt.

"Frank's gone" was all Jersey could think to say.

"Eddy, help Jersey. I'm going to find Frank," called out Mr. Clark, running out the door.

Mrs. Clark came into the kitchen, a shawl wrapped around her flannel nightgown. Her eyes narrowed. "Jersey Rohn, what have you done? Did you say something to him?"

"I didn't say anything!"

She advanced on him. "You scared him, I know it, with your war stories."

Jersey tipped his head back to slow the flow of blood from his nose and tried to calm his breathing. "He's heard 'em a dozen times before."

"He doesn't need to hear about soldiers and fighting. He needs his family."

"Whatever happened to him over there, it didn't involve his family. Maybe he needs to remember it, if he's to heal." Jersey was mad, and when he got mad, his grammar improved. His mother chided him about speaking like a farmhand, but most of the time the cover felt more comfortable.

Mrs. Clark glared like he'd dropped his britches in church. "I'll not have you poisoning his mind with war stories!"

What was she going on about? How was it his fault that Frank had gone off his rocker? Jersey gingerly pressed a sleeve against his nostrils. The taste of blood filled his mouth and his mind went to the field where Andy died. He grasped the table and drew himself to his feet. Shaking his head to clear it of the unwanted images, he reached for his crutches. "Could you get some cotton or a rag or something to stop me from dripping on the floor?"

Mrs. Clark's mind was clearly elsewhere. "I won't have it!" she said, hugging her arms to her chest.

"Christ, woman! Have you lost your mind?" He knew he shouldn't have said it as soon as he saw her face harden.

"Don't you dare cuss at me, you little German half-breed." Mrs. Clark took a rolling pin from a drawer beside the iron stove and advanced like she wanted to brain him.

Jersey straightened up. "Get out of my way." Holding one crutch in front of himself like a battering ram, he hopped to the front door. He made it out without further injury, but when he tried to hop off the porch, he slipped and fell down the stairs, landing on his face in the yard.

Eventually, he crawled to the barn, where he shivered in a pile of dirty hay and listened to the Clarks call for Frank.

MR. CLARK pulled up in front of Jersey's house and shut down the Model T. "I'm sorry things didn't work out, Jersey. It wasn't your fault, what happened with Frank. I don't believe he would have hit you, had he known you. But Eddy, well...." His gaze skipped over the barn and the house without meeting Jersey's eyes. "She is... she is my wife. I'm grateful for your help with Frank."

"How is he?" Mrs. Clark had not let Jersey back into the house after Charlie found Frank hiding in the toolshed and coaxed him out. Instead, Jersey and Charlie watched speechlessly as she packed up Jersey's trunk and dragged it out onto the porch, showing a vigor that belied the loose flesh on her bare arms.

Charlie frowned. "Hard to say. He didn't say much after we got him inside and into bed. He got pretty chilled before we found him."

"Will you send me a note? Tell me how he's doing?"

Mr. Clark put a hand on the back of his neck and frowned. "If I can figure a way without upsetting the missus. She's dead set against you. Can't entirely understand why. Sometimes, she just takes up against someone." He shook his head. "I best be going. Here, let me help you down."

Jersey's father came out of the barn about the time Mr. Clark set Jersey's trunk on the porch. Mr. Clark nodded but said nothing as he cranked the Tin Lizzy. Jersey's father watched the car rattle down the lane, then turned to Jersey, his smile not entirely hiding the question in his eyes. "*Mein Gott*! Were you set upon by Indians?"

Jersey's nose felt swollen and probably looked like a ripe tomato.

"What is this?" Jersey's father motioned to the trunk. "You didn't swear in front of Mrs. Clark, did you?"

Jersey laughed helplessly. Before long his gasps were indistinguishable from sobs.

"EDDY! HE'LL be all right. He just got a chill hiding in the shed all night. You mustn't worry yourself so!" Charlie wrapped an arm around her and pulled her against his chest as she tucked an extra blanket around Frank's bed.

Eddy stiffened against him. She tried to relax but found it near impossible. "Are you a doctor now, Charlie Clark? Joe's people said Adele died in two days! By the time you decide to do anything, he could be dead!" *Oh, why did we allow Frank to persuade us to take on that miserable little German?* She'd known it was a bad idea to bring a soldier into the house. Frank's mind should be on his family, not the war.

Frank had been overseas four years according to the AFAU, doing heaven knows what for the French army. Four years of worry for his mother. Adele had been so worn out she'd broken down and written to Charlie to confess her fears. She didn't write to her mother, of course. She'd die before admitting fear to Eddy. She *did* die first. She complained to her father that Joe's only response to her anxiety was to spout platitudes about God's will. That was one of only a few letters she wrote after running off with Joe.

After the letter, Eddy spent the next year waiting for the telegram informing them that their only grandson was blown to bits like the Franklin boy. The government telegram Mrs. Franklin received said only that her boy had been killed in action, but she'd received a letter from his commanding officer explaining that he'd been killed instantly by a shell and that there wasn't enough of him left to bury. Mrs. Franklin hadn't come to church for a month after that.

Only Joe's occasional notes kept her from losing her mind. At least Joe had the courtesy to write. In September, Joe wrote to say Frank had been wounded near the Front. Then came a terrible silence. Eventually, the Quakers wrote to inform them that Adele and Joe were gone—taken by the Spanish influenza. Almost 12,000 had died in Philadelphia that October and November.

The thought that Frank could have the same disease made Eddy want to scream.

Charlie looked at her in a way that made her want to slap him. "I am not hysterical, Charlie Clark!" She slapped the blanket into place instead.

Frank's eyes opened to focus on someone visible only to him. "Don't go back! They'll take the other one! Don't go back, Jersey, don't go back…."

Charlie leaned over the bed and brushed back Frank's damp hair. "Frank, you're here with us, your grandmother and grandfather."

"Give me your driving coat, Charlie Clark. If you won't go, I'll go myself."

Finally, her stubborn husband nodded. "Okay, Eddy. I'll go into town and get Doc Thierson."

THE DREAM was as vivid this morning as the first time it had woken him. The goddamned smell was strong in his nostrils, and his limbs wobbled like a colt's when he got up to bang his way outdoors into the diffuse predawn glow. He made too much noise knocking his crutches on the bedroom door and kitchen table on his way out, but he couldn't bring himself to wait for the shaking to subside. *Am I going to be broken for the rest of my goddamned life?* The thought rattled him.

It was too cold to sit on the porch without a blanket. He had not thought to bring one, so he swung himself across the yard and into the barn. Inside, it was still too dark to see much, but the old building was etched into his mind clear as a blueprint. He moved slowly to the stall of his childhood friend, Flash. Flash was getting on now and mostly retired from farm work. Jersey hadn't ridden him since before the war. But he still brought the horse an apple or a carrot whenever he visited. Flash blew curiously and shifted a little when Jersey leaned his crutches against the wall and hopped into the stall.

"Sorry, old boy, I ain't got nothing. You won't mind if I share a little warmth, will ya?" Jersey lowered himself onto the clean hay at the front of the stall. Flash blew again, his breath hot and smelling of fermented hay. Jersey made a fist and held it out in front of himself. He could just make out his trembling hand in the dark. *Some boxer you are. Camp Custer lightweight boxing champion and you're shaking like an old man.*

Jersey closed his eyes and breathed in the familiar smells of horse, hay, and manure. Andy had thought fighting was a sin—something you did when you had no choice. Consequently, he completed his fights with businesslike dispatch. *Boxing made no sense to you, did it, pal?* But the manly art had made Jersey feel like he could take care of himself. He saw Andy with that quizzical look—half-smiling, uncertain—he got when he didn't quite follow your English. Then his expression slid into the openmouthed horror of the dying Andy, the boy who had stared at the bloody holes in his chest and realized he was done.

"Goddammit! I will remember you how I want."

"You did not swear so much before the war."

Jersey started and banged his head on the side of the stall. "Hellfire! I'm sorry, Papa."

The morning light warming the barn made a silhouette of his father's head. "Is your leg hurting you?"

"No, not really." He wanted to explain why he was in the barn, but he couldn't think what to say to this gentle man who loved nothing better than to get down on his knees and work the dark soil of his vegetable garden, this gentle man who could not possibly imagine what his son had seen and done.

His father rested his arms on the top of the stall door. "Will you help with the milking?"

"Yes, Papa. I'll help with the milking."

AT BREAKFAST, his mother returned to her favorite topic since Jersey's latest homecoming. "Did you say something to offend him? You must have done something."

"Mama, I told you. I didn't do anything! Frank wasn't himself or he'd never have hit me. He's not like that."

"Then why'd they send you packing?"

"How should I know? Mrs. Clark got this notion that it was my fault Frank got upset. She's a hard woman—weeks I was there and she never once gave me a smile. She never would've agreed to hire me if it hadn't been for Frank insisting on it."

His mother set a plate of eggs and bacon in front him. His mouth watered at the smell.

"Would they take you back if you wrote out an apology?"

It was too much. "For what, Mama? Should I apologize for having a German name? For recollecting what Frank can't?" Spittle flew. "For losing only one leg, instead of two?"

"Son." His father's voice was low.

Jersey swallowed and wiped his mouth, ashamed at his outburst. "I'm sorry, Mama, but you gnaw at me so. Maybe when Frank starts recalling more, he'll wanna see me again."

His mother sighed and rubbed her hands on her apron. "It's just that you sounded so happy when you wrote to us."

Jersey clenched his fists. "I was happy."

CHAPTER 7

THE WAKING was a gradual shooing of pressing spirits, supplicating eyes and missing limbs fading as Frank transitioned from one world to another. He opened his eyes and rubbed the crud from the corners. He realized he was in Jersey's bed, in the spare room. Where was Jersey? Trying to rise, he found himself weak. How long had he been in bed?

Slanting rays from the window told him it was afternoon. *I've been ill.* He swung his legs off the bed and waited for the blood to reach his head. Sounds from the kitchen indicated he was not alone in the house. A stack of loose notepaper lay on the windowsill, anchored by a book. Seeing the notes reminded him that a gray-haired woman named Eddy should be in the kitchen.

"Grandmother?" he called out. "Where's Jersey?" A pan clattered to the floor.

"You're awake!" Eddy came into the room and stopped abruptly, her eyes on the notes, which remained on the windowsill. "Oh, Frank." Then she cried, her hands pressed to her breast. The tears ran down the deep furrows beside her mouth and dripped, unacknowledged, from her chin. Frank was unprepared for the display of emotion. He remembered his grandmother's existence better than her form. He rubbed his legs, gathered strength for a trip to the privy, and wished for something to say to stop the discomforting flood.

He asked for Jersey again after eating the meager dinner his shrunken stomach would tolerate. Eddy would not meet his eyes. Charlie, summoned from his toolshed for dinner, answered. "Mr. Rohn has gone home."

"Why? Is someone ill?"

Eddy answered, "He thought it—" At a sharp look from her husband, she started again. "We thought it best. You were very upset the night he left."

"I don't remember—I dreamt I was being chased by soldiers. They were all missing arms, legs, parts of their faces. I tried to run away, but they were all around, touching me." He shook his head, seeing the supplicating faces from his dream. "Did I do something silly?"

"You punched Jersey in the nose," Charlie said.

"Damn! Do you think he'll forgive me?"

"I'll not have that language in my house." Eddy's mouth pressed into a firm line.

"I'm sorry, ma'am."

IN THE week that followed, Frank found himself more and more frustrated that he could remember nothing of his life before the farm.

"You didn't have time to get frustrated before," Charlie grunted, as they pitched hay bales into a wagon, under the afternoon sun. "The problem was fresh every morning."

It was the first day since his illness that Frank felt strong enough to help with the heavy work.

"It would be easier remembering nothing at all. I get images like an overdeveloped photograph. I know something's there, but it's too faint to make out." Frank's movements ground to a halt as he looked at his grandfather. "Where are my parents? Why am I not with them?"

Charlie straightened his back and squared his shoulders. "Your grandmother and I, we thought we should wait until you were better before…." His gaze wandered over the stubble field to the line of trees on the ridge where red and yellow had begun to replace green. The flesh of his jowls sagged. "Your parents are dead, Frank. Adele and Joe died last October in Philadelphia from the Spanish influenza."

The sky darkened around Frank. A great wind ripped the strength from his limbs. He stumbled at a chasm's edge. Even as he tried to regain his footing, he wondered how it was that he could feel the loss of his parents so strongly and not remember their faces. Charlie spoke, but it was

Jersey's voice that called him back from the pit. He tried to hold that warm, half-joking voice in his mind. He turned away from his grandfather and jammed his fork into a bale.

He and Charlie worked for more than an hour, slowly becoming caked with dust and bits of hay, until it was too hot, and Frank went inside the barn to dunk his head in a bucket of cold water.

FRANK TOOK a last sip of iced tea and put down his glass. "I'm going to take a walk."

Charlie sighed. "I'll get my coat."

"Thanks, Grandfather, but I'd like to be alone. I'll be all right by myself." He patted the notes in his pocket. "You stay and put your feet up."

Charlie looked like he might protest, but Eddy cut him off. "What a good idea!" She smiled at her husband. "You rest while I put away the dishes. When I'm done, I'll come and read the paper to you."

Frank left the house and walked diagonally up the hill toward the tree line, where he hopped the low, split-rail fence surrounding the pasture. The field was green and dotted with cow patties and lichen-covered rocks. The cows and horses were in the barn for the night, but the air still held the scent of warm manure. With no particular destination in mind, he picked his way along the tree line, avoiding stray patties.

The sun dropped behind the low ridge that separated the valley from Taperville, the last rays setting a fringe of red and yellow leaves glowing on the crowns of the hills. The trees were on fire. His breath caught and his heart pounded. He told himself it wasn't true even as he spun around searching for... his truck? Before the thought could fully resolve, the sun went down and the ridge lost its glow. Weak-kneed, he dropped to the grass and concentrated on slow, even breaths.

Shaking off the odd panic set off when he'd thought the ridge was burning, Frank resumed his walk along the high edge of the pasture. The light faded to blue, and he searched for a familiar shape or clump of rock that could confirm that this place had once been significant to him, but the landscape remained strange. Had his parents ever brought him here? Grandfather and Grandmother always seemed too busy to tell him about his parents. Didn't they want him to remember? He resolved to read the letters that remained unopened on the writing desk in the attic room. He'd wanted some sense of his father and mother before he read the last words they addressed to him. He knew he'd loved them. His chest constricted painfully when he thought of their passing, but he could not recall their faces. In fact, the only person whose form he could fully resolve in his mind's eye was Jersey. But Grandmother had banished Jersey.

Charlie could be induced to talk when Eddy wasn't around. From his grandfather, Frank learned that his father, Joseph Huddleston, had been a Quaker, and that Frank had grown up in Philadelphia, near the Germantown Friends School where his father taught. But when Frank asked how his parents had met, Charlie only muttered, "No point in dredging up ancient history," and turned away to hoist a bag of feed. Frank was reduced to tiptoeing around his questions. If Eddy was around or if his questions were too pointed or too frequent, Charlie would clam up. Nevertheless, Frank turned back toward the house, determined to corner Charlie again.

Walking back amid the rustling grass was like being at sea. It was fully dark and the Milky Way was a diffuse white band across the sky. Why had his mother left this place? Nearing the porch, he could just make out Charlie sitting on the wicker love seat.

"Have a good walk?" said Charlie.

He sat down next to his grandfather. "Everything is so clear and sharp, but I can't remember ever being here."

"This is my favorite time of year."

Frank saw a pale flash as Charlie waved an arm to encompass the whole of the valley.

"The hills seem closer in the dry air, and you smell the fallen leaves when the breeze flows down from the ridge."

Frank ventured a question. "It's so beautiful! Why did my mother move to Philadelphia?"

Charlie sighed. "She and Eddy, they were all sharp edges and hard surfaces. She wanted a bigger world, or at any rate, one with more people than Eddy can tolerate. Adele was primed for it, when she met your father. He offered the big city, new people, a more exciting life. Joe was a steady fellow. She could go find her big world and feel safe with him."

"Why is this place so unfamiliar to me? Didn't my parents ever come to visit?"

"Your mother and Eddy fell out over her decision to follow Joe to Philadelphia. Joe never stopped trying to get them to reconcile, but he never convinced Adele to visit. Adele, she was a lot like her mother. Hard to shift once she set her course."

Frank closed his eyes and tried to picture his mother, this headstrong woman who'd left the family farm and never looked back, but her face was elusive as ever.

SATURDAY WAS market day. When Charlie went to get the Model T, Frank jumped up to give chase. "Grandfather, would you mind if I drive today?"

Charlie glanced around in surprise. "You want to drive? Do you remember how?"

"I'm sure I do. I started to remember something about an automobile the other night. I thought it was a truck, but I'm not sure now. Anyway, I'm sure I can drive."

"Well, then." Charlie put a hand Frank's shoulder and guided him toward the far side of the barn. "Let's check you out. I bet you do all right. When you get back from town, maybe we can take a walk together. There's something I want to tell you."

"You're not coming?"

"No, if you can drive your grandmother to the market, I would just as soon stay here and get some work done. I'm behind again since Jersey left."

"I want to talk to you about that. Jersey—"

"Let's talk about that later," Charlie said. "Right now, I want you to walk me through the start up."

Check flight successful, Frank took the wheel while Charlie installed Eddy in the front seat. As they left for town, Frank squeezed the horn's rubber bulb. Charlie jumped at the raucous sound, but he grinned and waved. Frank was comfortable in the car, his hands falling to the spark advance lever and steering wheel, his feet finding the pedals without thought. They passed through the hickories and over the ridge top. He let the car pick up speed as they rolled downhill toward Clear Creek.

"Frank, please slow down," yelled Eddy. "It's too cold for a swim in the creek."

Frank had never heard his grandmother joke, and he wasn't entirely sure that he hadn't imagined it. "Sorry, Grandmother."

He stole a glance at her. She faced straight ahead, one gloved hand resting in her lap, the other resting on top of the door. The leaf-scented breeze moved the single gray lock that had escaped her hat. The corners of her mouth pulled back in what might possibly be a smile.

"What will you get at the market?" Frank asked.

Eddy raised her voice without turning her head. "Butternut squash. We've eaten all of Charlie's. There will be apples this time of year. I want apples for pie and for sauce. If there are any tomatoes, I'll take some to can. Would you like an apple pie?"

Frank grinned. "I believe I would."

CHAPTER 8

"I'M GOING into town. Some boys are having a confab about a new veterans' group at the Grange Hall next Saturday." Jersey made the announcement at dinner, a couple of weeks after his ignominious return from the Clark farm.

Jersey's father speared a slice of carrot. "Got the hay to get in yet."

"I know, but I'm not much use beyond the milking—thought I'd ride into town so I wouldn't burden you."

Jersey's father put down his fork and glanced at his mother before responding. "You haven't been on a horse since you got home, son."

Jersey took pains to keep his tone conversational. "I know, Papa, but you ain't using Flash no more. I thought he might enjoy the outing."

This was too much for Jersey's mother. She bounced in her chair and practically stamped. "It's not Flash I'll fret about, Jersey. What are you going to do with your crutches? What if you fall off?"

"Mama. I've been riding Flash since he was a colt. I'm not gonna fall off. I figure I'll strap the crutches together and loop the strap over the saddle horn. I thought I might practice in the morning, to get the feel of it."

His mother rose and snatched his half-full plate. "I think it's a damn fool idea," she said. "But you'll do what you want, I suppose."

Jersey swallowed a complaint. "Mama, I've gotta start figuring out how to get along in the world. I can't spend the rest of my life on the porch." By the time he finished, he was talking to himself. His mother had gone into the kitchen. He didn't get to the real reason he wanted to go into town: to see if Mr. Clark had left news of Frank. It was just as well. He didn't need to remind his mother about the lost job.

Jersey's father took out his pipe, pouch, and matches. When his pipe was drawing properly, he removed it from his mouth. "You thought about how you're going to get him saddled?"

Jersey was grateful for his father's matter-of-fact tone. "After we finish milking, if you could get the saddle down from the peg and lay it over the side of one of the stalls, I bet I could swing it over."

"You're sure you don't want me to saddle him?"

"I wanna try on my own."

His father tried his pipe and found it had gone out. After lighting it again, he gave Jersey a direct look. "Okay, you fall off, I tell your mother you twisted my arm."

"Anyone want pie?" Jersey's mother called from the kitchen.

His father glanced toward the kitchen and raised his eyebrows. "Huh."

Jersey grinned. "Yes, ma'am!"

THE SUN balanced on the horizon like a cue ball on felt when Jersey watched his father hoist his saddle over the edge of the empty stall as instructed. His father stepped back to look and made a clicking noise with his tongue, then tightened the stirrup on the right side as far as it would go. He contemplated his work for a few seconds before turning to Jersey. "You want me to get Flash after breakfast? I could get him ready and leave him by the fence."

"No thanks, Papa. I've gotta learn to do for myself."

His father shrugged. "Okay, we do it your way."

After breakfast, Jersey walked side by side with his father across the yard. His father squinted into the bright sun. "Nice day for riding."

Without another word, he strode off toward the far side of the barn where he'd parked the Fordson Model F he'd bought in '17. He'd been so proud to get the first one in the county. Just about everyone had a tractor now, most of them Mr. Ford's.

Jersey went into the barn to get Flash. Getting the bridle on him wasn't too bad. Flash snorted and moved a little, whether surprised at Jersey's odd hopping about or at being bridled at all, Jersey couldn't tell. With Flash's reins in one hand and a handful of his mane in the other, Jersey hopped over to the saddle. He looped Flash's reins around the post at the corner of the stall. When in position, he grabbed the saddle and swung it off the top of the stall—and promptly lost his balance. He landed on his back with the heavy saddle on top of him.

"Son of a bitch." After he pushed the saddle off, he used the slats that formed the side of the stall to pull himself back up. He hoisted the saddle again and hopped to Flash. After swinging the saddle up and onto the horse, he hung on and caught his breath before tightening the cinch. "Good boy. Been a while for both of us, hasn't it?"

What now, genius? Flash had never seemed so tall. Jersey looked around the barn in desperation. Hopping again, he led Flash over to the ladder to the hayloft. "Stay, boy." Flash's ears twitched as he considered Jersey's request. Blowing slightly, he lowered his head to get some loose hay near the base of the ladder. "Good boy!"

Jersey pulled himself up rung by rung, until he was even with Flash's back. Leaning out, he took hold of the saddle horn and pulled Flash closer. "Come on, just a little bit more." When Flash was as close as possible, he launched himself into the saddle, almost sliding off the far side.

Breathing hard, Jersey pulled up the reins and turned Flash toward the front of the barn. Only then did he notice his crutches where he'd left them, leaning against the side of the empty stall. "Damnation."

He leaned over the right side of the horse to grasp one of the crutches, forgetting the empty stirrup on that side, and promptly slid off the horse, landing painfully on his shoulder. Flash sidestepped daintily and snorted.

Jersey lay on his back and ran his hands through his hair. "Son of a bitch!"

"Are you okay?" said his mother, sticking her head around the barn door.

"Get out!" Jersey struggled to get up. "Get out!"

She flinched and retreated swiftly.

Jersey fell twice more as he learned to balance without his right leg. At dinner, he mentioned the problem to his father.

His father nodded. "I have an idea about that. You leave it to me." After dinner, he took a lantern and strolled out to the barn, humming to himself.

Jersey followed his mother into the kitchen. "Mama, I'm sorry." He put an arm around her.

"Served me right for poking my nose where it wasn't wanted."

That night, Jersey was so stiff it took him ten minutes to work his shirt off.

JERSEY MADE his way to the barn to find his father waiting with a sly grin. It might have been Christmas morning.

"Come into the tack room." His father led the way to the converted double stall they used for tack. Mounted on pegs in the wall were saddles, halters, bridles, and other equipment. A solid handmade table held odd bits of leather, a set of punches, stamps, a mallet, rivet setters, and various specialized cutting tools. The room smelled of saddle soap and lemon oil, with a faint underlying hint of horse sweat. His father had installed a potbellied stove in the corner so he could stay warm as he made repairs during the winter.

"What about the milking?" Jersey asked.

"Cows will wait. I want to show you something." He pointed to where he'd laid out Jersey's saddle on a block. Attached to the stirrup leather on the right side was a leather cup the size of Jersey's stump. "I've made it adjustable for height. It's lined with wool from a blanket, but I expect you'll have to experiment to get it comfortable. You can try it after breakfast."

Jersey dropped his crutches and hugged his father, grunting at the pressure on his bruised shoulder.

"Maybe you better wait a few days—"

"The devil I will."

JERSEY AND Flash set out for Taperville on Saturday. The ride would take an hour and a half if he didn't push. They would pass three miles of recently harvested corn and wheat fields, now stubble, then follow the river road into Taperville. Neither was predisposed to hurry. The day was crisp and clear. Jersey was certain, were it not for the curvature of the earth, he could see all the way to the Czar's former home in St. Petersburg. Why hurry on such a day? Flash seemed agreeable, as he was only inclined to haste when his stall was in sight.

The day had started out poorly. The dream had left him shaking and ready to bolt, though he had no notion where. But the shaking had passed, and his heart, racing like a motorcycle on a board track, eventually dropped to a slower circuit. Maybe it was the good weather or maybe it was the thought that he might find news of Frank that buoyed him. Perhaps it was all the gabbing he'd done when it had been like dropping pennies in a well, but Frank was the only man in whose company he'd ever felt comfortable talking about Andy or the fighting in France. What had prompted Frank to punch him? Had his memory returned? The child in Jersey preened at the thought he'd been the first person Frank remembered—until shame caught up and banished the spoiled brat.

Jersey shivered down to his toes as he pictured Frank's piercing gray eyes and the endearing flush that played on his cheeks when he was excited. He'd considered sending him a letter, but he knew of the pile of unopened letters on Frank's desk. Moreover, Eddy would likely confiscate a note before it reached his friend. So he pinned his hopes on Charlie and his halfhearted agreement to send news if he could do it without alerting the missus. Nothing had arrived by mail, but letters to local folk were as often entrusted to the Grange as the Post Office.

The veterans' meeting was an excuse to visit the Grange Hall. He'd heard about the meeting from Lars Rasmussen, a soldier who'd also grown up in the Taperville area. They'd met in the hospital.

The purpose of the meeting was to discuss the organization of a new veterans' group. *What could they want with a runt like me?* The regular army officers had an agenda, of course: continued employment in a permanent, federal army. They probably sought to enlist the support of their former troops. Jersey had little use for officers. They were mostly good for getting people killed. Aside from the boxing and occasional opportunities to get blown to bits, army life had been composed mostly of tedium and endless jawing among the enlisted men.

Not that Jersey minded talk, but it had been a picture of a soldier running across a grassy field on a recruiting poster, his muscular forearms bare, his face flushed with exertion, that had caught Jersey's imagination toward the end of his senior year in high school. Up to that time, soldiers had been tin figures spread out on the cellar floor, engaged in bloodless maneuvers. (The night his parents first read about the "Rape of Belgium" in the papers, Jersey had enacted the Battle of Waterloo, since it had taken place in that country.)

Some of Jersey's schoolmates signed up as soon as they were old enough, egged on by their girlfriends and fearful of being branded with the white feather. Jersey had no girlfriend to goad him to action. German soldiers shooting unarmed hostages, burning towns, and pillaging museums didn't arouse interest in a military career.

The war remained distant even after Wilson declared war in April of '17. Not until Uncle Sam—in the guise of the Local Board—pointed his bony finger at the young men of Taperville did Jersey's attitude change. That was when the poster went up outside the County Courthouse. The soldier looked manly. Jersey wanted to feel that way.

At Camp Custer, Jersey's stature was less a problem than he'd feared. If small, he was used to constant physical activity on the farm. Moreover, by the time he arrived at the camp for training, General John "Black Jack" Pershing, Commander of the American Expeditionary Force, needed men acutely. Conscripts who would not have been considered fit for duty in less pressing times crowded the camp. There were sallow clerks from the city, railroad workers with missing fingers, and miners who coughed and spit black gobs when they got out of breath. When the NCOs lined them up one morning and informed them that they were going to learn to box, Jersey was optimistic. *I ain't hardly the worst of this lot.* The day turned out to be a good one, for that was the day he met Andy.

JERSEY LURCHED back to the present when Flash sidestepped to avoid a Garter snake sunning itself in the lane. "Damn you! Give me some warning next time." Flash flicked his ears and resumed his lethargic pace. There had been little rain to keep down the dust since the storm that had prompted Jersey's fit at the Clark farm. They turned to follow the river road. Dry rock protruded from the water in places where gentle swells were typical. Nearer town, he passed the spot where rocks sliced across the flow like a line of battleships. Playing here as a child, he'd imagined himself an admiral of the line setting course to destroy the enemy fleet. He could not remember which fleet he'd thought the enemy to be. The Spanish? He would not have thought of the German.

As he neared the outskirts of Taperville, Jersey encountered Model Ts and farm wagons loaded with produce for the market. Twenty minutes later, he plodded along Main Street. The Grange Hall had a watering trough and hitching post where he could leave Flash. More importantly, it had a porch under the portico that he thought he could use to get back onto his horse when it was time to return home.

Jersey stopped outside the Hall, keeping an eye on the Model T he saw coming down the street, a plume of dust following like a tame genie. As it neared, the front wheels twitched as though the driver were not quite sure where he was going.

"Hey, Jersey, you made it! Get down off that beast and meet the guys."

CHAPTER 9

THE AFTERNOON breeze kicked up a dust devil on Main Street as Frank aimed the Tin Lizzy, with its load of market goods, toward home. Up the block, he saw the Grange Hall. A group of men lounged on a bench by the hitching post, some of them in uniform. Two worked at attaching a United States flag to the columns supporting the portico.

"I wonder what they're up to?"

Eddy frowned. "It's no concern of ours."

A horse and rider trotted toward them, apparently headed for the Hall. Frank slowed the car to keep from frightening the horse.

"Why are you stopping?" said Eddy sharply. "I want to go home!"

"I'm not stop—wait, that's Jersey! I want to say hello."

"Frank Huddleston! I have groceries to put up and canning to finish. Please continue driving."

"Grandmother, please, it will only take a second. I owe Jersey an apology."

"You owe that boy nothing."

Frank slowed the car further. Jersey had reached the Hall, but remained atop his horse as they rolled up.

Eddy grabbed the wheel and attempted to turn the car away from the Hall.

"Hey, quit that," Frank said, straightening the wheel.

One of the men called out, and Jersey twisted in the saddle to greet him.

"Don't you dare stop!" Eddy reached past Frank and gave the horn a firm squeeze.

Before Jersey could react, Flash reared and bolted.

Jersey lost his balance and his seat on the horse. He slid off the animal to land flat on his back in the dust. Flash's hooves kicked up football-sized puffs of dust as the horse galloped down Main Street. Horrified, Frank pushed his grandmother roughly away from the controls, brought the car to a halt, and jumped out. "Jesus, Jersey! Are you all right?"

Jersey gasped like a fish out of water. "Goddammit! You... tryin'... t' kill me?" His lean frame swam in his coat. His dark mop was speckled with dust from the road.

"I'm sorry. I didn't mean to... I mean it was—" Frank said as he crouched by Jersey's side.

"That was a damn fool thing to do!" the man who had called out to Jersey yelled. "Boys, see if you can catch that horse." Two of the men jumped up and chased the horse down the street.

Mortified to see his friend struggling for air, Frank spun around. "Grandmother, why'd you do that?"

Eddy's face could have been set in concrete. No answer forthcoming, he turned and lifted Jersey to his feet, surprised at the dense muscle he found strung on the thin frame. "Are you all right?" he asked again.

"Dandy," Jersey gasped. "Just need... catch my breath."

The man who had called out to Jersey came over. "Who the hell are you?"

"Simmer down, Lars. He's... friend of mine," Jersey said.

"Some friend! You should know better than to startle a horse like that."

"I'm very sorry," Frank said. It was pointless to explain that Jersey was the last person he would try to hurt.

"I'm perfectly all right," Jersey said, having regained his breath. "Lars Rasmussen, this is Frank Huddleston. He's Charlie Clark's grandson." He nodded toward the car. Eddy stared straight ahead, refusing to acknowledge anyone. To Frank's discomfort, Jersey continued, "He was in France too."

"What unit?"

"I'm not sure that I—" started Frank.

"You must have served in a military unit to join the American Legion," Lars said, pointing at the group of men who were putting up a banner next to the flag.

"My grandson served in France. He has as much right to join your club as Mr. Rohn." Eddy's voice shook.

"Christ, Grandmother! I just wanted to say hello to Jersey."

"Looks to me like you owe him more than a hello." Mr. Rasmussen nodded toward Jersey's empty pant leg, which had come unpinned. "Unless those boys get 'hold of your horse, Jersey, I'm thinking you'll be needing a ride home."

Eddy gave an audible hiss from the Model T.

"Flash'll be back, once he gets tuckered out. Pity he took my crutches with him."

"I'll help you," Frank said. He continued to hold Jersey's arm, restraining an inexplicable impulse to caress it. "Put your arm around my shoulder."

Jersey frowned, but he let Frank guide him to the bench.

The protective instinct that Jersey brought out in Frank unsettled him. *I'd carry him around like a puppy if he'd let me.* The thought was absurd, even insulting. Jersey would never tolerate treatment as anything less than a full-grown man and former soldier, so why did he feel this way?

"Make way for the walking wounded!" Lars called out to the men milling about in front of the Hall. "Man got a Croix de Guerre and DSC fighting the Huns. Give him some space."

"Button it, Lars. I just wanna sit down for a second."

CHRIST, I'M tired of being carted around like a goddamned sack of feed. Once he got over the shock of landing on his back and figured out that Eddy had honked the horn, Jersey was delighted to see Frank. Even as he swallowed his embarrassment at having fallen off his horse, he was acutely aware of the size and strength of Frank's hands as he was lifted to his feet.

Frank insisted that he and Eddy wait until after the meeting, or until Flash was found, before leaving. Livid at the delay, Eddy refused to get out of the Model T, but she didn't argue, apparently resigned to the fact that Frank's sense of responsibility would require him to see Jersey home.

Jersey would have fallen over dead rather than admit he didn't want to ride home. His shoulders were stiff, and he could feel new bruises where he'd landed on his back. The ride home in the Model T would be uncomfortable enough. Then it hit him. *If Flash gets home before I do, Mama will have a fit!* Concern for his mother's feelings warred with his desire to be with Frank. Guiltily, he allowed Frank to usher him into the meeting, determined see his friend even at the risk of worrying his mother.

When they were seated thigh to thigh in the packed room, the close quarters prevented them from exchanging more than whispered greetings. Jersey wanted to ask Frank if he had remembered any more of his family or service in France. Eddy's obvious sensitivity on both subjects made him doubly curious, but he didn't want to yell his questions in the noisy room.

They listened to an army officer from Detroit address the assembly about the new veterans' group. Jersey closed his eyes. He was used to the harsh stink of unwashed men, but Frank's scent was subtle and distracting. Frank smelled of soap, leather, a hint of lubricating oil, and clean sweat. He swallowed and tried to concentrate on the man on the podium. Congress had chartered the new organization in September. *Pack of old men! They gonna conscript us into this as well?*

Frank must have sensed his irritation, because he put a hand on Jersey's knee and squeezed. Jersey's attention focused on the warmth and gentle pressure of that hand. He shifted in his seat to keep Frank from noticing the erection that threatened to tent his trousers. Jersey opened his eyes and tried to focus on the speaker. The man finished his spiel with words he said were from the organization's new constitution: "For God and country." A man could get behind a phrase like that, even if he questioned the God part.

"Are you sleeping with your eyes open, Jersey? Let's get going. Let me give you a hand. Think they've found your horse? I'm really sorry about that." Frank was uncharacteristically loquacious.

Jersey rolled his eyes. "Quit apologizing! I know it was Eddy blew the damn horn. Who put the bee in her bonnet?"

"Put your hand on my shoulder," Frank said.

While they waited for the men to clear out of the Hall, Lars ushered the afternoon's speaker over. "Wait up, Jersey. I want you to meet Colonel Martin. Colonel, this is Jersey Rohn. I know you don't like to talk about the war, but the Colonel was at Chateau-Thierry."

"Howdy, Colonel. You'll have to excuse me. I was a mite distracted about the time we hit town. Not much chance to socialize outside the squad."

The colonel's eyes widened briefly, and then he laughed. "I'm sure you were. Nonetheless, I'm very pleased to meet you now, Jersey. I understand you acquitted yourself very well. You're exactly the sort of person we want to have in the Legion."

Shows what you know. "Thank you, sir. Pardon me, but I really gotta see about my horse."

"You rode here?" The colonel gestured at Jersey's empty pant leg. "You don't find it hard to keep your seat?"

The colonel just made polite conversation, but it wasn't a topic Jersey wanted to explore. He glanced impatiently at the door. "I managed fine until Frank showed up." He wanted to bite his tongue as soon as the words left his mouth.

Frank didn't try to hide his wince or the blush that darkened his face. "I'm so sorry, Jersey—"

"Christ! Will you quit that? It wasn't your fault. Let's go. I'm tired of hopping around like a one-legged jackass."

"But, Jersey, I hoped that you might join the colonel and myself for dinner—"

"I'm sorry, Lars. Colonel." He snatched the colonel's hand to shake it again. "I really must be getting home." He all but shoved Frank toward the door.

There were no signs of Flash or the men who'd run after him on the street. Jersey waved off Frank's help and hopped onto the running board and from there into the back seat of the Model T. He nodded at Mrs. Clark. "Good day, ma'am."

Mrs. Clark's head remained pointed forward. "Put on your gloves, Frank. I have waited long enough."

Frank leaned into the car and set the ignition, then drew on his gloves before cranking the engine. When it started, he turned to Mrs.

Clark. "Yes, you have. With Jersey's permission, I'll take you home first, then return Jersey."

"You'll do what you want with no regard for me."

Frank flushed. "I said I'd take you home first. If you hadn't blown the damn horn—"

"I'll not hear that kind of language from you, Frank Huddleston."

Jersey listened with his own misgivings. Enticed by the notion of time with Frank, he was also desperately afraid Flash would arrive home without him.

"Frank, maybe I should go—"

"Please, Jersey." Frank's tone was soft, but the set of his shoulders was eloquent.

It was the second time Frank had asked for him. Jersey had no will to resist.

THEY BOUNCED to the Clark farm in frosty silence. Frank helped Eddy down and unloaded the day's shopping as efficiently as he could manage. When he came out of the house the second time, he found Jersey breathing audibly but resting in the front seat.

"You all right?"

Jersey's face predicted a sharp retort, but his answer was merely curt. "I'm fine."

Frank suppressed an impulse to apologize again and went to spin the crank. "Jersey, would you retard the spark?"

Jersey gave him a blank look.

"It's the lever to the left of the steering column. Set it on the fourth notch."

"Got it."

The engine turning, Frank ran back to the driver's side. "You ought to think about getting one of these. Might be easier than getting around on that horse."

Jersey shrugged. "No money. No leg."

"But you can get a leg, right?" Frank adjusted the throttle and got the car moving. "How are your parents?"

Jersey's Adam's apple bobbed visibly. "Fine. Or they were when I left. This rig go any faster?"

Frank negotiated the narrow lane through the trees at the top of the ridge.

"How's your noggin? Forgotten my name yet?" Jersey asked.

"No, Gerald."

Jersey's jaw dropped. "You know my real name?"

Frank chuckled. "I asked Grandfather."

"You will *not* call me that." His tone brooked no argument.

"I prefer Jersey," Frank said, grinning.

Jersey's expression softened. "What about your kin? Your ma and pa, I mean. You recollect anything yet?"

Frank chased the beams of his headlamps from tree to tree. He hadn't, in fact, remembered anything new. Not one thing. He knew Jersey would understand, but it embarrassed him anyway, as if it were his own fault. "You know those letters I've got?"

"The ones you've been putting off reading?"

"They're addressed to me. It's silly, but I don't feel like they're mine. It hasn't felt right to open them." He struggled, trying to order his jumbled thoughts. "I'm afraid I won't recognize the writers."

"Have you remembered anything from before you was hurt?"

Frank patted the steering wheel. "I know I've driven one of these before."

"Your grandparents rich or something?"

"What do you mean?" They picked up speed as they began the downhill stretch toward Taperville.

"Not so many folk 'round here got an automobile. They're mostly still paying off their tractors."

"I don't think my parents owned a car," Frank said. "I want to ask you something."

"Fire at will."

Frank slowed the car before forming his question. "Will you do me a favor and read the letters with me?" What he really wanted was for Jersey to read them *to* him. He wanted a familiar voice, even if it wasn't one of his parents.

"With you? What for?" Concern clouded Jersey's expression. "Your head injury…."

"No, it's nothing like that. I just…." Frank shrugged.

"Well sure, if that's what you want."

Frank was relieved Jersey didn't push for an explanation.

"You think Eddy's gonna let you drive her into town anytime soon?"

What was his grandmother's beef with Jersey anyway? "I'm not much of a horseman or I'd ride over," Frank said. "To be honest, I'm not even sure I know how to ride—not like you do."

"Some jockey, I am! Didn't take much to send me arse over teakettle. Hey, you serious? You don't know how to ride?"

"Not like I know how to drive." Frank tried to imagine himself on a horse, but the image that formed in his mind was of steel rails. "I don't recall riding… but I think there was a train, no, a streetcar in front of the—"

"Hey, watch it!" Jersey dived for the wheel and yanked the car back onto the road and ended up draped over Frank's lap.

"Sorry!" Frank grabbed the collar of Jersey's coat and lifted him, one armed, back into place, noting with disapproval how light he was.

"That's something. You recall a streetcar," Jersey said. "Hey, you were a city boy! How'd you get so good at farm work?"

"Must have been from helping Grandfather. I couldn't retain names or faces from one day to the next for the longest time, but my body remembered how to do things."

"That's mighty peculiar, when you think of it."

They passed back through town and made their way south along the riverbank. The afternoon slid rapidly toward dark as it does in autumn. Frank shivered in the open car, the breeze off the water cool. He'd been in such a rush to get away from the house that he hadn't thought to get a heavier coat. No doubt the air would chill him through going home. "I remember what *you* say," he said.

Jersey laughed. "See! Nothing wrong with your head."

Frank wrestled the car's wheels across rutted road as he turned onto Swift Lane. When he straightened the wheel, Frank saw a horse rider's canvas jacket glowing red in the warm rays of the lowering sun. The man rode toward them at a trot, holding the reins of a second horse in his free hand.

Jersey stiffened and started to wave, but aborted the movement with a glance at Frank. "Hey, that's Papa—with Flash!"

Frank pulled the car to the side of the lane and stopped the engine, not wanting to risk disturbing the animals. Mr. Rohn brought the horses to a halt.

"Papa! Bet you were measuring me for a casket! I'm okay. Flash got spooked and caught me with my britches 'round my ankles. Frank offered me a ride home. Mama isn't too worried?"

Mr. Rohn might have been a Kansas farmer watching the approach of a tornado. "You know better, son. She's like to jump the fence. Thank the Creator I caught Flash before he found his way home. Your mother, she knows only you are late. Are you fit to ride?"

Jersey hesitated. "Sure, I guess I—"

"No, he isn't, Mr. Rohn," Frank said. "He's moving like a nob-kneed granny."

"Good to see you again, Mr. Huddleston."

"We've met?" Frank didn't hide his interest.

"Sorry, I guess I should…." Jersey caught Frank's attention. "Frank, this is my father, Gerald Rohn, Senior. You met when I started at your grandpa's place, but you wouldn't remember that."

Mr. Rohn nodded. "Mr. Huddleston, I thank you for looking out for my son. Now, I ask again, are you fit to ride, son? We mustn't keep your mother waiting."

"Uh…." Jersey glanced at Frank and frowned. "I'd rather not, Papa."

"So." Mr. Rohn looked from one boy to the other. "I will take the horses back and tell your mother you are on your way. Even Flash will be faster on this road than that automobile." He turned in his saddle to face Frank. "Mr. Huddleston, you will drive that thing as quickly as you may? Jersey's mother frets."

"Yes, sir."

Mr. Rohn wheeled the horses and spurred them to a canter.

"I'm going to catch hell for this," Jersey said.

"It's my fault."

"If you keep saying that, Frank, I might start believing you."

FRANK AND Jersey stepped onto the porch. Jersey could hear his mother scolding his father inside the house. "Gerald Rohn! You actually thought you would sneak those horses into the barn without my noticing? If you had gotten them past me, what then? Were you even going to tell me you found Flash? I waited through a year of nothing but 'Hi, Mama, I'm fine,' every couple of weeks from my soldier son. Am I such a child that you think me unable to bear this? Gerald Rohn, did you marry a child?"

Jersey winced and shot a glance at Frank. His letters might have been on the short side, but he'd done better than that! He heard the low rumble of his father's responses through the open door, but he couldn't make out the words.

"Mama? I'm home and we have company," Jersey called out. "Frank is here."

There followed a dead silence, followed a second later by an anguished cry. "What! You worry me half to death, and then you bring home company without warning me? Gerald Rohn, Junior, are you trying to kill me?"

Jersey's mother marched out the front door, followed quietly by Jersey's father. The tips of his father's ears were pink. He met Jersey's gaze with one that seemed to say, *She's your problem now.*

"Mama, please! This is my friend, Frank Huddleston, the Clarks' grandson. Frank, this is my mother, Marta Rohn."

"Good evening, Mrs. Rohn."

She turned to Frank with all the warmth of an eagle tracking a rabbit. "Pleased to meet you, Frank."

Frank's smile became a little fixed. "I'm sorry to have caused you worry. You see, it—"

Jersey delivered a sharp jab to Frank's left kidney. "What Frank is saying is that he was kind enough to give me a ride home after Flash wandered off from the Grange Hall."

"The only way that horse wandered off from anywhere is with an apple in front and a stick behind. How did you fall off?"

Frank's cheeks darkened. Fortunately, his mother was too focused on Jersey to notice Frank's reaction. Unfortunately, he hesitated too long trying to think up some excuse that wouldn't sound dangerous.

His mother scowled. "I thought so. I suppose you tried to jump a fence or some fool thing."

"Well, actually—" said Frank.

"Can it, Frank. It was something like that, Mama. I don't wanna talk about it."

"Jersey! That's no way to speak to company! Frank, you must be freezing," she said, softening a little. "Come in and get warm by the fire. Gerald, put another log on. Would you like something to eat, Frank?"

"Mrs. Rohn, I would be delighted to have something to eat," Frank said. Jersey gave him a high sign from behind his mother's back.

His mother went into the kitchen. While she was getting the food, Jersey told his father about the veterans' meeting and the Colonel who'd wanted to take him to dinner.

His father grimaced. "I hope you were polite to the officer."

"What do you take me for? Of course I was polite to the officer."

"But you refused him, yes?" His father shook his head.

"Well I had to get home before Mama had a conniption, didn't I?"

After serving sandwiches and hot cocoa, Jersey's mother decided Frank would stay the night. "I'm sorry we don't have a spare room for you. Jersey took the guest room after... anyway, Gerald moved the bed from his old room, and I've got my sewing things in there now, but Jersey will share with you. Jersey, get a clean towel for Frank from the linen closet."

"Yes, Mama." As Jersey swung across the room to get the towel, the muscles of his back spasmed. He froze and hung on his crutches for a moment until they loosened enough for him to continue. When he turned from the cupboard, the towel in his teeth, he caught his father watching him. His father raised his eyebrows, his face serious. Jersey continued into his room. "Good night, Papa."

"Good night, my son."

Frank splashed himself with water from the basin, washed, and dried his face.

"You don't mind sharing?" Jersey asked. "I could sleep on the sofa."

Frank laughed a little too dismissively. "And come morning, be laid out stiff as a corpse? You're already moving like you fought at Gettysburg instead of Chateau-Thierry. I appreciate the thought."

"Thank you for your consideration." Jersey knew he sounded as stiff as he felt, but Frank had the most irritating smirk.

Jersey's last thought as he lay beside Frank was that he would never be able to sleep with Frank's body putting off heat like a furnace a few inches away.

CHAPTER 10

FRANK DROWSED between the contradictory states of relaxation and arousal. As a clearing draught of consciousness washed over him, he realized his cock pressed through the thin cotton of his drawers against the knobs and indentations of Jersey's back. Before he could move away, Jersey whimpered, rolled toward him, and flung out an arm that struck Frank in the nose. He freed a hand from the covers and raised it to his face. "Good morning to you too!"

Breaking his other arm loose, he tried to catch Jersey's hand. Jersey's movements escalated to inarticulate yells and flailing arms. Frank grappled with him, making calming sounds as he tried to avoid being hit.

JERSEY WOKE, his heart racing, held firmly in the arms of a ghost. "No, Andy, no!" He struggled to free himself.

"Shh, it's Frank."

Jersey redoubled his efforts to escape Andy's reanimated corpse, twisting from side to side.

"Jersey, wake up! You're hurting me," Andy said in Frank's voice.

The terrible face suspended above Jersey transformed into Frank's. The fear drained slowly out of him, and he stopped struggling.

Frank let go of Jersey's arms and relaxed back onto his side of the bed.

Jersey's breathing slowed. "I thought you were Andy come back from the dead to get me."

"You're not dead yet. Nor am I, no thanks to you. I think my nose is bleeding. Come here, you're shivering." Frank pulled Jersey into his arms, until the length of Jersey's back rested against Frank's chest. "Shh."

Frank held Jersey until his shaking stopped. Eventually, with a faint sound that might have been a sigh, Frank rose from bed and turned his back. He stepped into his trousers, and, hopping for balance, pulled them up.

"You are very tolerant," Jersey said, examining Frank's muscular backside through his loose cotton drawers. Despite his embarrassment at displaying weakness, he wanted Frank to get back into bed so he could kiss him.

Trousers on, Frank turned around. "I have bad dreams too."

Jersey schooled his expression to friendly indifference. "Papa will be down soon." Jersey sat up. "I gotta help with the milking."

"Chores everlasting," Frank said, his expression uncharacteristically intense. He looked like he wanted to say something more. What finally came out was "I'll help."

Frank left after breakfast, having agreed to meet Jersey in two days' time at the battleship rocks. He would bring the letters.

"GRANDFATHER TOLD me they died of the Spanish influenza."

"Where were you?"

"In the hospital. I don't remember it." Frank balanced on a rock a few feet out into the river.

Jersey sat on a fallen log and repressed an urge to throw rocks at Frank. It had been all he could manage to climb down the bank to the water's edge without falling headlong into the river. How in hell was he getting back up the slippery bank without asking for help? He did not wish to discuss hospitals or think about his own stay in one. He wanted to return to the time before the war, when the future had been as open as the western horizon and all he'd needed was to find the right companion with whom to explore it. Frank would have fit the bill, but what would Frank want with a friend who'd tie him down, a friend whose disability would always be a cage around them both? He stared at Frank's broad shoulders and wondered what it would feel like to trace his fingers over them. "Wish I didn't."

"My hospital discharge papers say head injury. That could mean anything, but Eddy tells everyone I was caught in a shell explosion. I don't know whether to believe her. The discharge papers don't say anything about a unit or rank. I don't think they do, anyway. I picked up some spoken French when I was there, but I'm adrift reading it."

Jersey tried unsuccessfully to skip a rock across an eddy. "I didn't think much of the French officers. Stuck-up boobs who treated us like *we* didn't know what we was doing. The *poilus*, on the other hand, they were friendly. Course, it was officers gave me those tin medals. Shows what they knew."

"Why do you always act so peeved about the medals? Do you regret what you did?"

"I didn't deserve any medals. Other guys were better soldiers."

Frank hopped to another rock and smiled at Jersey. "Surely not."

"What in hell do you know? You don't know what *you* did, much less what *I* did." Jersey hurled a rock into the river, splashing Frank's boots.

"What are you so hot about? I can't believe you did anything to be ashamed of."

"You wanna know? To remember?" Jersey batted his stump. "Just after I got mine, the Germans opened up with a machine gun and cut down my best pal and the sergeant while they were finishing off the jerry who shot me. It was my fault! I knew the kid was still breathing, and I knew what I ought to do, but I looked at his face, and I couldn't do it. Then he up and shot me, and my buddy and the sergeant stopped to do what I couldn't do, and they got killed for it. I was soft and my friends got killed for it."

"Come on, Jersey. You can't think it was your fault. You couldn't know what would happen."

"It was my fault—my leg, their lives—because I was soft."

Frank jumped back to shore and sat down next to Jersey. "Don't you think there's something to be cherished in that kind of softness?"

"Not when it gets your friends killed."

"But you couldn't know that would happen."

"It doesn't matter what I knew or didn't know."

"Okay, so you're soft. I don't think I was even a soldier. I don't know what I was doing in France, but I doubt I was sticking people with bayonets."

Jersey watched a turtle snap at a water bug as it walked across the surface of the eddy. "Why hold off? Give me the damn letters, if you won't read 'em yourself, and let's see what we can find out."

Frank stood up again and stared out at the rushing water. "I'm afraid I won't recognize my mother and father."

"You sure won't hear them. Christ! You'll be hearing me. Sit down already!"

Frank turned to look at Jersey, his expression serious. "That's why I want you to read them." His face colored. "I mean, I like your voice."

Jersey rolled his eyes. What was the big deal about hearing him talk? Anybody could talk. "Give me the damn letters."

Frank pulled the letters from his shirt and handed them to Jersey. He opened the oldest of them.

"Dear Francis—"

"My God, Eddy even changed my blasted name!"

"Put a sock in it, Frank."

Germantown Friends School

June 2, 1918

Dear Francis,

> *I am pleased to learn that thy ears are not closed to God, even as thee provide service in support of the war effort.*

Jersey stopped. "Why does he talk funny? It's like that confounded Shakespeare Miss Roberts made us read in school."

Frank swallowed a couple of times as he stared out over the river. "It's called plain speech. Quakers don't believe in differences of caste or class. It is a testimony—a way of showing one's beliefs in one's actions."

"It don't sound plain to me. Was your father religious?"

Frank pulled each word as from a well. "We went to Friends Meeting… I don't know. I don't know how I know about the plain speech. Everything's so… it's there and then it's not."

"What's Friends Meeting?"

"That's what Quakers call their religious meetings. Keep going, would you?"

> *Thy feelings regarding the treatment of Negro soldiers show that thy inner light shines untarnished. Keep listening to thy heart and thee will find the right path.*
>
> *Your mother and I walked in the park today where we spent so many hours when thee was small. We were reminded of the time thee found a fallen nest containing a newborn chick. Thee insisted on attempting to nurse it to maturity. Thee failed, of course. A chick that young could not survive without its mother. But we were proud of thee for trying.*
>
> *We may not always agree, son, but we love and respect thee for thy convictions and thy testimony.*
>
> *In Truth and Love,*
>
> *Thy Father*

"I hope you got more from that than I did," Jersey said. "What does he mean by 'thy service in support of the war effort'? It's a queer way to talk about soldiering."

Frank's eyes narrowed. "I don't know. I still can't remember anything of that time. What was that about Negro soldiers, I wonder? The Friends are pacifists. It is one of the testimonies: the testimony of peace. He would not have approved of soldiering in any form."

"Anything else tickle your gray matter?"

"I remember the park he mentions. I think so, anyway. There were trees and flowers and paths and"—he waved at the river—"a creek or river. It has been in my head since we got here. I thought it was just an imaginary place, my private Xanadu, but when he mentioned the chick, I knew it was real." The sides of his mouth twitched. "And the plain speech. That rings familiar."

"I'm glad this ain't been entirely fruitless," Jersey said. "Want me to read another?" Now that they were making progress, he was eager to see what else Frank might remember.

Frank didn't answer, but continued to stare out over the river.

Jersey lost patience. "Watson, come here!"

"What? Yes. Please read another."

Jersey looked down at the thin paper in his hand. "Okay, this one's from July. It's kinda scribbled."

Dear Francis,

It is beastly hot today. I long for the past when I could sneak down to the creek near my father's farm and swim. Girls were not supposed to do such things, of course, but that part of the county is nearly devoid of people, so the chances of getting caught were small. My mother rarely left the house on a hot day, preferring to sit in the shade of the porch and fan herself during those rare moments when she wasn't cooking or cleaning. I only had to watch out for Papa. He caught me once when I was about twelve. I don't know who was more shocked, him or me. He waited until I came home—fully dressed, of course—and beat me black and blue.

I hope conditions there are more bearable and that the Huns are quiescent. Do be careful and don't spend any more time at the Front than you must. I know your work is important. Someone must help those poor men who have been so horribly maimed, but don't let yourself catch a wild punch from standing too close to the brawl.

Mrs. Newton says that I am altogether too fancy of dress for the wife of a teacher at the Friends School. I am going to try to make amends by baking her an apple pie. I am not, however, taking the lace off the frock I just finished. It is much too pretty! Your poor father is so earnest in his attempts to explain to me the testimony of simplicity, but I remain incorrigible.

Your loving
Mama

"Now that's more like it," Jersey said, laughing. "She sounds lively."

"Yes, she does." Frank smiled, but Jersey saw the shine of tears in his eyes.

Jersey looked through the letters in his hands. "There's another in the same hand."

Frank pounded his forehead. "I can't see her face—nor my father's. Am I to know her only from her letters?"

"Give yourself time. You've only just started to regain your memory." Jersey held up another sheet. "Do you want me to read this?"

"No, put it away. I can't do this anymore."

Jersey handed the letters back. They sat in silence on the riverbank, and Jersey watched the stone battleships of his childhood, their bows thrusting aside the rushing water, making their steadfast way to glory.

"WHAT HAVE you got against him?" Frank railed at his grandmother. "He's my friend. I will see him if I wish."

"Not in my house, you won't!" Eddy's face was red, but her pursed lips looked like dried onion.

"Then I will leave *your* house." It was early in the afternoon, and he had sidled into the kitchen to catch Eddy before she began dinner. Clearly, he'd chosen a poor time. He stamped out, rattling the plates in the glass-fronted cabinet where Eddy kept her best china. The argument had started when Frank raised the idea of inviting Jersey to dinner. He'd known that Eddy would resist, but he had not expected her to refuse outright. How was it that they saw such different things in Jersey? He saw laughing eyes and wild energy, motion caged in an uncooperative body. Grandmother saw Jersey as a threat.

Outside, the sky faded to a permeable gray that seemed to absorb all light. He headed toward the barn to find Charlie.

"Grandfather, you there?" he called out.

"In the tack room."

Frank found Charlie at the table with his leather tools laid out before him. Charlie motioned him to pull a stool over from the corner. "What can I do for you?"

"Grandfather, why is Grandmother so aggrieved about Jersey?"

Charlie took a punch from the row of tools on the table, placed it carefully in the center of a long strap, and hit it lightly with a mallet. "I can't rightly say, Frank."

"But you must have some idea."

"Maybe." Charlie carefully measured an inch from the hole he'd just punched and placed the punch in position. Frank, usually content to watch Charlie work, found the experience like waiting for a hen to lay. "She's not one to question her feelings."

"What does that—"

Charlie hit the punch with his mallet. "What does Jersey mean to you?"

"Jersey is my friend... my only friend."

Charlie grunted. "It's likely her own words that are stuck in her craw. It's all over town and circulating among the church ladies that Jersey was a big hero in France—won medals and all. I never heard a word of it from him, but I guess the Rasmussen kid mentioned the medals when they were planning the veterans' meeting and word got around. Whereas you—it's not your fault, seeing you were brought up along your father's kin down in Philadelphia—but you being a pacifist and a conscientious objector was hard for her to explain. I'm talking about 1917, with the flag waving and all the boys joining up. Eddy was uncomfortable with you being a conscientious objector and she kind of let people think her grandson was a soldier. You were over there, after all. Then you got hurt, the Spanish flu came along, and your parents passed...." Charlie cleared his throat and looked down at the punch in his hand. "Well. Here you are, word gets out that you might not actually have been a soldier, and Eddy's caught in a lie."

"None of that is Jersey's fault."

"Nope." Charlie picked up his mallet again. "But that boy is salt to Eddy's wounds."

"What am I supposed to do? Jersey and I are friends." Frank picked up a bit of leather and twisted it in his hands as the import of Charlie's words hit him. "What was I doing in France if I wasn't a soldier? Surely my parents told you."

Charlie finished measuring for the next hole, marked the spot with an awl, then put down his tools and looked at Frank without speaking. Red scalp showed through his thinning pale hair.

"Actually, they didn't," said Charlie finally. "Your mother and grandmother, they didn't get along. Adele gave up on Eddy, and Eddy pretty much disowned Adele. Called her a tra—said some pretty mean things about her, said she wasn't a fit member of society." He picked up his awl again. "Her society."

"What about you? She was your daughter. Didn't you stay in touch?"

"I wrote her pretty regular, but she blamed me for not standing up for her enough against her mother. Leastways, she didn't often write back."

"Did she tell you I was a conscientious objector?"

"Nope. We got a letter from the local board in Philadelphia asking about your religious beliefs when you applied for CO status. We told them we didn't know anything."

"THEY REALLY got no notion what you were doing in France?" Jersey was incredulous.

"Nope. Grandfather said he hoped we could figure it out from the letters. To be fair, I don't think he expected I'd sit on them so long."

"Me neither."

The day was cool. Jersey and Frank lounged in the hayloft at the Rohn farm. They'd retreated there for privacy after Jersey rode Flash into town with a spare horse for Frank.

After greeting him, Frank had smiled shyly and admitted that he'd brought his kit so he could stay overnight if that was okay. Jersey had flushed from head to toe, glad he was up on Flash so Frank couldn't see the effect on him.

"What did Eddy say?"

"Didn't talk to her. I left a note saying I was going visiting and would be back in a few days."

"Bet she's steamed."

"I don't care."

On the way to the house, they'd been mostly silent, Frank apparently content to enjoy the ride without conversation, his gaze shifting from side to side as he pointed, without comment, to birds or trees that interested him, confident that Jersey would understand what had caught his interest. Jersey was content to watch Frank. When they reached the house Jersey had suggested the loft for privacy.

"You ready to read 'em now?" Jersey said, pointing at the letters stuffed in Frank's shirt pocket.

Frank leaned back against a bale, his expression unreadable. "Not really."

"But you're gonna do it anyway, ain't you?"

Frank handed the sheaf of letters to Jersey. Jersey looked over the first letter briefly before clearing his throat. He recognized the same precise handwriting he'd seen in the first letter.

> *Dear Francis,*
>
> *We've heard from the AFAU that thee have been hurt. The telegram says only that thee have sustained a head injury, but it says nothing of thy condition or prognosis. Your mother and I pray this note finds thee recovered. I beg thee, if thee is able, write with news of thy health. There is surely no more humbling condition than the impotence of a father who knows his son to be in jeopardy and cannot help. I know thee to be secure in God's keeping, but God has seen fit to separate many fathers from their sons this year.*
>
> *Your mother paces from kitchen to parlor and back like a caged lioness, her mind occupied with thoughts of thee.*
>
> *Thy Loving Papa*

Jersey waved the letter like a pennant and tossed hay into the air with his free hand. "I know what you did! The AFAU, that's the American Friends Ambulance Unit. I heard of them, but I didn't realize they were Quaker. I didn't connect it up until just now. They operated a *Section Sanitaire*, an ambulance unit, for the French army." He shook Frank's shoulder. "You were an ambulance driver. No wonder you know the Tin Lizzy. You might have carried me to the hospital when I was shot. How your mother must have fretted! I wrote to my parents about my missing pin myself, so they'd know I was all right, but you couldn't because of your head injury."

"I doubt they would have used *all right* to describe your condition," Frank said. "At least they were not held in suspense as my parents were. How fierce my mother sounds! There is another letter, isn't there? I wonder if they found out what happened to me before they…." He fell silent and dug a small trench in the hay with his boot.

Jersey held out the last of the letters. "You want…?" He was still unsure why he was doing all the reading—not that he minded—but it was strange Frank didn't just read them himself.

"No, you read it."

"Okay, this one's dated September 28, 1918."

Dear Francis,

O darling! How dare you wait so long to write! You have spoiled us with regular missives. Your father is bereft as a hound locked in the yard while his master strolls the park. We have written everyone we can think of for news. The AFAU tell us only that you are not ready to leave the hospital where you were taken after your adventure. The hospital authorities tell us that you are "dans les mains de Dieu." Between those fools and your father, with his talk of God's plan, I want to rend napkins with my teeth. If we do not hear something soon, I shall set sail for Europe to retrieve you myself.

In the meantime, to fill the hours, I have volunteered at the school infirmary to help nurse children who have fallen ill with the Spanish flu. We have so many sick, there is talk of canceling classes. Frankly, I hope they don't, for I don't know what I should do with your father moping around the house all day. He loves you so and worries that he was too harsh when you announced your plan to drive an ambulance.

I took the streetcar downtown this morning, quite forgetting in my state of distraction that there was to be a great parade and rally to sell Liberty Bonds. It was so crowded, I turned back without purchasing a single thing.

*Please write and tell us that you are all right and will return
soon to*

Your loving, impatient Mama

"I can't comprehend how she can touch me so, yet remain a shadow in my mind." Frank hunched his shoulders and picked at the hay between his legs.

Jersey could see he'd teared up again. "Quit that." He threw a handful of stalks at Frank. "I'm like to bawl myself if y' keep that up. Ain't nobody with a mama could read that without leaking some."

Frank snorted. "I expect you were too busy looking at pretty girls to listen when they were teaching grammar?"

"It wasn't the girls I was eyeballing." The words emerged from Jersey's mouth before he could stop them. *You moron! What's he gonna think of you now?*

Frank smiled. "Some of us grow up more quickly than others."

"It ain't that I...." Jersey wanted to make a joke of it, but the dishonesty of it stopped him. "I ever tell ya 'bout my friend Andy?"

"He was the one killed when you were shot." Frank regarded him with disconcerting fondness. "You cry out for him at night."

Jersey felt blood heat his face.

IT WAS the best day of his life—so Jersey thought at the time. Their unit was taking possession of a sawdust-filled barrack that would be their home for basic training. They marched past a long row of identical two story buildings that still smelled of tar and fresh-cut lumber, a ragged line of greenhorns hauling stiff canvas duffels. The sergeant barked an order and they filed into a building distinguishable from the others only by the number stenciled on its side.

Jersey claimed a cot and stowed his gear, then looked up to notice a blond giant on the other side of the room. The giant was a head taller than the men around him, with a glowing corona of hair from the sun streaming through the open windows. He threw his head back to laugh at something and caught Jersey staring at him. His laughter died and he stared back for an instant, then grinned. Jersey grinned back, amazed.

A few days later, the army decided that boxing was good for morale and fitness. They counted off into groups for instruction and Andy and Jersey got the same number. Jersey shoved his way up to the blond giant where he waited for his turn to spar with the instructor and poked him in the side. He nodded toward the short fellow who was up first. "Mama didn't feed him enough beefsteak."

Andy turned and grinned. "Gotta be a miner—pale as a mushroom. But look at the arms, like pile drivers."

"That one ain't done growing," Jersey said, pointing at another.

"His shoulders aren't as wide as my hips," Andy countered.

"Long arms, watch out for his cross."

"Listen to you! You didn't know a cross from a jab until five minutes ago."

When it was his turn, Jersey was conscious of Andy's grin from the sidelines spurring him on. From that day, he and Andy sought each other out in the rare moments of leisure that camp life permitted. They sat together at meals. Later, when Jersey began fighting in the camp boxing competitions, he always looked to see if Andy was among the yelling men crowding around the makeshift ring. If he questioned why it should matter to him so much whether or not his friend cheered him on, it was not a matter to which he devoted much thought. When they talked about boxing, Andy said that he didn't really understand what made men want to fight when they didn't have to. Jersey didn't mind, so long as Andy watched him.

"WHAT ABOUT Andy?" Frank said.

Jersey lurched into motion and threw a handful of hay at Frank. "I dunno. I was just thinkin' about him."

Frank retaliated with more stalks. In an instant, they filled the air with debris like an autumn gale.

CHAPTER II

FRANK AND Jersey hoisted Mama's German-style apple pancakes like a matched pair of steam shovels. Jersey's father put down his coffee cup and stilled in the way that meant he had something serious to say. Jersey glanced at Frank and found his friend's attention already focused on his father.

"Jersey, it's time we talk about your future."

"Now?" *With company in the house?* His mama slipped through the door from the kitchen and perched on a straight-backed chair next to the door.

"You have been home with us now for eight months, and while your mama and I thank God—" He cleared his throat. "—thank God for returning you to us, we worry about your future. A day will come when I can no longer work the farm, but it seems God does not mean for you to be a farmer."

"Yeah sure, Papa, I know I gotta figure something out, but why bring it up—"

"Son, is it not right that such things should be discussed with your family?"

Jersey glanced at Frank again. Frank seemed transfixed by his father.

His father nodded toward Frank. "Family. When we went to the hospital to bring you home, they told you that you should return in six months to see about getting a pros—" His gaze slid to Jersey's mother.

"Prosthetic leg," she said.

"A prosthetic leg. We see how the crutches hurt you, how they leave you bruised and sore. Don't you want a better way to get around, one that might open doors for you?" Jersey's father reached into his vest pocket to pull out his pipe and tobacco.

"Sure, I guess." Reeling from his father's admission that he would not always be able to manage the farm and his decision to treat Frank as family, Jersey shifted uncomfortably in his chair, plucking at his pant leg where it was pinned below his stump. He'd meant to go back to the hospital. He'd been distracted.

Jersey's father methodically loaded his pipe and struck one of the wooden matches he carried in his pockets. He held the flame to the bowl until the pipe drew to his satisfaction. "Have you considered what work you might do?"

Such thoughts had Jersey rattling around looking for something to do with his hands. The only time he'd ever felt confident was boxing in the army. But there was no living in that, even if you had a full complement of limbs.

"Perhaps you will do that while we plan a trip to the hospital."

FRANK CONCENTRATED on the white smoke curling out of Mr. Rohn's pipe and willed the confusion from his face. His mind whorled. He was family now? Surely, Mr. Rohn couldn't know what Frank felt when he looked at Jersey. Even *he* wasn't certain why he wanted to protect Jersey. What did Mr. Rohn mean by including him in this way? He probably just meant to acknowledge their friendship.

As his face cooled, Frank's thoughts cleared. *He's Jersey's father, right? So it's not you he's concerned about, you dolt, it's Jersey. He thinks you can help Jersey get moving again, and he wants you to understand the stakes. He wants you to know you're at bat and the bases are loaded. Jersey's been on the porch since he returned from France, and the first thing that got him off it was the job working for my grandparents. Maybe he thinks I had something to do with that.*

But he had to leave! He had to go to Philadelphia to find out more about his family. He had known it would be necessary since Jersey read the last letter from his mother and she referred to his letters from France. His letters would help him remember. But he couldn't help Jersey if he left now. "Where does one get a prosthetic leg?" he asked. "Who makes them? They don't make them at the hospital, do they?"

"I dunno," Jersey said. "Before I left the hospital, they took me to this workshop where they fitted all kinds of braces, artificial legs, and even mechanical arms for people. That's when they said I should come back in six months, after my stump was healed. But I don't think they made 'em there." Jersey seemed to warm to the subject. He probably wanted to shift the topic away from what he was going to do for the rest of his life. "Some had a manufacturer stamped on them. I saw this one that bent at the knee. It was spring-loaded so that—"

"All right, all right," said Mrs. Rohn, glancing at her husband. "You've got a lot to say for somebody who can't be bothered to get a leg of his own."

Jersey shrugged. "I've been distracted."

THE NEXT day, Jersey convinced Frank to let him help with his riding. Frank wasn't sure he really wanted to be perched on the back of a horse, clutching the saddle horn in one hand and the reins in the other, but it was important to Jersey, and it gave Frank a chance to try and convince Jersey to accompany him to Philadelphia.

"Like this. See how I move when I wanna go this way?" said Jersey.

"Kind of. Have you thought about Philadelphia?"

"Focus on what you're doing, Frank! We can jaw about Philadelphia later."

"I've got to start home pretty soon."

"What's everyone in such a damn hurry for?" Jersey shifted his weight and circled Flash around Frank and Stilts, Frank's loaner for the day. "You got someone special waiting for you back on the farm?"

"You know I don't, but Grandfather and Grandmother will worry if I don't get back. I told you I planned to go home today."

"What difference will a few hours make? The sun is out, the clouds are floating along like dandelion seeds, and all you can think of is leaving." While he talked, Jersey guided Flash around in tight circles.

"You've gotten better since you fell off in the middle of Main Street."

Jersey grinned. "Been practicing. Gotta be ready when I see you coming. Jeez, you're holding those reins like they're snakes."

Frank tried to get his horse to follow Flash. Jersey looked over his shoulder and grinned. "Riding Flash is about the only time I do get around easy. That's why I'm not fired up about going to Philadelphia. How am I gonna get around there? Ya see me climbing onto a streetcar? Like as not lose my other pin."

"We could get an automobile."

"Right. Then you'd have to drive me everywhere."

"I wouldn't mind."

"I sure as heck would. Where'd we get the money for an automobile anyway?"

"You ever apply to get your veterans' bonus from the state?" Frank asked.

Jersey turned his horse again. "Y'know, there was this French staff officer who used to drive his Renault to our division to deliver written orders. He had a wooden leg, but he could drive all right."

"I thought not." Frank's horse took advantage of his distraction and drifted to a halt.

"Funny how you can remember how to drive and all. Makes you wonder, don't it? Maybe it'll all come back someday." The excitement in Jersey's voice had Flash's ears twitching.

"Don't you see? That's why I have to go to Philadelphia—to find the letters I wrote to my parents. Think about what might happen when we read them."

"We? Still can't recall how to read for yourself? Anyway, they've probably thrown them all away."

"Goddammit, Jersey!" Frank swung a leg over and slid off Stilts, who had already put his head down to nibble the grass at the base of a fence post. "I'm going home." He headed toward the house.

"Frank, I'm sorry," Jersey called. "I didn't mean—how're you getting home anyhow?"

"Rather walk than listen to you," Frank said under his breath as he mounted the steps to the porch.

Jersey caught up to Frank in the little bedroom off the kitchen and in his hurry banged the doorframe with a crutch. Frank flinched.

"Come on, Frank. I'm sorry! It was a stupid thing for me to say. I wasn't thinking."

"Thinking isn't your strong suit, is it?" Frank gathered his possessions and stuffed them into his duffel.

"I said I was sorry." Jersey leaned on the wall behind him.

"So you did." Frank's heart pounded and his face felt like he'd leaned over an open stove. He picked up his bag and walked out the door.

JERSEY LAY face down in his bed and pounded the pillow. *I am so stupid.* He'd been having so much fun. Then he'd gone and gotten carried away. He knew how much recovering his past meant to Frank. It was as important to Frank as getting a new leg was to him. If only getting the leg didn't mean visiting a hospital—worse, visiting a hospital in the middle of the city where people would stare at his empty pant leg. There would be streetcar rails to trip over and automobiles and wagons and horses and children to avoid. He hadn't felt so jittery since they'd formed up to run across that stupid field in France. Why hadn't he just told Frank? The guy already knew he was soft. He knew the answer. He liked showing off in front of Frank. He had to be the big man. *See what it got you, stupid.*

Jersey came awake in the usual way, gasping like a diver who'd stayed under too long. He concentrated on his breathing and waited to regain control of his limbs. He did not understand how his dream could be so familiar and at the same time so terrifying. The war had rent his mind and body. To the body he inhabited but did not control, the dream was no less horrific than the actual events that were its origin. His wayward limbs shook as much now as the first time he relived Andy's death at the whitewashed hospital in Nantes. It did not matter that the events he dreamed about had already taken place and couldn't be helped.

In the hospital, floating on a cloud of morphine, he'd been unable to take in the loss of his leg. It didn't matter that the men in the ward around him had similar injuries—missing arms or legs. One man even had a missing jaw. Jersey still pictured himself walking out of the hospital intact, stopping at beds here and there to drop words of encouragement like a visiting general. He'd tell a joke or two and wish the man a speedy recovery, and then walk out on two good legs. His mind and body were one in the delusion of wholeness: the phantom pain was a persistent assertion that his leg was still attached.

Missing Frank's steady breathing to set a tempo for his own, Jersey finally rose and went into the kitchen. He pulled his bathrobe tightly around himself, huddled in a chair, and waited for the thump of his father's boots to signal the beginning of the day.

He started awake for the second time with the clunk of a plate on the table where his forehead rested. The smell of bacon set his mouth to watering. "Smells good." He rubbed grit from his eyes and looked around. "Where's Papa?"

His mother set down a second plate of eggs and bacon and sat across from him.

"Finishing the chores. I wanted to wake you, but he said to leave you."

"I should help him."

"Eat your breakfast. He'll be back in a few minutes. I want to talk to you." She wiped her hands on her apron and took up the gauntlet. "Have you thought about what your father said to you the other day?"

"I am not a child anymore, Mama! Leave me alone!" Ambushed, his resentment came out shrill.

"You've no call to snap at me, Jersey."

Jersey lowered the pitch of his voice. "I don't need you or Papa to tell me what to do."

"We're not telling you what to do." She rested her hand on Jersey's arm, her gentle touch shaming him. "We just want you to find a life that will make you happy."

He snatched his arm away and pulled his robe tight. His mother flinched. "I'm sure enough not gonna find it here. That's why... that's why I'm going to Philadelphia with Frank." It wasn't until the words came from his mouth that he realized he'd made the decision.

His mother's eyes widened. "Philadelphia? Why Philadelphia? What could you possibly—"

"That's where Frank grew up. His parents died there. Frank sent letters to Philadelphia from France, and he thinks we might be able to find 'em. They might help him remember stuff. I can go to a hospital there to see about a leg."

He watched his mother's face pass from worry, through surprise, to interest. She never could resist a story.

"When Adele Clark ran off with that Quaker fella who came to speak at the Grange Hall, she went back to Philadelphia with him? Is that where his family came from? Did they get married there?"

"They must've. Frank's people, they're called Friends, even speak funny, like in olden times. Frank calls it plain speech, but it sounds more fancy than plain to me."

"Has Frank been in touch with them? Does he know their names?"

"Frank's last name is Huddleston, and we know his father taught at the Germantown Friends School in Philadelphia. That should be enough to get us started."

She leaned forward, her eyes wide. "They're not German, like our people?"

"How should I know?"

Dear Frank,

Did I stick my foot in my mouth! What I said about people tossing away your letters was thoughtless and stupid. Please forgive me. I want to be a better pal. Whatever the chance those letters are still sitting in a drawer somewhere, you should look for them! Likewise, you have every right to ask that I—as your friend—help you find out more about your life before the war, and that I take seriously your notion that we go to Philadelphia together.

What I'm trying to say is that I have come around to your way of thinking. The truth of it is, I've been nervous about the trip because of my leg, and because I find the noise and crowding in cities wearing. But that's of no account. I've decided that I want to go to Philadelphia with you.

Did I tell you the Red Cross hospital in Nantes where they took me to recover after I lost my leg was organized by the Jefferson College and Hospital? That's in Philadelphia. There's a doctor I'd like to look up if he's back from France.

Your sorry friend,

Jersey

Dear Jersey,

Sorry you may be. A sorry friend you are not. I got upset because I was worried that you were right. Why would strangers save my letters? You are not a thoughtless person, even if your mouth does sometimes get a little ahead of your head. I was trying to hurt you when I said that. What kind of person does that make me? I'm sorry too.

Are you sure about the trip? I know it's a lot to ask.

Frank

CHAPTER 12

CHILL AIR flowed from the open window when Frank rolled out of bed. He dressed in traveling clothes—the same wool suit and vest, white shirt, and black tie he wore to church. Moving precisely to keep from making any sound, he picked up his shoes and the carpetbag he'd packed after Charlie and Eddy went to bed. He tiptoed down the stairs to the kitchen and took a half loaf of bread from the breadbox. Ripping off a hunk, he chewed while he knelt to put on his shoes. The remaining bread went into his pocket where it took the place of a letter, which he set on the kitchen table.

His breath steamed in the faint, predawn light as he trudged up the hill toward the top of the ridge. He did not look back, but he did briefly imagine himself the star of a different departure, one that took place in bright sun and featured Eddy and Charlie waving from the porch. Eddy's attitude prevented that leave-taking. She countenanced neither Jersey's participation in the trip, nor the idea of Frank traveling without first contacting his remaining family in Pennsylvania. Frank wasn't waiting. Who knew how many months and how many letters it might take to track down Frank's remaining family? Frank had the name of the Germantown Friends School and its location in Philadelphia. That was enough. Inquiries would be easier in the city where he'd lived—and he wouldn't have to spend the winter in the chill of Eddy's disapproval. The letter explaining his decision would do. His only regret was that his abrupt departure would hurt Charlie.

At the top of the ridge, he switched his bag to his other hand. The plan was to meet Jersey and his father in Taperville. Jersey's father would give them a ride in his wagon to Kalamazoo, where they would catch the train to Fort Wayne. From there, the Pennsylvania railroad would take them through Pittsburgh and Harrisburg to Philadelphia—in about sixteen hours. The fare would take almost all their pooled resources, but he thrust that concern aside. He thought, instead, about Jersey's letter and the value Jersey seemed to place on their friendship. He began to whistle.

FRANK COULDN'T tell what seemed odd about the man in the silk top hat and yellow waistcoat. The old fellow had to be seventy or more. Lank white hair, as thin as his mustache was luxuriant, escaped from under his hat. The man leaned back on the bench in front of the station with his legs stretched out, his eyes invisible under his wide-brimmed hat. Presently, he took out a long black cigar. He put it between his teeth, unlit, and worked it ruminatively. Maybe the oddness came from the way the man kept one leg stretched out straight as a ruler, while he kept the other one bent.

Frank and Jersey sat on their carpetbags in front of the former Grand Rapids and Indiana Railroad terminal in Kalamazoo. They waited for the train that would take them down to Fort Wayne, on the first leg of their journey to Philadelphia. When they had purchased their tickets, the stationmaster told them the GR&I was part of the Pennsylvania Railroad. The GR&I might be Pennsylvania owned, thought Frank, but the government was still running the railroad, as it had since the war.

The old fellow sighed, lifted his hat, and placed his unlit cigar underneath. He leaned forward and grasped his left ankle with both hands, then pulled his leg into a bent position. After planting his boot firmly, he crouched over his knees and popped upright like a jack-in-the-box. Jersey gasped. Once the man stabilized himself, he gave Jersey a slow examination that terminated at Jersey's empty pant leg. "Good luck to you," he said, tipping his hat. Jersey's mouth dropped open. The man lurched out of sight around the side of the building.

"Don't worry, Jersey, your new leg won't be like that fellow's." Frank paused dramatically. "You lost your *right* leg."

Jersey closed his mouth with a click.

Frank held his breath. After a tense couple of seconds, he was relieved to see a quiver around Jersey's shoulders, and then they were laughing like kids at a circus.

"His leg must be spring-loaded!"

"That man—" Frank gasped. "—put his... cigar... in his... hat!"

WHEN HIS hilarity subsided to an occasional hiccup, Jersey heard a distant whistle—two long, one short, one long—the engineer's warning before a crossing.

"Suppose that's ours?" he said, struggling to stand.

Frank jumped up to peer through the window into the depot's waiting room. "It's time. I'll grab the bags. You just get yourself on board."

"Quit worrying. You're like an old woman. I'll be fine."

Jersey heard chugging and the clang of the train's bell before the locomotive came into sight. He flinched at the sudden noise and checked whether Frank had noticed, but he needn't have worried. Frank watched the train with a silly grin on his face, their bags in his hands. Eventually, the locomotive passed and the cars came squealing to a halt. A long burst of steam and wet ash signaled the release of pressure from the boiler. As if to drive the point home, the engineer let off a final scream on the whistle.

The conductor swung down from a car's vestibule. "All aboard for Fort Wayne!"

They waited for a man and woman to get off the train. The man wore a tweed jacket and jodhpurs and carried a long set of fishing poles. Frank raised his eyebrows and tried to catch Jersey's eye, but Jersey ignored him, his attention on the steps leading to the car's vestibule. Jersey swung into motion as soon as the way was clear, but Frank reached the car first. The conductor motioned him up, but Frank put down the bags and turned to Jersey. "You go ahead."

Jersey handed his crutches to the conductor. "Hand me those when I get up."

"Yes, sir, I will. Watch the steps! You don't need a boost?" said the conductor.

"No, thanks." Jersey grabbed the metal railings and hopped up a step at a time.

The conductor handed up the crutches. "Find yourself a seat quick as you can. You don't want to be maneuvering when we start out."

Frank leaped up the steps into the vestibule. "I'll get him situated."

Jersey turned his back to Frank and moved down the aisle. "This do?" He threw his crutches onto an open seat and sat without waiting for a response.

Frank stowed their bags and slid in next to Jersey. "What's eating you?"

"You don't have to be so goddamned helpful. I'm not a child."

"Sorry, pal. I know you can take care of yourself."

Jersey grunted and looked out at the yellow brick depot. A porter rolled a handcart stacked with expensive leather cases toward the depot. "Those've gotta be for the fella with the fishing poles."

Frank grinned. "I expect so."

THE TRAIN rattled south to Indiana. Jersey thought they must be going thirty miles an hour—a lot better than Flash could do. He squinted at a flash of sunlight off the rails where a gondola sat in a siding by a grain elevator. The country was mostly flat fields of stubble or raw earth, punctuated by the occasional creek or small river, but the speed made the view exciting. Frank extracted a hunk of bread from his pocket and offered it to Jersey. It was fresh, and the smell—even competing with steam, lubricating oil, ash, and worn upholstery—set Jersey's mouth watering. "Hey," he said, chewing, "we'll have time to get something to eat in Fort Wayne, right?"

"We will," Frank said. "The station master said the Broadway Limited has to pass through before we can catch the local. That's the way to travel! They've got no coaches at all on the Limited, just sleepers and a dining car. They get from Chicago to New York in twenty hours. I'm surprised they're still running it, what with the Feds in charge."

Jersey laughed. "Rich folks always gonna find a way to their pleasures. That train's not for the likes of us."

"Maybe not," Frank said. "But I intend to watch her go by."

IN FORT Wayne, they bought sandwiches from a vendor near the station and returned to wait for the Limited. Frank got a good look when it glided in, steaming like a thoroughbred, the K4 "Pacific" locomotive pulling gleaming Tuscan-red cars. It was dusk and the cars brightly lit. In the dining car, men in black suits and starched shirts escorted women in elegant gowns. One man lifted a lady's hand to his lips.

"That's class!" Jersey said, smoothing his curly hair into place.

"Too flashy for my taste," Frank said. It was fun to catch a glimpse of another world, but the truth was that plain suited him better.

Their train was due at 8:03 p.m. Jersey fell asleep on a bench in the barrel-vaulted waiting area of the Pennsylvania Railroad terminal. Frank watched the comings and goings of the passengers, their voices and leather-soled shoes echoing in the stone and marble room. Although the war had been over for months, there were still many soldiers in khaki uniforms and Western-style service hats. He jerked out of a doze when he heard Philadelphia mentioned on the loudspeaker. It was dark, the lamps forming yellow pools on the boarding platform.

"Jersey, wake up. They've announced our train."

"Whasamatter?" Jersey rolled upright and rubbed his eyes.

"It's time to go outside. Our train is coming."

They stepped onto the platform and got a blast of cinders and steam from the passing locomotive.

"I think I got something in my eye," Jersey said, blinking. "Christ, that burns."

"Hold still. Let me look." Frank took Jersey's head in his hands and angled it toward the light. Jersey's right eye streamed, but there wasn't enough light to see the cause of the problem.

"Can you wait until we get on?"

"Got no choice, do I?" Blinking furiously, Jersey swung down the tracks toward the open vestibule.

"All aboard for Lima, Crestline, Pittsburgh, Altoona, Harrisburg, and Philadelphia!"

Jersey reached the end of the car. Frank followed, carrying their bags. The conductor was speaking to another passenger, his back to them. Before Frank could say anything to get his attention, Jersey put his arm through the center of his crutches, took hold of the metal handrails, and hopped up to the first step. A crutch caught in the steps and pushed him off balance. Swearing, he let go of the handrail to free the crutch. Trying to grab the rail again, he missed and fell backward with a cry—into Frank's arms.

"Careful there, sir," said the conductor, turning around.

"It's a good thing you don't weigh much," Frank said. "You all right?"

"Goddammit!"

"There's no call for that, sir. Your friend's got you," said the conductor.

"Why don't you let me handle your crutches, this time," Frank said. "Just get yourself up."

Jersey would not look at Frank, but allowed him to take the crutches before hopping up the steps a second time. After they found seats, Jersey excused himself to go to the toilet and see to his eye. Mutely declining an offer of help, he left his crutches and hopped down the aisle, holding the seats on either side.

Frank waited, gazing out the window into the darkness. After some minutes, when Jersey had not returned, Frank got up to investigate. He stopped outside the toilet, poised to knock. Hearing sniffling from inside the compartment, he returned to his seat to wait and to stare out into the night.

JERSEY WOKE to find he had hoisted a tent pole, as his army buddies would have said. His erection pressed uncomfortably against his trousers. Frank slumped, his knees pressed against the seat ahead, his head resting on Jersey's arm, his mouth open. Jersey considered a trip to the toilet, but he hesitated to move lest he wake Frank. Instead, he sleepily admired Frank's muscular thighs. His prick strained harder, intent on producing the most mortifying display possible.

It was familiar torture. The barrack showers at Fort Custer had afforded no privacy. He'd managed with cold water and eyes focused on the tile floor. His interest in men's bodies was wrong. He knew that. As a kid, it had been a mystery, one of many mysteries centering around his own and his schoolmates' bodies, such as why Jimmy Talbot grew bright red pubic hair at age thirteen, while Jersey did not grow his own dark, tightly curled patch until he was fourteen, or why Judy Weiss had a noticeable bust at twelve and Margot Canning didn't. He hadn't needed the other boys' talk to know he was expected to show an interest in girls. He'd seen a stallion covering a mare. He knew what a penis was for. An interest in women would come in its own time, like his pubic hair had.

In the army, he'd discovered the variation in men's penises. They were long and thin, short and fat, pale or brown, veiny or smooth. Some curved up, some curved down, and some cut to the right or left. His own aimed upward when confined in his drawers and tended to stick straight out and bounce annoyingly when unrestrained. Frank's was thicker than his own. A delicately curved hat brim was clearly outlined through the wool of Frank's left trouser leg.

They neared Philadelphia and he would have to move soon. Before he got around to it, Frank yawned, stretched, and glanced at Jersey. "Chilly in here." He spread his overcoat over their laps. "Wake me when we get to Paoli. I want to see the city as we come in."

"PHILADELPHIA! NEXT stop, Philadelphia, Broad Street Station!" announced the conductor, rushing through the car. The train creaked and swayed over switch after switch as it made its way into the center of Philadelphia.

"Will you look at the size of that train shed! There must be fifteen tracks leading in there." Jersey pressed his face against the window to get a better view. "What's the tower behind the station?"

"City Hall."

"Do you remember it?" Jersey said, glancing back at Frank.

Frank shrugged. He hoped his face did not betray his growing anxiety as he listened to Jersey's chatter. He'd succeeded in getting Jersey to come along. Now they had arrived in the city, he could think of nothing but where they would sleep and what they would do for money, while Jersey seemed oblivious to any practical concern. "Not really. That's what it is."

"Have you ever been inside? It must be amazing. Can we walk by on the way to… where are we going anyway?"

"Me? Inside? I doubt it." Frank wanted to laugh. He was obsessed with where they were going to get their next meal, and Jersey wanted to tour City Hall. "I thought we would start with the Germantown Friends School. Do you want to see to your leg first?"

The train lurched and slowed. The windows darkened as they passed under the giant metal ribs of the train shed.

"I didn't mean we should... hullo, looks like we've arrived," said Jersey. Frank gathered their bags and followed Jersey onto the platform. Jersey made it down without incident, then stopped to gawk. "It must be five hundred feet!" Passengers, porters, and luggage crowded the long platform.

Jersey's mood shifted abruptly when they reached the stairway from the elevated tracks down to Filbert Street. He stopped at the top of the steps, which cascaded to the street like a human waterfall.

"Watch out! What's the hold up?" a man called out as he thrust through the surge of people heading down the steps.

"I can't do it." Jersey's tone was bleak. "Not with all these people."

"Yes, you can," Frank said as he fought to hold back the press of people from behind. "Give me one of your crutches. Hold onto the railing and go slow. I'll be right behind."

Jersey was frozen in place like a pylon in a rushing river. "Jersey! You can't stay there," called Frank as he got buffeted from behind.

"I can't." Jersey clutched the handles of his crutches with white-knuckled fists.

"I can't carry you and the bags at the same time. Please, Jersey, move over to the railing." Jersey didn't move. "Jersey!" Frank yelled in desperation. Finally, Jersey lurched over to the railing. "Give me that crutch. There. Hold the railing. Would you rather hop?" Jersey shook his head. "All right. One step at a time."

By the time they reached the bottom, they were both wrecked. Handing Jersey his other crutch, Frank surveyed the street. The cobblestones were little improvement over the crowded staircase. Jersey still wasn't getting steam to his cylinders. "There!" Frank pointed. "Head for that bench."

Jersey made his way to the bench and collapsed. "I'm sorry I'm such a burden."

"Nonsense. We can rest here while I figure out where we're going."

Jersey, his eyes wide, panted like he'd hopped up the stairs instead of down. Frank had never seen Jersey this rattled in daylight. "You all right?"

I have got to get him someplace safe.

A TRAIN whistle pierced the air like a demon's howl. Jersey saw Frank's lips moving, but he couldn't make out the words. He couldn't slow his breathing. He twisted around. Everywhere he looked, people, delivery wagons, automobiles, and trolley cars rushed up and down. The air vibrated with a great din of clanging bells, honking horns, and shouting. Then Frank put his arm around Jersey's shoulders. Jersey closed his eyes, took a long breath, and held it. For an instant, there was nothing but the comforting weight of Frank's arm. When he drew a breath again, it was ragged, but no longer a pant.

I'VE SEEN men panic before. Frank could not remember the men or the circumstance. He could summon no faces to justify his body's dumb recognition, but men cried out behind the closed borders of his past. A phrase formed in his mouth: *Les soldat blessé.* Wounded soldiers. Watching Jersey struggle, he wondered for the first time if he might be better off leaving the gates of his past closed.

"You shouldn't have brought me with you," Jersey said in a low voice. "I'm nothing but a burden to you."

Words hastily crowded Frank's mind, all of them impossible. He pressed a fist to his forehead. "Jersey, I have no one else. No friend, no father, no mother, no past. I know things about this city. I feel something. But you are the only friend I have. You. Would you abandon me?"

Jersey looked up, startled. "Abandon you? Christ, Frank. There's no part of me could do that."

"Then listen to me. Stop feeling sorry for yourself. It isn't healthy. I will carry you to Germantown if I have to and think myself lucky for the chance, but I will not listen to you speak poorly of yourself."

For once Jersey seemed to have nothing more to say.

Frank turned away to save them both from further embarrassing disclosures. "I've got to ask for directions to Germantown." He marched rapidly in the direction of a street vendor.

FRANK RETURNED to the bench with the information that the Number 23 trolley ran north to Germantown along 12th Street, just a couple of blocks on the other side of City Hall. They set out toward the ornate building, and Jersey asked about the fellow perched atop the highest tower.

"William Penn!" Frank replied, as if all the world should know it.

"Odd hat."

Jersey craned his neck to look, as they made their way past the building. He took in carved stone and statuary. His gaze flew up column to capital, past the portico, and paused on the mansard roof, before finally climbing to the top of Penn's hat.

"You'll trip over your crutches if you don't quit gaping," said Frank.

Jersey didn't reply. The architect of the building must have thought himself deficient in his duty should he design any feature that was not entirely covered in fancy stonework.

THE TROLLEY to Germantown left them off at a corner where a number of old buildings were visible, any of which could have held classrooms. Jersey looked around in confusion, but Frank started out toward a cluster of plain, clean-lined buildings as if he'd visited just last week. They were of two stories, constructed of wood, with sloped roofs, and regularly spaced, unadorned windows. A loggia surrounded each building on the ground level.

A gray-haired man raked leaves from the grounds.

"Excuse me, sir," asked Frank, as they came up behind the gardener. "Is this the Germantown Friends School?"

The man turned and leaned on his rake, his smile broad. His face was round and lined, not so much weathered as creased. "It is."

Frank hesitated. "Could you direct us to the… headmaster's office?"

The man's face took on a quizzical, though still welcoming, expression. "If it's the Head of School thee is looking for, Francis, I might do so, but he would not be there."

Frank's mouth opened in surprise, and he flushed.

Jersey knew Frank must be mortified at his failure to recognize the man. Frank seemed unable to say anything, so Jersey leapt into the gap. "I see that you know Frank—Francis—sir, and that's good. I'm sure he'll tell you so, when he's got his words back. My name's Jersey Rohn, and I'm a friend of Frank's. I reckon you may already know this, but Frank was injured in the war. What you mightn't know is that his memory's not entirely restored yet. I hope you'll not hold it against him that he doesn't know you. That's why we're here, to help him remember. We'd sure welcome any help that you might—"

"Let the man get a word in, Jersey, would you," Frank murmured.

A rake of lines formed across the man's brow, but he thrust out a hand. "I'm pleased to meet thee, Jersey. An unusual name, that. Thee is from Michigan, I take it? I recall that Francis's mother was from there."

"That's right. Pleased to meet you, sir."

"I am sorry to hear thee is not entirely recovered, Francis, but I thank God to have thee with us again." Glancing back and forth between their faces, he added, "I don't know your plans. Will you join us for a meal at least?"

"We would be honored." Frank's tone was polite, but Jersey saw an instability around his mouth that worried him. "Will you tell us your name?"

"Please forgive me. I am Head of School Robert Underwood."

CHAPTER 13

"HE CAN'T have been more than six years old. He sets himself down on the bench with the most serious expression, his little legs swinging, as though determined to engage in the deepest examination of his inner light. Now, Jersey, thee is not a member of the Friends? It's quite all right, we believe that all men share in God's light. Thee may not be aware that we spend much of our meetings in silent reflection, children for a period suited to their age, adults longer. Now Francis was of an age to sit for at least ten minutes—well he knew this. But not more than two minutes after he sat down, little Francis pops up and is halfway to the door before his father can ask where he's going. With the most beatific smile, the boy announces that his inner light has informed him that there is a lonely puppy in the yard and that it would be cruel to leave him alone. 'Since you have taught me that cruelty to man or beast is wrong,' he says, 'my duty is to play with him.' 'Oh,' says his father, and before the man can say another word, the boy is out the door. Thy father got a ribbing for that, Francis."

They had finished dinner at the head of school's house and were seated in the parlor, dessert plates balanced on their knees. Jersey was getting used to the simplicity of the furnishings and lack of decoration. It was clearly not poverty that kept the head of school's house plain; the house was meticulously maintained.

Jersey had expected, or at least recognized, the plain speech, although he had not expected its intimacy and warmth. But the simplicity of the Underwood home took him by surprise, after the cluttered velvet and lace of the Clarks' parlor.

"If *I* left church in the middle of the sermon, I'd likely get a solid cuff on the head," Jersey said.

"Thy father practiced corporal punishment?" Mrs. Underwood asked. She had followed them into the parlor after the meal, apparently expecting to join in their discourse. Jersey's mother would have been in the kitchen clearing up the dishes. Weather permitting, male visitors would have gone to the porch to smoke and talk. Ladies would have helped with the cleaning up, then settled in the parlor with coffee. Mrs. Underwood's presence after the meal felt strange and made him shy.

"Corporal punishment?" Jersey had not heard the term before.

"Violence toward children," clarified Mrs. Underwood. She was tall and willowy, with brown hair gone nearly as gray as her husband's.

"Jersey's father is the gentlest of men," Frank said.

"Wouldn't be my father that cuffed me, but my mama," Jersey said. "She's the one gets exercised about the state of my soul." Watching Mrs. Underwood's eyes widen, Jersey quickly added, "She hardly ever hit me—only when I cussed or something."

"I see. Many do worse."

Jersey wanted to defend his mother, but Frank's pensive face distracted him.

"What are your plans, boys? Will you stay in Philadelphia for a while?" said Mr. Underwood.

Jersey glanced at Frank, but Frank seemed lost in reverie. "Frank wants to find his family. I don't suppose you know where they live?"

"I believe they hailed from New Jersey," Mr. Underwood said.

Frank must have paid some attention because his shoulders sagged at the news.

Mr. Underwood hastened to add, "I'm sure we have an address somewhere in our files. I'll ask our registrar to look tomorrow morning. Have you a place to stay? You are welcome to rest here."

"We do not want to impose on you," Frank said.

"Francis, thy memory of it may be impaired, but thee grew up at the school. There are many here who would be pleased to see thee. Stay as long as thee would."

"Thy friend is welcome as well," said Mrs. Underwood, inspecting Jersey as a sergeant would a recruit.

"We ain't hardly in a position to refuse," Jersey said.

"We have a guest room on the second floor you may share," said Mrs. Underwood. "I'm sorry there's nothing suitable on this floor," she added, frowning at Jersey's empty pant leg. "Will that be all right?"

"The world's made of stairs today," Jersey said. "I reckon I'll manage."

"Thank you, Mrs. Underwood," Frank said.

The stairs proved too narrow for crutches, so Jersey hopped up all fifteen steps, holding the banister and counting silently as he went. When he and Frank reached their room, he was secretly pleased to find only one bed in the room—and ashamed of the feeling. Breathing hard, he took in the gauze curtains, simple quilt, wardrobe, and walnut dresser. Frank put the bags down and slumped on the bed.

"What's the matter?"

"I tried all evening, Jersey. I tried and tried. Mr. Underwood must have mentioned ten people I ought to remember. Not one name meant a thing to me. Not one! It's not coming back. Nothing's ever coming back."

Jersey wanted to tell him to be patient, that it would come back in time, but he couldn't bring himself to make such an uncertain prediction. Frank had recovered so little of his past. Instead, Jersey leaned his crutches in the corner and put his arm around Frank. He was taken aback at Frank's raw and hungry answering look. Was it possible Frank's feelings mirrored his own? He recoiled at the thought that Frank might share his affliction. He let his arm fall away, but he stayed where he was, his thigh touching Frank's, until a knock on the door made them both flinch. Frank fairly leaped to the door.

Mrs. Underwood delivered fresh towels and wished them a good night.

JAMES SPALDING rushed his morning lessons as if talking fast would move the hands of the clock more quickly. Francis was alive and had come to visit! Along with his elation came a nagging question. Why hadn't Francis written to tell him of his visit? His last news of Francis had come a year ago, in September, just before the Spanish influenza outbreak. They had lost Francis's parents in the pandemic—they had been his informants since Francis's injury. An ominous silence had followed their deaths. Inquiries with the American Friends Ambulance Unit had suggested that Francis might be with his maternal grandparents. However, the man with whom James had corresponded had written regretfully to inform him that any record of an address in Michigan had been lost in the confusion surrounding the influenza outbreak.

Things had remained in that unsatisfactory state until this morning, when he received Mrs. Underwood's strangely worded invitation to lunch. She broke the wonderful news, but warned that Francis was not entirely himself and that James should come fortified with patience and his faith in God. Patience? What could she possibly mean? What had happened to Francis? He imagined gruesome disfigurements or a speech impediment.

At noon, James ran across the grounds to the head of school's house. His rapid progress elicited laughter from his students, who were unaccustomed to seeing a faculty member behave with such a wanton disregard for his dignity. He leapt up the steps of the house, thrust his fingers through his hair, then straightened his tie before knocking vigorously. Mrs. Underwood came to the door herself and greeted him warmly but with a disquieting seriousness.

"James, I'm so glad thee could join us. Please come in. Hang thy overcoat there. James?"

"Mrs. Underwood?"

She spoke in a low tone that would not be audible in the dining room. "Be patient. He needs thy support."

There was that word again—patient. "Of course. He's my friend. I would never—"

"Just so. Come in, James, join us in the dining room," she said, more loudly.

James expected to embrace his friend with the warmth and familiarity of an intimate. He was unprepared, despite Mrs. Underwood's warnings, for Francis's greeting. Francis turned to meet him with the polite smile of a perfect stranger.

"Francis," said Mr. Underwood, "this is James Spalding, our newest faculty member. You grew up together here at the School." Francis's gray eyes narrowed, but that was his only visible reaction.

"Francis, I'm so glad to see you! I didn't know what to think after your—after I stopped hearing from your parents. I'm so sorry for their loss."

"Thank you, Mr. Spalding. I'm pleased to—to see you too." Francis flushed. "I regret to say that I'm not able to remember our past association. If circumstances permit, I hope that proximity and conversation may restore some of our mutual history."

For the rest of the lunch, James strove to retain his composure. He'd expected the conversational shorthand of old friends. Instead, he strained for small talk. The effort tired him beyond measure.

AFTER LUNCH, Frank announced he was tired. Jersey was happy for a break, for his arms were bruised from the crutches. They'd spent the morning touring the school, shaking hands with a long procession of former acquaintances, none of whom Frank appeared to recognize, although he stopped telling people so after the painful luncheon with Spalding. Instead, he limited himself to exquisitely polite small talk of the kind Jersey imagined suitable at the embassy of a foreign nation. Jersey was relieved to make excuses and return to their room.

Frank sat on the bed and put his hands to his face. "I didn't know it would be so hard. I imagined seeing a person and the memories fitting into place like, well, like pegs in a cribbage board."

"You didn't remember anything?"

"No. It's infuriating. I don't recognize them, but I sometimes feel something. I know that I like a fellow." He snorted. "Or that I don't. But I have no idea *why*. It's damn frustrating!"

"They seem to like you."

"That's as much a mystery as anything."

"Not to me," Jersey said. They sat side by side on the bed again. Frank leaned forward, rubbing his face, the knobs of his backbone visible through his shirt. Jersey wanted to run his fingers along them. "Relax. You're trying too hard. Here, sit on the floor."

He pushed Frank down to the floor and kneaded his neck and shoulders, gradually increasing the pressure to loosen the rigid muscles. It was like trying to smooth knots from a tree. "You're very stiff," Jersey said, his traitorous mind flying immediately to the previous morning on the train. His cock thickened at the memory.

Frank hunched his shoulders and crossed his legs as though he were thinking the same thing. He pulled away and put a hand on top of Jersey's.

"Thank you, Jersey, but a nap is more what I need right now."

They lay down on the quilt. Jersey basked in the heat of Frank's body. He let it expand around him like a blanket, until Frank's breathing was all he heard.

HE FLOATED in a fetid pond, the air dense and humid. A rumble of thunder signaled an approaching storm. A gust of wind set the branches of the great willow tree that shaded the bank into motion. Alternating stripes of hot and cold marked sun and shade on his sweat-beaded skin. He heard the rasp of breathing in the water next to him.

Frank drifted in the no-man's-land between dream and waking. Beside him, Jersey shifted and mumbled something unintelligible. He smelled faintly of musk and hair tonic. Frank wanted to touch him, but he knew that it would be wrong, that it would corrupt their friendship. Maybe this was who *he* was, but he wouldn't believe it of Jersey. He'd thought it more funny than erotic on the train when he'd woken to their mutual state of arousal. But now, his need for comfort made Jersey's closeness unbearable. *Did Jersey know how I felt when he touched my shoulders?* Impossible. That would mean that Jersey too felt the obscene urges. Was this heat what drove men to seek out prostitutes? He imagined Mr. and Mrs. Underwood humping sedately under a quilt. Did sex leave them damp and gasping for breath? What if it were he and Jersey under the quilt? His cock, already hard, strained at the idea, but only shame and condemnation waited, should he touch Jersey's hot skin. He'd seen a painting of cavorting fiends once in a museum, the burning orgy that awaited sinners below the surface of the world.

The people he'd met today were so happy to see him—until they realized he couldn't remember them. Had something happened in France to heat him to this boil of corruption? Or had he always been a hypocrite, a dissembler who fooled people into believing him virtuous? If only he could find some piece of himself in a letter. He risked disappointment. The letters might reveal little, being composed by a young man for his parents. There were things no man told his parents. But there might be a clue to his true nature.

THAT EVENING, Frank drew a design on the table with a finger while he talked about his parents' letters and his hope they might find more correspondence. "They are crucial!" he said, glancing at Jersey with burning eyes. "I would be grateful if any could be found."

"We will ask," said Mr. Underwood. "Thee does not recall thy home in Germantown?"

"Not really. I get only the vaguest images—shadows on a wall."

"I will help in any way I can. Thy family lived in a house near here, owned by the school and rented to faculty. Our maintenance staff may have saved something—it was a terrible time. So many dead, so suddenly. Our meeting lost twenty-two, altogether. Has thee had no contact with thy father's family, Francis? Thy father spoke often of his parents."

"I received no letters from them in Michigan." Frank flashed a smile before continuing to draw his designs on the table. "I have no names or addresses."

"We have had difficulty finding the records… my secretary was one of our losses. But we may yet be able to help," said Mr. Underwood, compassion deepening the creases in his face.

PERHAPS IT was the rain rattling against their bedroom window, perhaps it was anxiety about Frank, but Jersey woke in the early hours with his heart racing and the nightmare stink of blood and gunpowder in his nose. He had not woken to the dream since their departure from Michigan. He wished Frank would wake and hold him, but Frank snored gently on. Jersey tried to imagine telling him what he needed, but he couldn't compose a request that didn't sound weak and womanish, so he rose instead, and went out to patrol the wet school grounds.

He was not the only early riser to challenge the light rain and shifting wind. As Jersey dragged along a gravel path, James Spalding stepped from behind one of the school buildings. Spalding had struggled so much for words during the meal the previous day that Jersey had wondered why the Underwoods invited him. The young man still wore the same brown suit from the day before, only now it appeared slept in. His tie was loose and the top button of his shirt was undone. His unbuttoned overcoat blew out behind him like a cape.

"Good morning, Mr. Spalding. You're out early." Jersey meant only to be polite, but Spalding offered a hand to shake.

"Mr. Rohn, isn't it? Good morning. I'm glad to run into you. I don't want to impose, but do you have a moment?"

"Sure, but you'd better call me Jersey. Mr. Rohn's likely to have me checking for my father."

"Then you must call me James. My father lays first claim on Jim."

"James it is. Should we get out of the rain, or are you out for a constitutional?"

"No, I...." Spalding hesitated, looking around at the darkened buildings. "Let's go into the meeting house."

The meeting house held only wooden benches—no altar, podium, statuary, or stained glass. A potbellied stove and neat stack of firewood awaited the next meeting. The simplicity of the room's furnishings gave it an ascetic air. *What happens here, happens in the mind,* they seemed to say. *Decoration only distracts.*

James must have seen Jersey's thoughts in his face. He chuckled, "I see you are not a member of the Friends."

"That obvious? Yeah, the family's Lutheran, but my Papa's more likely to get exercised about his tomatoes than Heaven or Hell."

"I suspect I would like your father. I have started an experimental patch behind our house, although there's not much to do this time of year."

Jersey stared out at the gusting rain. "Do you get much snow here?"

"I've never lived anywhere else, but I don't imagine it compares with Michigan."

"No." What did this fellow want from him?

His thought must have shown on his face again. James sighed. "Have you known Francis—Frank—long, Jersey?"

Jersey counted on his fingers. "I reckon it's been about six months. I've never met a fellow I feel closer...." He hoped the collar of his overcoat hid his burning ears.

James didn't seem to notice his confusion. "I grew up with Francis. We were close. It was a shock he didn't know me. I didn't know what to say."

Jersey tried to smile reassuringly. "It ain't personal. Ain't nothing he wants more in the world than to remember."

"Of course. It's just that I feel his loss so keenly. When I didn't know if he was dead, there was at least a chance. Now, I feel he is truly gone."

"Just you wait a minute!" Jersey banged a crutch on the floor. "He might not be the Frank—Francis—you remember, but he isn't dead, not by a long shot."

"I'm sorry." James smiled ruefully. "I didn't mean to offend. I see you care for him. Perhaps I'm selfish."

Jersey cooled as fast as he had heated. He waved his indignation away. "It don't signify. What was he like when you knew him?"

"He was a natural leader, not loud, but the other boys always listened to him. He had a certain authority...."

"The two of you grew up here at the school. How come you don't speak funny, like Mr. and Mrs. Underwood?"

James raised his eyebrows. "You mean the plain speech."

"Sorry, why don't you use the plain speech?"

"Not all Quakers do. The practice is dying out, even among those who have grown up among the Friends. Francis and I had that in common. Our mothers weren't raised Quaker. Since they didn't use the plain speech, we didn't either. It set us apart from the other children, the opposite of how plain speaking is supposed to work, really. It drew us together."

"Mrs. Huddleston didn't use the plain speech in her letters."

James looked surprised. "You've read her letters?"

"Frank likes me to read his letters to him." Jersey wished he'd kept his mouth shut when he saw James's reaction.

"He's not—I mean, he can still…?"

Will you ever learn to think before you blabber? "He can read fine. It's just a thing we've done."

"I see." James paused, apparently wanting to hear more.

Jersey wasn't about to explain. "I ought to be getting back. Don't wanna miss my chow."

"Thank you for conversing with me, Jersey. I hope to see you and Francis again soon."

Jersey thought about how he'd feel if Frank forgot him. "Sure, that'd be peachy."

Making his way through the rain on the way back to the house, Jersey gritted his teeth with every step. At home, he realized, he'd mostly stayed on the porch or ridden Flash. He wasn't accustomed to so much walking on crutches. He was raw and bruised under his arms. He hoped they would stay at the school for a spell so he could heal. *What'll I do if Frank wants to go hunting for his family?* He'd cross that bridge when he came to it. Maybe he could look up that doctor at Jefferson Hospital and see about his leg. Rupert Constantine, that was his name, Connie, when the boys were joshing him about the way he mothered the soldiers under his care.

He glanced up as he passed under the Underwood's bedroom window. Mrs. Underwood stared down at him from the window, her mouth open in surprise. He managed what he hoped was a jaunty wave with one of his crutches. Unfortunately, the effect was probably ruined when he put his weight back on the infernal thing.

ANNE UNDERWOOD arrived home on Wednesday to find the guest bedroom of her parents' house occupied by a pair of exotic visitors. Frank Huddleston was a Quaker, which was not interesting, but the fact that he was an amnesiac who could not even remember his own family, now that was intriguing. Anne dreamed of leaving her family, particularly her mother. What more thorough break from your family could you make than to forget them completely? To be so unencumbered! It would be like throwing away your corsets and going around in short dresses like the flappers.

Jersey, on the other hand, was a little on the small side, but he had absolutely dreamy long eyelashes and dark curls. His missing leg excited her in a way she did not dare examine. She imagined Jersey taking her to a club like the ones her brother had told her about. They would dance to the syncopated beat of a piano rag. Jersey would throw his crutches aside and spin in her arms like a top. It would be smashing.

"Anne! What is thee staring at? Come along while I get dessert. We have cherry cobbler today. I want to hear about thy brother and his school friends. We must remember to send your uncle a note to thank him for escorting thee to Swarthmore." When Anne did not move, Mrs. Underwood's tone sharpened. "I'm sure our guests have better things to do than entertain a gawping schoolgirl."

"Mother! I am not gawping, and I don't want to go with thee." Anne, her parents, Jersey, and Frank were in the dining room. A pot roast congealed on a platter on the sideboard amid the remaining pieces of carrot and potato. "I want to stay with Frank and Jersey," she continued. "I can tell thee about Bobbie's stupid friends later." She kept her bottom pressed firmly to her chair.

"Go with thy mother, dear. I must talk to Frank about his family. They are none of thy business."

Her father sounded amused, she couldn't imagine at what.

"But I want to hear more about France from Jersey!"

Jersey glanced at Frank before turning to her with a grin. "I reckon I've got stories to tell, if Frank doesn't need me…."

Frank blinked and moved his head ambiguously.

"Oh for heaven's sake, Anne!" said her father. Shaking his head, he smiled at Jersey. "Thee is too kind. Let's go to my study, Frank. I believe we may have found something for thee."

Frank rose so slowly Anne was tempted to poke him to see if he was still awake.

Anne gave Jersey her most beguiling smile and leaned ever so slightly in his direction. "Was it terribly gruesome in the Army?"

"Jersey—we'll talk later?" said Frank.

"Sure thing, Frank." Jersey waved distractedly and grinned at Underwood's daughter.

FRANK DID not want cherry cobbler. Apple would have suited him better, although he could not remember the last time he'd eaten cobbler. He'd been sure the visit to the school would tease out new memories, just as his father's letter had reminded him of walking in the park. So far, his visit had consisted of a series of frustrating and embarrassing interviews with strangers.

Yesterday's experience at lunch had been particularly horrifying. What could he possibly say to the childhood friend of whom he could produce no image, not even a fractured glass plate? He had been painfully stiff and formal with Spalding. Without meaning to, he had hurt the man. Now he wanted to retreat to the safety and comfort of his friendship with Jersey, but Jersey was clearly enjoying the attention and inane questions from their host's pretty young daughter.

The study to which Mr. Underwood led him was warm and smoky from the fire, but comfortably furnished with walnut furniture and bookcases. A Persian rug and matched pair of leather armchairs showing the creases and scars of long use were arranged before the fireplace. Frank selected one and watched Underwood sink into the other with a contented sigh. A few of the books that Frank could see from his low vantage point were religious. A broad selection of history, philosophical thought, and natural science filled the shelves. Conspicuous for their absence were novels or stories of any kind. Mrs. Underwood probably thought them frivolous.

"Thank you very much, Mr. Underwood. I'm eager for your news."

Underwood leaned forward and spoke with some excitement, his eyes bright. "Our secretary found an address in thy father's file. It's in Plainfield, New Jersey. There are many Friends in that area."

"I'm grateful for your help," Frank said. He would have to go there. But the prospect was less exciting than the trip to Philadelphia had been. What if he didn't recognize anyone there either? "You found no letters?"

"I'm sorry." Underwood plucked a piece of paper from his breast pocket and passed it to Frank. "Perhaps this will mean something to thee."

The address meant nothing to Frank. He closed his eyes and tried to quell his disappointment. When he opened his eyes, the letters scattered across the page, their shapes as random as sticks on a forest floor.

"Is thee well, Francis?" Underwood leaned forward, the vertical lines between his eyes deepening.

"I wish you would call me Frank, Mr. Underwood. I like Francis, it feels softer than Frank, but until Francis holds some meaning for me, I must be Frank." Underwood raised his eyebrows at the pun, seemingly ready to laugh if that were Frank's intent, but Frank could not muster a smile of encouragement.

Mrs. Underwood carried in a tray of dessert plates, forks and napkins. She handed each of them a plate of cobbler and placed the tray on the small table between their chairs. "May I get you anything else?"

Frank pictured a scrapbook pasted full of photographs of strangers, each labeled with his or her name.

"Thank thee, dear." Underwood smiled at his wife and waited until she left. "Will thee go to New Jersey, Francis?"

"I said to call me Frank," Frank said sharply.

Underwood's eyes widened. "I did not mean to offend. I will amend my habit."

Frank rubbed the top of his head. "I'm sorry, Mr. Underwood. I am out of sorts and behaving badly. I should go to bed." He rose and placed his untouched cobbler on the tray. "Will you tell Jersey I've gone up?"

JERSEY WAS tipsy with the newfound pleasure of entertaining an admiring female. "Ain't Anne a peach?" He tossed his crutches into the corner and bounced on the bed.

"She's pretty enough. It's obvious she finds you attractive as well."

As well? What is Frank on about? "You know I can't resist an audience. You've heard a parcel of my yarns."

Frank's shoulders were hunched as he sat cross-legged on the bed.

"What's wrong? I thought Mr. Underwood had good news. Didn't they find any letters?"

"No, they didn't find any letters." Frank plucked at a loose thread in the quilt in front of him. "Just an address for my grandparents—in Plainfield, New Jersey."

Jersey glanced at his crutches where they leaned in the corner of the room. "Do you mean to go there?"

Frank spoke without looking up from the quilt. "We leave tomorrow."

Jersey rolled his shoulders, feeling the stretch of stiff muscles. "Tomorrow! Jeez, Frank. Do what you want, but I'm not goin' anywhere tomorrow."

Frank raised his head sharply, his eyes red-rimmed. "I suppose you want to stay and puff yourself up in front of that little hen."

"Suppos'n I do? What's wrong with that?" Jersey could not bring himself to mention the bruises under his arms. He did not want Frank to see him as weak. Anne's calculated blushes were laughable, but they were better than pity.

"I liked you better when you refused to tell war stories to strangers."

"I wasn't—she just wants to hear about the good stuff. It's not like I'm telling her about Andy and the sergeant." Frank was the only person to whom he'd ever described those horrors.

"You were quite the little Napoleon, strutting your stuff."

Now that's over the top. Jersey felt his face heat. "I was not strutting."

"Whatever that was, it sure worked."

"You're just jealous because she liked me better 'n you."

"I couldn't care less what that girl thinks about anyone."

"Well, I liked her. And she's isn't the one handing out orders, without so much as a by-your-leave." He mimicked Frank's crisp tone. *"We leave tomorrow.* Hell if I will."

"You wanted to come on this trip." Frank's tone was frigid.

"Yeah, so maybe I've changed my mind. Maybe it's just as well you go off to New Jersey by your lonesome, if you're gonna be a jackass every time I chat up a gal."

"Fine. I'll go by myself," Frank said, pulling the quilt around himself like a cocoon. "I don't need you."

JERSEY BANGED and clattered down the stairs to the first floor. The things he'd left unsaid worried him like a loose saddle. He told himself that Frank had no right to talk to him like that, that Frank's failure to grasp his simple joy in telling harmless stories to an appreciative audience was ridiculous and unfair. Nevertheless, he wished he'd said what he'd wanted to say, which was that he didn't want Frank to go to New Jersey without him. He wanted Frank to wait a few days for his arms to heal. He flopped into one of the armchairs and picked up a book from the coffee table in front of him. *A History of the Religious Society of Friends, with Extracts from the Writings of George Fox.* Jersey opened the book, randomly picking a page from the middle.

"Is thee interested in learning more about the Friends?" Mrs. Underwood smiled from the doorway.

"Frank explained about the plain speech. I'm afraid I'm not very religious."

Mrs. Underwood stepped into the room. "I could teach thee—"

"That's very nice of you and all, Mrs. Underwood," Jersey said. "Maybe some other time. I thought I wanted to read, but I'm tuckered out." He grabbed his crutches. "I'll go up."

Mrs. Underwood pursed her lips, but nodded. "I'll wish thee a good night, then."

FRANK WASHED and dressed for the trip in silence. It was not until Jersey had followed him out to shuffle awkwardly on the front stoop that he finally spoke. "You have any money?"

"A little."

"You can stay here until I get back. Mrs. Underwood has taken to you."

"I'll be fine," Jersey said. "I'll poke around and see what I can find out about your—"

"Don't put yourself out." Frank picked up his bag.

"Frank! Why're you acting so mean?"

Frank would not look at him, but he put down his bag and gazed out across the brown grass and leaves of the school grounds. "Jersey, you have your life to live. I must not get in the way."

"You aren't—"

"You cannot imagine how painful it is for me to find no connection, no feeling of familiarity here. I am adrift. If I can find one person from before the war…."

"Christ!" Jersey knew he should be feeling compassion for Frank. But anger, not compassion, made him yank open the door and slam it between them. Why couldn't Frank focus on the present for once, instead of the damn past?

CHAPTER 14

1965

THE DOCTOR sank into his usual chair with a sigh. The young man in the hospital bed grimaced. "You're not going to take it off again? That was disgusting."

"Not if you don't want me to, Sergeant." The doctor stretched his leg out in front of him.

The sergeant muttered, "Since when does what I want enter into it?"

"We must all learn to accommodate."

"What if I can't?"

The doctor examined the young face. The eyes were raw. There were dark circles underneath them. Gaunt cheeks broadened slightly to fit chapped lips. Faint parentheses surrounded the mouth. "Does that worry you?"

"I don't want to talk about it."

The doctor wrote a note on the clipboard in his lap.

"What are you writing?" the sergeant asked.

"A shopping list for dinner."

"How do you get away with being such a smartass? If I spoke to an officer like that, I'd be busted to private before I finished the pushups."

"I'm a consulting physician, not a member of the military. Won't be long before you're outside too. Have you thought about what you're going to do with yourself?"

The sergeant turned his head away. "Killing is the only thing I'm good at."

"Not a very transferable skill, is it? You thought about going back to school?"

"Me and school didn't get along."

The doctor laced his fingers behind his head. "Do you think it might be different if you were studying something you cared about?"

"Like what?"

"We've got some aptitude tests that might help you figure that out. I'll make you a deal. You tell me what happened to you, and I'll help you figure out what you might be interested in."

The sergeant turned his head away. "I don't want to talk anymore."

"Is there someone else you would prefer to talk to?"

"Yeah, but he's dead."

The doctor made another note.

The sergeant craned his neck to see. "Goddammit. What are you writing?"

"I take notes to help me do a better job, Sergeant. They're for me, not for you. Who's dead?"

"Nobody."

The doctor shuffled through the papers on his clipboard. "That's not what your after-action report says. Were you talking about one of the men in your squad?"

"I'm not speaking to you."

"Do you know that psychiatrists have the same rule as priests do? We can't repeat anything you say unless you give us the all clear."

"Yeah, right. Does the Army know about your little rule?"

"I'm not in the Army. Nor will you be for much longer."

The sergeant turned his head away. "Fuck you."

"I'm sorry, but I'm out of time for today. Maybe tomorrow."

CHAPTER 15

1919

JAMES THREW the note from Mrs. Underwood with the news that Francis had left into his wastepaper basket. Unsatisfied, he swept the schoolwork he was grading off his desk and onto the floor. He then spent the next ten minutes carefully collecting and reordering the papers. When he finished, he went out.

A light fog flirted with the tops of the street lamps on Germantown Avenue, leaving their ornate housings surrounded by diffuse, yellow halos. He walked up the street toward the school with no more intent than to replace the smell of coke from his grate with something that didn't leave him nauseated. As he neared the school, he became aware that his steps were echoed by the distinctive cadence of a man on crutches.

Jersey swung rapidly along the other side of the avenue, the sleeves of his greatcoat bunched under his crutches.

"Mr. Spalding… James?"

James stopped to wait while Jersey crossed the street. "Hello, Jersey. I thought you were on your way to Plainfield."

"Frank left this morning. We—I decided to stay and see to my leg." Jersey moved the crutches from under his arms and balanced on his good leg.

"Does Frank plan to return? I was so lost the other day—I hoped to speak to him again."

Jersey shrugged, panting. "Most likely."

James took in Jersey's wild curls and disordered collar. "Are you out for exercise?"

"I guess. It was a damn fool idea."

"Perhaps you would like to warm up? My rooms are not far."

Jersey glanced toward the school and rolled shoulders. He sighed. "I'd like that. I'd like to ask you about Frank—if you don't mind."

As they walked back toward his rooms, James noticed Jersey grimaced when he put weight on his crutches. When they reached the rooming house where he boarded, James stopped in confusion and looked up at the window to his sitting room.

Jersey followed his gaze to the window and laughed softly. "World ain't made for one-legged fellers, is it? Don't concern yourself. I reckon I'm getting used to it."

"I'm so sorry. I didn't think." James's rooms were on the third floor.

"Lead on, man. I'll manage. Your neighbors won't be in bed, will they?"

James didn't figure out what Jersey meant until they reached the stairs. Jersey calmly handed his crutches over and proceeded to hop up the stairs with the energy of a child at hopscotch. The neighbors would think James had invited a herd of schoolboys for tea. He laughed out loud. "You're very fit."

"It's level ground that's a challenge today." Jersey nodded at the crutches James carried. "I'd like to burn the infernal things."

"They hurt you?"

They reached the top of the second flight. "I figure I'm not used to them yet. Which way?" Jersey gasped.

"To your left and up again."

"Good thing I like you."

"Indeed," said James, laughing.

When Jersey was settled in the armchair by his grate, James went to get water. "I'm afraid I don't drink coffee, but I can get you water or milk."

"I'm okay. Never did take to the black swill."

"Tell me," said James, returning with water anyway. "How did you and Frank meet?"

Jersey leaned back, his smile fading. After an instant, he blinked and his smile broadened. "That's a story, isn't it? Since the war, I've had this thing about loud sounds like thunder. Well, Frank's grandparents put this notice up in the Grange Hall...."

"HE PUNCHED you in the nose?"

"Yessir. Good thing I'm a boxer—was a boxer." Jersey sipped from his water glass. "Amazing what you can get used to." *Stairs, for one thing.*

"It is."

"Now it's your turn." Jersey leaned forward. "I wanna know about Frank. You were his pal. How'd he end up in France? I mean, we figured out that he drove an ambulance...."

"He didn't tell you?" James's glass dropped to the carpet without shattering. He bent down to snatch it up.

"He doesn't remember anything before Michigan, not really. He gets flashes, but that's about it."

James looked like he might be sick.

"You all right?" Jersey asked.

James shrugged, helplessly. "I told you, Francis and I were close. I feel I've lost a limb."

After a second, James's ears reddened. Jersey grinned. "Don't concern yourself. People say stuff like that all the time. They don't mean nothing by it. Tell me something about Frank."

Nodding eagerly, James asked, "You know he was in the American Friends Ambulance Unit?"

"Yeah, we got that from the letters, but that's about the extent of it."

James put down his glass. "How much do you know about the Friends?"

"Frank's told me a little. I've had my eyes open since I got here. Why?"

"Do you know what the testimonies are?"

"Not really. Frank said that plain speech is a testimony. I'm not sure what he meant. What does this have to do with what happened to Frank?"

James smiled. "Sorry. I'm a teacher. I can't help myself. It's just that Francis—Frank—felt that driving an ambulance was a kind of testimony. Friends believe that we should live out our beliefs in our actions, that our lives—everything we do—should testify to our beliefs. Frank's belief in the testimony of peace made it impossible for him to join the army or to fight in France, even though he was appalled by what the Germans did in Belgium. We all read about it. They murdered ten civilians if one German was shot, burned homes and museums. The stories were awful, and Francis was never one to sit around waiting for someone to tell him what to do."

Jersey grimaced. "He's more inclined to do the telling."

James laughed. "I gather you've some experience of that. In any case, in 1915, when we were reading about new atrocities every day, he fixed on the idea that he must act. He thought by driving an ambulance he could help the victims of the war without killing anyone or violating his beliefs. But it bothered him. He feared that transporting the wounded helped the French army, because many of the soldiers he carried were sent right back to the front as soon as they were well enough. Truth be told, his father was dead set against it."

Jersey lifted his empty glass, but put it down again with a frown. "I joined up because I wanted to feel—well—the local board would've got me sooner or later. All the boys in my town signed up. I didn't think what it would be like to kill someone until I came to it."

James pursed his lips. "How did you feel then?"

Before Jersey could concoct an answer to the uncomfortable question, another thought hit him. He leaned forward. "How do you *know* it bothered Frank that the soldiers were being sent back to the front?"

"Why, he wrote to me, of course. I've kept all his letters."

JERSEY LAY shaking, trying to expel the battlefield stink from his body. He asked himself again whether he would ever finish with Andy's death. He knew this: he did not like to be alone to wait out his terror. When he was with Frank, the warmth of Frank's body and the steady rise and fall of his breathing shortened his recovery time. Tell Frank what he needed or stay silent, which was the greater risk? In the brief time they'd shared a room, this calculation had become as much a part of the predawn hours as his dream.

When he thought he could get up without dropping a crutch or knocking over the night stand, Jersey put on a robe and went down to the kitchen to get a drink of water. He waited for the plain linen curtain to brighten until his exhaustion overcame him and he put his head down in his arms.

"Jersey, wake up." Mrs. Underwood's voice broke through a gentle dream in which he and Frank rolled in fragrant hay.

He cleared his throat, blinking. "Must've dozed off."

Mrs. Underwood examined him silently for a moment before announcing, "Thee look terrible. Thee do not sleep. Is thee in pain?"

"No, ma'am. Least ways, not much." Some explanation for his sleeplessness was needed.

"Lift thy arms," ordered Mrs. Underwood.

He stared, the demand incomprehensible.

"Come on, young man. Lift them up." She gestured, making her desire plain if her reason less so. He complied, grunting as he stretched sore muscles. Mrs. Underwood nodded. "I thought so. Take off the robe. I want to see your arms."

He was shocked. Even his mama hadn't seen him naked since he'd started taking baths on his own. "What? I'd rather—"

"For heaven's sake, give me the robe."

Jersey complied reluctantly, still uncertain whether or not he should flee.

"There isn't an ounce of meat on you. Is thee eating?"

She'd added insult to injury. "I eat plenty, Mrs. Underwood. God made me skinny."

"Thee should try extra helpings of meat before thee blame God for thy condition." Mrs. Underwood freed the buttons of Jersey's union suit in order to bare his chest and arms. "Look at those bruises! It's no wonder, the way thee has been gallivanting all over the place. How does thee plan to treat these?" she demanded, peering at the bruises on the insides of his arms.

"Treat them?" They were only bruises.

"Mother! Leave him alone. He's not your responsibility."

Jersey looked around to find Anne Underwood standing in the doorway. From her posture, she had been there for some time. While Mrs. Underwood glared at her daughter, Jersey took the opportunity to cover himself.

"That's not for thee to say, Anne." Mrs. Underwood turned back to Jersey. "I think thee ought to consult a doctor. I have seen men with false legs. Have you looked into getting one?"

"They told me to wait until my stump healed." *She'll probably demand to see that as well.*

Mrs. Underwood made a clicking noise. "How long ago was that?"

"Eight months, more or less."

"And?"

"I figure on seeing this doctor I know at the Jefferson Hospital."

"I'd say it's high time."

"Yes, ma'am," said Jersey, as he headed for the stairs.

AFTER BREAKFAST, Mrs. Underwood cornered Jersey again. "What do you want to do after thee get thy leg?"

She followed him to the coat stand and inspected him as he prepared to go out. She was worse than his old sergeant. He said the first thing that came into his head. "I wanna read more books." His answer had the virtue of being true, which might have been a good strategy, but it was a tactical error.

Mrs. Underwood leaned forward eagerly, her eyes bright. "Thee should go to college."

"Me?" Jersey decided he would get invited to dinner at James's place if he had to set up camp on the front stoop.

"WHY ARE all women so confounded obsessed with my future? It's all my mother goes on about. Where will you live? What will you do? It ain't no good to tell them the truth, neither. *I dunno* is catnip to a tabby."

James laughed and handed Jersey a plate. "It's the mothering instinct. Your emaciated frame and waiflike aspect inspire it."

"Oh, don't you start. Some pal you are. Mrs. Underwood is probably fuming because I ain't eating her double portions of beefsteak. I was a boxer, y'know, in the army."

"Bantamweight?"

"Lightweight, thank you very much. I've lost a few pounds since then."

They ate perfectly good roast chicken with green peas. Jersey gnawed a drumstick and wondered how James would react if he knew how Jersey felt about his boyhood friend.

THE CLINIC at Jefferson Hospital smelled of wet wool and soiled diapers. Jersey made his way to the reception desk, past a young mother with two children—a crying baby of indeterminate sex and a brown-haired boy who sneezed on Jersey and then stared, wide-eyed, at his pinned-up trouser leg. The woman held her baby loosely and looked right through Jersey. At the desk, Jersey asked for Dr. Constantine.

"Dr. Constantine is busy. What is your complaint?" said the nurse on duty, fountain pen poised.

"Complaint? I wanna see Dr. Constantine. I met him at the hospital in Nantes."

The nurse pointed her pen at the ledger on her desk. "If you want to see a doctor, you must have a complaint."

"I really don't got a complaint. I just wanna see Dr. Constantine."

The nurse sighed. "Dr. Constantine is busy. I must have a complaint."

A white-haired crone spoke up behind Jersey. "If you don't have any complaints, mister, I can share a few. My knee hurts, my hips hurt, and my hands are swollen."

Jersey held up his crutches. "The doctor cut off my leg. Will that do?" Another doctor had actually removed his leg at a hospital near the Front. He hadn't met Connie until the army moved him to the American hospital for recovery, but Jersey was desperate. Connie would forgive him for the falsehood.

"Does it hurt?"

"Only when I try to walk on it."

"Complaint: pain when walking," intoned the nurse. "Name?"

"Christ almighty!"

"If you speak the Lord's name in vain, I'll ask you to leave," said the nurse, pointing her pen like a lancet. "Name?"

"Jersey Rohn."

"Spell it."

"MR. ROHN," called the nurse.

Jersey took a long breath and opened his eyes. "I'm here."

"The doctor will see you now."

Jersey's rear end had fallen asleep in the hard chair. He nearly landed on his face when he tried to get up.

The nurse waited, arms folded.

"I'm coming," he said. He followed her into an examination room, which he was relieved to find smelled of carbolic instead of dirty diapers.

"Remove your trousers and underclothing," said the nurse, handing Jersey a gown. She closed the door firmly behind her.

A few minutes later, a knock sounded. Before Jersey could respond, the door opened wide. Jersey tucked the gown around his thighs.

"Jersey!"

Connie was olive-skinned, with a high forehead and crooked nose. Jersey remembered he had a habit of pinching it when he thought, as if a straight nose might bring order to his deliberation.

"Hi, doc." Jersey started to get up.

"No need to get up," said Connie, putting out a hand to shake. "I'm surprised to see you in Philadelphia. I thought you were from"—he frowned—"somewhere west?"

"Michigan," Jersey prompted.

"That's right. How's your leg?"

"Missing."

"Ha, ha!" Connie peered at his clipboard suspiciously. "Your chart says you are having difficulty walking."

Jersey shrugged. "The nurse insisted I have a complaint."

"I see." Connie chuckled. "What really brings you here?"

"At Walter Reed, they told me I should wait for my stump to heal before I tried to fit an artificial leg. It's been a while...." Jersey rubbed his stump.

"Let's take a look." Connie pulled a clean sheet from a cabinet and spread it out on the examination table. "Hop up." Jersey got onto the table and pulled up the gown. The doctor examined the stump carefully, probing gently with his fingers. "Any pain?"

Jersey thought about the past few weeks. Mostly, it hadn't been his leg that hurt. "It aches some."

"Any bleeding, discharge, red streaks?"

"Not since the hospital."

"It looks good. I'd say you're ready for a prosthesis. Why don't we have a look at the rest of you while we're at it?"

Connie checked Jersey's pulse, listened to Jersey's breathing, and tested his reflexes. "Those are impressive bruises," he said, lightly touching the black-and-blue area under one of Jersey's arms.

"I've been traveling—lot of walking."

"Where are you staying? Can you get ice? It would help reduce the inflammation."

Mrs. Underwood would move mountains to get him ice if he asked, but.... He shrugged.

"Are the crutches the right height for you?"

"Seem to be."

"I wonder if we might...." Connie made a note. "How are you sleeping? Still having bad dreams?"

"Just the one."

"I could give you something to help you sleep," said Connie, watching him intently.

"Nah, I don't care for that stuff."

Connie grinned. "Just as well." He put his hands on the back of the chair. "You can put your clothes on now." Jersey dressed while Connie sat down to make some notes on Jersey's chart. "Where are you staying? Do you have family in Philadelphia?"

Jersey finished tying his shoes. "I'm staying at the Germantown Friends School."

"You're not...?"

"No, I'm not Quaker—raised Lutheran, actually—but I'm traveling with a friend who is. He knows the head of school."

"That's handy." The doctor reached for the doorknob. "Is there anything else I can do for you?"

Jersey was ready to tackle Connie to keep him from escaping. "What about my new leg?" he burst out.

Connie broke into a grin and winked. "Ha! Knew I was forgetting something! Actually, I made an appointment for you at two tomorrow with our prosthetist when I saw in your chart that you were still on crutches. It's high time, I should think. Mr. Gould will measure your legs and make a cast of your stump. We keep catalogs of prosthetic devices. Mr. Gould keeps a few on hand you can try out. When you've chosen, he'll send your particulars to the manufacturer."

Jersey tried to keep the disappointment out of his voice. "I've gotta wait for one to come from the manufacturer?"

"I'm afraid so." The doctor touched his nose. "Stumps, like noses, come in all shapes and sizes. You'll be more comfortable if your leg is made to fit."

"How do I know which kind of leg to get?"

Connie pinched his nose and drew his fingers down its length. "Mr. Gould may recommend something. He knows as much as anyone about these things." He paused, eyes unfocused, face solemn. "Jersey, I have to finish up here, but there's something else I may be able to do for you. If you meet me at the corner of 10th and Chestnut at six, I'll have something for you. You can get something to eat while you wait."

Jersey wondered what Connie had in mind, but the doctor left before he could ask.

AT SIX, Jersey hopped slow circles around a crutch in the pool of light from the street lamp at 10th and Chestnut. Connie was nowhere in sight.

However, there were plenty of people around, so Jersey watched them. If he was sly about it, he could catch them looking too, like the young man in a butcher's apron who passed him without acknowledgment, but threw a dark look over his shoulder, only to retreat hastily at Jersey's fey grin.

In Taperville, he would have been making a spectacle of himself. Here, his was one of many small performances. One man had caught his attention as Jersey passed through Washington Square earlier in the afternoon: a grizzled fellow in the blue coat and cap of the Union Army. He was blind and sat on a bench with his head tilted toward the sun. Whenever a lady passed—Jersey had no idea how the man always knew it was a lady—he would creak to life like an automaton, tip his cap and announce, "Fair day today, ma'am." He wished Frank was here to share his impressions. It was odd how he'd come to take as much joy from Frank's reactions to people as his own.

Jersey was dizzy from his circuits when Connie finally appeared. He carried a long canvas sack. "Sorry to keep you waiting, Jersey. I went to check on a patient...." He shrugged. "You weren't bored?"

"Not me. Too much to see." Jersey swung a crutch in an arc to encompass the street, nearly bashing a sober-suited businessman in the face.

"Pardon me," said the man, glaring.

"Sorry, sorry!"

"Careful with that thing!" said Connie mildly. "I don't suppose you visited Paris before your injury?"

"Marched through a corner of it once. We was so tired...." He shrugged.

"That's a city to walk in, along the Seine, where the booksellers have stalls, up the Champs-Élysées!" Connie's face lost a little of its tension.

Jersey pointed. "What's in the sack?"

Connie's gaze drifted over Jersey's shoulder. "Have you eaten?"

Jersey wondered what was on the doctor's mind. He wasn't usually so distracted. "Got me a pretzel. Never knew they came so big."

His attention returned to Jersey, and he smiled. "Will you join me? I'm buying."

"Sure, doc, but I got a few clams left. You don't gotta carry me."

"It's a couple of blocks this way."

When the waiter had seated them, Connie ordered a beer and raised his eyebrows. Jersey shook his head. The doctor raised his glass. "Missing friends."

"Missing friends," echoed Jersey, lifting his water glass. "Guess you're getting it while you can."

"Damn drys! Thanks to them, I'll have to start carrying my own hooch next month. Prohibition is a joke. It'll never work." The doctor took a long pull. "It defies human nature." He wiped his mouth and settled his shoulders before lifting the sack. "Okay. This is a special pair of crutches that I had made for another patient." He loosened the drawstring and pulled out what looked to Jersey like a matching pair of walking sticks, each with a perpendicular handle and a leather loop at the top, like a belt. "Stand up and put your forearms through the loops. Good. Now grab the handles. You'll work harder holding yourself up. But"—he touched Jersey's side—"no more bruises. Now let go of the handles and lift up your arms. See, there's a hinge where the strap attaches, so they hang straight down when you let go. It frees your hands."

Jersey grabbed the handles and swung himself around the table. "Wow! They're perfect. But you could have given them to me before we walked over here."

"Nothing's free, my friend." Connie took another pull on his beer. "I want to tell you about Jeff Conroy."

Jersey nodded and sat down again, but he held on to the new crutches.

"Conroy was a patient. Lost a leg in France like you did, only he wasn't so lucky. His leg was blown off in a mine explosion. He spent a night in the crater covered in every kind of foul—you know what it was like. It was a miracle he made it back to the States." He drained his beer and waved for another. "Anyway, I'm getting ahead of myself. At Nantes, they cleaned him up as best they could and sewed up the stump. Got him on a ship. Only they hadn't gotten all the muck out, and he got an infection. Had to take off more leg halfway across the pond. Eventually, he ended up in my care. It seemed for a while like he might make it. That's when I had him measured for these. He was wiry, with strong arms like you. I caught him trying a handstand in the ward once." He smiled. "Idiot nearly fell on his face." His smile faded. "But the infection was just biding its time. We had to take off more leg. I did it myself the last time. Cleaned everything out. Poured in so much carbolic, I was afraid I'd poison him." He turned his head away. "It was all for naught, and he died of blood poisoning. Don't know quite why, but I've kept these with me since."

Jersey was ashamed at his cheeky comment about the walk over. He swallowed. "I'm sorry about your friend."

Connie rapped the table top sharply, his eyes hard. "He wasn't a friend. He was a patient."

Jersey looked him in the eye. "Right."

The doctor drew his fingers down his nose. "It was probably unfair to tell you about Jeff. Use them well."

CHAPTER 16

FRANK DIDN'T have enough money for the train to Plainfield. He knew it when he left the school. He told himself that was the reason why he hadn't tried harder to get Jersey to come along. He planned to hop a freight, so Jersey's crutches would be a liability. Short of walking or bumming a ride, it was the only way he could think of to get to the far side of New Jersey, almost to New York City. So he took the trolley to Market Street and asked around until someone told him about the big railroad yard south of the city. A trolley to the naval shipyard got him pretty close. It wasn't long before he found other would-be travelers who knew the ropes and could show him how to identify the freight trains that were going to New York (and would pass through Plainfield) and how to avoid the railroad detectives.

That was how he came to be peering from behind a clump of tall brown grass at the edge of the railroad yard where trains passed slowly enough for a man to run alongside and grab hold. All he had to do was spot an open car, preferably in the middle of the train, not too near the engine or the caboose. He wished he had a rucksack instead of his carpetbag. The sun was gone and the temperature had fallen, but the yard was bright enough from the arc lights; he'd be able to see the next train.

He was shivering by the time he heard the chuffing of a steam engine and a set of muffled clanks. A locomotive was taking up the slack between cars. The pitch of the engine increased as the train accelerated slowly through the yard. Soon he saw the yellow light of a headlamp playing on the brown grass above his head. He waited until the locomotive and tender were past and all he could hear was the screech of metal on metal and the clacking of the wheels hitting joints in the rails, then he stuck up his head.

Here we go. An empty boxcar with a partially open door neared his hiding spot. He grabbed his bag and ran, reaching the tracks just as the boxcar swayed into position. He swerved to run parallel to the car, then heaved his bag into the open door. He was committed, at least if he wanted to see his clothes again. There was a ladder up the side of the car, so he slowed and grabbed for the steel bars as they came along side. His legs swung free, and he thought for a second they would go under the car, but then he got a knee onto the ladder and pulled himself up. *Now what?* How was he supposed to get inside? The sliding door was at least fifteen feet away and there was nothing to hold on to between the ladder and the opening. Not knowing what else to do, he climbed the rest of the way up and slithered onto the top of the boxcar. There was a narrow platform for walking along the top, but he was afraid to stand or sit for fear the brakeman or conductor in the cabin car might see him. It was going to be a cold trip to Plainfield if he couldn't find some way of getting inside the swaying box.

FRANK SOLVED the problem of getting into the boxcar when the train squealed to a stop at a signal. He slid down the ladder, jogged to the open door, and climbed in without difficulty. Using his carpetbag for a pillow, he lay down on the rough planks and looked out at the passing night. Soon the train was crossing the Delaware River. A barge passed under the bridge piled high with dark mounds of coal. Was this the life he was supposed to be living? Lulled by the rhythmic clacking of the rails, he was content to let the question pass unanswered.

He woke abruptly when a bundle of some kind landed on his legs. Startled, he scrambled to get out of the way. Seconds later, the bundle was followed by three men who pulled themselves into the boxcar. Their faces were hidden in the dark interior of the car, their bulky shapes silhouetted against faint starlight.

"Lookee here!" said one, tripping over Frank. "Seems there's already a bum in this 'un."

"Hello, my name is Frank."

"We've a swank 'ere, boys," said the first.

"Should we show 'im the ropes?" said his companion.

"Be a public service."

There was a sudden movement in the dark, and Frank's head burst into pain.

FRANK CAME to with a throbbing head and no coat, shirt, shoes, or pants. Before he could come to terms with his predicament, his self-appointed instructors grasped him on either side and sent him flying headfirst into the night. Sharp rocks and skull-crushing bridge abutments filled his mind before his outstretched arms hit the ground with a sound like the crack of a baseball bat.

HE CAME to for the second time shivering in a muddy ditch. To this point in his life, he had not known that mere shivering could cause excruciating pain. Stiff and bruised as he was, he knew instinctively that he must move or die of exposure. When he tried, he discovered the source of the crack when he'd landed. His left arm burned with white heat when he tried to shift it. He lay in mud, racked with convulsive shudders until the cold began to feel warm and he knew it was now or never: he must move if he wanted to see Jersey again.

He tried to sit up without jostling his arm. A wave of dizziness and nausea nearly put him back in the mud. Taking deep breaths, he got to his knees, swaying but upright. Trying to stand made him vomit. He spat bile and stayed on his knees until he heard the high shriek of a train whistle. It screamed salvation. He waited until the headlight was too bright to look at directly, then stood and waved his good arm like a drunken supplicant. He thought at first he hadn't been seen and that he would die in the mud of the ditch. But the pitch of the engine changed, and he heard the squeal of brake shoes on steel wheels.

AN ANGRY man in a cap yelled at him. The man grasped his arm. Frank screamed.

HE WAS in some kind of bunk bed. He was warm, but jerking from side to side. His arm burned fiercely. He tried to tell the man in the cap to quit shoving him, but he wouldn't listen.

SOMEONE WAS in the room with him, smoking. Bright light turned the inside of his eyelids red. He didn't care to speak to anyone, so he kept his eyes closed. But the man did not leave—or stop smoking. Frank cleared his throat. "Not supposed to smoke... in hospital."

"Ain't no hospital."

"Where?"

"Doc Jones's surgery. Bound Brook, New Jersey."

Frank took stock. Unfortunately, his arm was still attached. The fierce burn had transformed into a deep ache that was almost worse. In addition, the limb had grown a couple of sizes.

"Doc set that for you. Says you'll be in the cast for six weeks."

"You're not the doctor?"

The man hooted. Frank's head exploded. "Sorry, fella," the man said. "Guess your head still hurts."

"Please go away," Frank whispered.

"Got to ask you a few questions."

Frank opened his eyes in resignation. It was a mistake. "Christ!"

"Blasphemy won't get rid of me. Answers might."

Frank sighed. "At your service."

The man chuckled softly. "Now that's better. How'd you come to flag down a train in your drawers—with a lump on your noggin?"

"Had to get to Plainfield. No money. Hopped a freight in Philadelphia."

"I don't imagine you fell off by yourself. Leastways not in your drawers."

"Got jumped." Frank saw there were crow's feet around the questioner's eyes, the kind of lines you get from looking at the world a little sideways. "Said they'd show me the ropes."

"They mention to close the door of the boxcar after you climb in?"

"Nope."

The man stubbed out his cigarette. "Might have done."

"Thanks."

The man stood and stretched. "The railroad don't take kindly to trespassers. On the other hand, they was more eager to be rid of you than to press charges. I wired the bulls in Newark to be on the lookout for a gang on one of their trains, but there ain't nothing likely to come of that." He sighed and put on a wide-brimmed hat. "Got a name and address—in case I need to get in touch with you?"

"Who are you?"

The man laughed again. "My apologies. John Bloom at your disposal, Union County Sheriff."

"Pleased to meet you, Sheriff. I'm Frank Huddleston, currently residing at the Germantown Friends School in Philadelphia." *The address in Plainfield!* It had been in his coat pocket and was probably in New York by now.

"Well, Mr. Huddleston, I suggest you walk next time."

"Yes, sir."

"The doc'll know how to reach me, if you need anything."

"Thank you."

The sheriff left. Frank closed his eyes. It occurred to him that he could have hitched with Jersey. Crutches probably would have helped attract a ride.

FRANK SHIFTED restlessly under the bedclothes. It was not that he was ungrateful for the care he received. But he'd been lying around for two whole days, effectively tethered to the bed by a complete lack of clothing, and he had yet to actually meet the mysterious doctor who had set his arm.

Lying about with nothing to do, his mind consistently returned to Jersey and the stupid fight that had led to this ridiculous predicament. If he hadn't been so hot to leave Philadelphia, if he hadn't let his jealousy of that silly girl get between him and Jersey, he'd never have hopped the freight and he wouldn't be in this mess.

The short, beaming woman who came in to change his dressings and replenish his pitcher of water appeared to be some sort of housekeeper, judging from her black dress and white apron. If she knew how to speak English, she declined to share her knowledge with Frank. Despite repeated tries, including a recent attempt to mime dressing while remaining under the sheet for modesty's sake, he had been unable to make her understand that he wanted clothes. Having only one working arm with which to demonstrate did not help.

Her response had been an even broader smile accompanied by a distinct facial tic, which might have indicated a nervous disorder, but looked suspiciously like suppressed laughter. When sufficiently recovered, she made a series of gestures that conveyed little except that he should rest, possibly until five o'clock. If five o'clock was what she meant, it was no comfort. He had no watch, nor was any clock within view. He was certain he could negotiate suitable compensation for whatever clothing might be found, if the doctor would stop to check on his patient.

Frank had just decided to get up, wrapped in a blanket if necessary, and explore his prison, when the door opened to admit a very large man in a spotless white coat. The man was not only fat—certainly he was that— but also tall and possessed of a very large head. His gray hair was unevenly cropped. Frank wondered if he'd cut it himself. More likely, he'd tried to explain what he wanted to his housekeeper.

"Well! At last I find you awake," said the man in a velvet basso profundo. "Henry Jones, at your service." Doctor Jones extended an enormous hand to shake. The man could have juggled watermelons for Barnum & Bailey.

"Pleased to meet you, doctor. I'm Frank Huddleston."

"How do you do, Mr. Huddleston? The arm hurting you much?" The doctor leaned over to look into Frank's eyes. His looming bulk was disconcerting. "Fortunately, you had a clean break, with no protrusion through the skin. It should heal in about six weeks."

"It aches. But it's nothing I can't live with. Listen, I'm very grateful for the care you've shown me, but I'm eager to be on my way. Do you think it might be possible to find some clothes? I'll compensate you for them—and for your services—in any way I can."

"Dear me, Mr. Huddleston, you are in a rush. Agrippa tells me you've been making the most amusing attempts to communicate. You must not think her dull. She's been acting on my orders—although I was unaware of her method until this afternoon. I had a difficult birth to attend. Baby insisted on coming into the world feet first. In any case, I told her to keep you in bed for a day or two, if at all possible. I gather she found it convenient to keep you in a state of undress. She says it would have been almost as fun to give you some of my old things and see what you did with them."

He chuckled softly, his low rumble evoking a lion's purr, measuring with both hands his impressive girth and height. Still rumbling, he folded down Frank's cover and inspected the cuts and bruises Frank had received upon ejection from the boxcar. "You appear to be healing well enough, Mr. Huddleston. However, I recommend another day of rest, if you can bear it. You'll find the arm aches less after the first week."

"But I must get to Plainfield as soon as possible." Another day of solitary bed rest would be unendurable. He would start gnawing his limbs.

The doctor straightened, put his knuckles on his hips, and blew out his cheeks like a petulant monarch. "That certainly won't take long. Wherever you go, I trust you will not try the railroad again? Should you jar that arm, you'll regret it. On the other hand, it is no business of mine what you do once you remove yourself from our care." He leaned over again and enveloped Frank's shoulder in his giant hand. "You must follow your own road."

Intended or not, the gentle pressure on his shoulder was a mildly painful reminder of his fresh bruises. The examination had tired Frank. "Might I have a robe at least? Is there a place I might sit and read?"

"A reasonable man! How delightful!" The doctor's enthusiasm brought the deep vibration back to his voice. "I believe we can accommodate you, Mr. Huddleston, if you are reconciled to another day with us. Agrippa might even remember a few words of English, should you grant her a smile. By the way, you are invited to supper, if you feel up to it."

It was pathetic how grateful he felt. "I would be delighted to join you, Doctor."

CHAPTER 17

JERSEY ARRIVED for his appointment with Mr. Gould on his new crutches. His muscles might be tired by the end of the day, but he was delighted to walk without aggravating the raw skin and bruises under his arms.

The nurse showed him into a room like a chemist's shop. The cabinets that covered the walls contained a selection of artificial arms and legs rather than a chemist's jars and bottles. On the left side of the room, maple-framed, glass-fronted cabinets above a counter contained a selection of carved hands and hooks. A taller set of cabinets on the right side contained lower limb replacements, some carved to the likeness of a human leg, while others were little more than metal braces riveted to a pair of shoes. A workbench with hand tools and plaster casting supplies occupied the back of the room. In the center, a table held a set of bound volumes. A chest-high folding screen stood in one corner.

"Mr. Gould will be with you shortly. While you wait, you may examine the catalogs in the binders. The legs are in the green volume," said the nurse, as she ushered him into the room.

"Thanks." Despite the invitation, Jersey wasn't ready to look at pictures. Too many interesting devices lined the cabinets. The hands particularly fascinated him. Most appeared to be simple plaster casts or carved hands that had no function, but an information sheet from the D.W. Dorrance Company, which someone had posted next to a hook, explained how the device opened through the use of a strap across the back so one could grasp objects with it.

"I thought I'd find you looking at the legs, Mr. Rohn. My name is Gould."

Jersey turned around to find a narrow man with a long face and workman's apron holding out a hand to shake.

"Pleased t' meet ya, Mr. Gould. Actually, I like the hands the best. That one is very fine, like a sculpture." As he examined the large, finely detailed hand, Jersey realized with sudden horror why it had caught his eye; it had long, strong fingers remarkably like Frank's.

Gould held his long head at a slight angle, brows furrowed. "Yes, it's pretty, but it has little utility. Now, the Dorrance hook—a man can use that."

Not to touch a person. Jersey's face heated at the thought.

Gould frowned and turned briskly away as if he could read Jersey's mind.

"It's a leg you're needing. We'll start by making a cast of your stump. I'm afraid you must disrobe, Mr. Rohn." He handed Jersey a flimsy gown and a pair of cotton shorts much like a boxer's. "You may wear these. They are too short to interfere with the plaster." He motioned to the screen in the corner. Jersey undressed while Gould continued. "We'll start with some measurements. In a few minutes, I will wrap your stump with strips of cloth dipped in plaster. You'll feel some heat as the plaster sets, but it should not be too uncomfortable."

In all, Jersey spent about two hours with the prosthetist. While Gould finished the cast, Jersey tried on various legs and shuffled through pictures of more. Connie had warned him that they would likely have to send away to a manufacturer, but he was disappointed that none of the legs fit properly. One was too long. Another pinched his stump painfully. None were close enough to encourage walking unaided. By the time Gould wrapped up, Jersey was thoroughly discouraged. He was buttoning his shirt when a knock sounded at the door.

The door opened slightly and a man peered in. "Pardon me. I'm looking for Mr. Gould. The nurse said I'd find him…."

"I'm Gould. You are?"

"Martin Greenleaf, at your service. I represent the Ohio Willow Wood Company of Mt. Sterling, Ohio. We make legs." As he spoke, the man nudged the door farther open and extended a hand to shake. "I'm pleased to meet you, Mr. Gould." Catching sight of Jersey, he added, "I see that I'm intruding."

Intruding or not, Mr. Greenleaf did not withdraw. His gaze traveled down from Jersey's face to rest on his stump. "I see you're missing a pin, sir. I'm sorry for your loss. You were overseas, I'm thinking? Dear me, so many of our boys lost parts there. Terrible thing."

The man's sentiment seemed a mite overplayed. Jersey was suspicious until the man stepped into the room. Then he noticed the man's stiff-legged movement. Maybe he had cause for his feeling.

The man smiled broadly. "You're a sharp one, yes sir. I lost it to a train, a few years back." He advanced, hand out.

Jersey balanced on his good leg and put out his hand to shake, the new crutch hanging free from his wrist, as designed. "I'm Jersey Rohn."

"Pleased to meet you, Mr. Rohn. Now that's interesting. Never seen a pair o'crutches quite like those."

"Dr. Constantine designed them," Jersey said.

"I made them here," said Gould tightly.

"Then I owe you, Mr. Gould. They're a far sight better'n my old ones," Jersey said.

Mr. Gould made a small sucking sound. "I believe the straps could be made easier to adjust with one hand."

"You're a perfectionist, Mr. Gould."

"Perhaps. What can I do for you, Mr. Greenleaf?"

"Mr. Ambrose—he's our founder, lost both his legs in a railroad accident—has designed a new leg. Since you're the prosthetist to see in these parts, I was hoping you'd share your views on it." Glancing at Jersey, he added, "I've one with me, if you've a moment to spare."

The leg was beautifully made. Even Gould said that it resembled nothing so much as the remnant of an ancient Greek statue. Finely carved of willow and designed to flex in the knee and ankle, its human shape made Jersey think of Frank's hands again. He did not have to be asked twice if he wanted to try it out. Unfortunately, the example Mr. Greenleaf had with him did not fit his stump. Greenleaf had an answer for that: if Jersey would travel to Mt. Sterling they would fit the leg themselves. If travel was impractical, he would make a cast and measurements himself to send to Mt. Sterling. Greenleaf would be staying in town for a week.

"If you'd care to take my card, I've written the name of my lodgings on the back."

After Mr. Greenleaf left, Jersey asked Gould what he thought.

"Hard to say, until you've tried to walk with it."

"Is there one you'd recommend more?"

"Not really."

Jersey was tired and Gould taciturn. "Mr. Gould, what aren't you saying?"

Gould sucked his teeth. "Willow Wood legs are pretty, there's no denying it, but they're expensive. I don't rightly know whether the government will pay for one."

JAMES WATCHED Jersey mount the stairs to his apartment. "The new crutches seem to help."

"Save me having to hop all the way. Still leave me puffing."

"Do you want me to carry one?"

Jersey held the bannister with one hand and a crutch with the other. "Nope, wanna see if I can do this by my lonesome. Not always going to have a body to carry my crutches."

"It's certainly a quieter operation."

"Neighbors squawk?"

"Not at all." Actually, they had, until James explained the cause. After that, only Mrs. Waversack complained, suggesting James ought to be the one to go visiting. "Let the cripple stay at home," she had grumbled.

"How did it go with the prosthetist?" asked James.

"Well enough." Jersey flopped down into the armchair. "Whew."

"Lemonade?"

"Sure." Jersey examined the bookshelves that lined James's walls.

"You were going to tell me about the prosthetist," James called from the kitchen.

"I was?"

"You'd better, if you want anything to drink!"

"THEN THIS salesman comes in. You know the type: a little pushy, apt to stick his foot in the door if you ain't quick enough t' stop him. Well, this fellow got his foot in the door all right, only it was made of wood. Turns out he sells legs, fine things carved out of willow. That's the name of his company, the Ohio Willow Wood Company. He persuaded me to try one, only it was too long and didn't fit right."

"You're telling me there are people who make a living selling prosthetic legs?" James laughed.

"Yep." Jersey grinned. "They got whole catalogs of spare parts."

"I had no idea. So you liked this fellow's leg. Will you order one?"

Jersey looked out the window toward Germantown Avenue. "Nah."

"Why not?"

"You got any more lemonade?" Jersey planted his crutches and stood. Balancing on his heel, he used his crutches to spin around.

"Watch it, you'll knock over the lamp!" James hovered as Jersey spun faster and faster, his dark curls glinting in the sunlight, until he collapsed, laughing wildly.

"You're worse than my twelve-year-olds, Jersey. I don't think you need any more sugar!"

"Sorry. Don't know what to do with myself."

"Anything I can do?"

"You're the only thing keeping me from flying out the window, James. Tell me about your books. Have any about a body like me?"

James looked at his tattered collection. "Francis and I spent hours talking about stories we read. We acted out scenes, played our favorite characters. When we were in college, we went for walks at night. Francis said he wanted to write after college, but—"

"Frank went to college?"

"Sure, we were at Swarthmore together before the war."

Jersey hunched his shoulders and rubbed his stump. "A college boy. I might've known."

SARAH UNDERWOOD heard a sound from the parlor below her bedroom and wondered who could be there at this time of night. Before she could investigate, a flash of lightning lit her bedroom window, followed quickly by a crack of thunder. *That was close. I hope we've not lost a tree.* She heard a thump from the parlor. Someone was down there. She sat up and looked at her husband, confirming what his drone already told her. He slept soundly, his mouth open. Disinclined to wake him, she got out of bed, put on a robe and soft slippers, and went down the stairs quietly.

From the foyer, one could not go directly into the parlor. The only access was via the dining room. A pair of heavy sliding doors, rarely closed, connected the rooms. The doors were open now, so she padded into the dining room and stopped to listen. Another flash of lightning lit the room and she saw her own shadow against the wall. Her sleeping gown and robe in silhouette made her look like a nun. Irritated, she brushed the thought aside. Another crack of thunder rattled the house. A series of rumbling aftershocks died away slowly and she heard sobbing from the parlor.

She rushed into the room to find Jersey on the floor by the sofa. He shook violently, his hands clasping his ears, his eyes squeezed shut. "Frank," he cried out, "where are you?"

She did not speak, but knelt by his side and touched his hair. When he did not respond, she gathered him in her arms and dragged him onto the sofa, where they sat until the shaking subsided and he stopped gasping. Eventually, his body stiffened, signaling the return of his self-possession, so she released him and moved away. The storm front had passed. A steady rain drummed against the windows, but the thunder merely rumbled distantly.

Jersey licked his lips. "You oughtn't to have seen that."

"Nonsense." She peered at his face, which was barely visible in the pale yellow light from the streetlamp outside the windows. Dark rings highlighted inflamed eyes. The rings had grown more pronounced in the last week. "Thee did not acquire the rings under thy eyes from one night's adventure."

"Rings?" He raised an unsteady hand to his face. "No."

"Thee is not sleeping."

"I've had nightmares since the war."

"Would thee tell me about them?"

"You mean well, Mrs. Underwood, but they're unpleasant. I don't like to talk about 'em."

She clasped her hands in her lap. "It might help thee to speak of them."

"I don't talk—I told Frank," he corrected. "But he and I...." He shrugged.

"Francis always inspired confidences. I'm glad he has not lost the knack. Perhaps a doctor might help—"

"No offense, ma'am, but I don't think you know...." He took a breath. "I know you mean to help. It's just there's nothing to be done. You know how a chick will fix on the first person it sees when it's born? Follow him 'round like he was its mam? Something happens to that chick when it sees that first living being, it don't matter whether it's a chicken, whether it makes sense at all. There ain't nothing can be done to change it. That's how it is for me. I got these things fixed in my head and there ain't nothing gonna shake 'em loose. I just gotta live with 'em, jus' like I gotta live with this." He raised his stump and waggled it, then held up his hand. "See, all steady now. It ain't killed me yet."

"Thee have a strong inner light, Jersey Rohn."

"I don't entirely know what you mean by that, ma'am, but I'll take it as a compliment."

"Will thee go back to bed?"

"No, but I best go dress."

"Can I make thee breakfast?" she asked, a little desperately.

The taut lines of Jersey's face stretched into a toothy grin. "That, ma'am, you can do for me."

IT WASN'T true, what Jersey told Mrs. Underwood. He painted a picture of an accommodation that was, in fact, still in negotiation. When Frank was around, he could delude himself into thinking he was better. With Frank gone, his hope that the nightmare would lose its grip on him diminished along with his capacity for sleep. The part of him that watched his panic from outside suggested he might, in time, come to terms with his condition—if he didn't drown first, some night when frantic exhaustion swept him over the falls. In the meantime, he had to leave Philadelphia.

He put on a face for Mrs. Underwood, pretending nothing had happened, and ate oatmeal and sausages like a firstborn son. While he might have the strength to go on despite his terrors, he did not have the strength to share his infirmity with a stranger.

He would go to Mt. Sterling, Ohio, and put himself at the mercy of the owner of the Willow Wood Company. Mr. Greenleaf had told him that the owner had lost both his legs. Maybe the man would let Jersey work off the cost of his leg. He might have to accommodate his ghosts, but he did not have to live with crutches. He would get the leg he wanted.

"NOW WHO can that be from?" said Abigail Huddleston. Betty probably thought she was mad. Since her husband's death, she had developed an embarrassing habit of vocalizing her thoughts. Apparently, she required a voice in the house, even if it was only her own.

She plucked the letter from the tray on her husband's massive plantation desk and carried it into the parlor, still avoiding the desk two years after her husband's passing. She would read awhile before dinner. The return address was the Germantown Friends School in Philadelphia. They probably wanted money. Her husband had studied there as a boy. "They never forget you," she said, addressing the portrait of her husband that hung over the mantelpiece. It had been commissioned to commemorate the christening of her husband's last ship. By then, his hair was the same white-flecked gray as the sea on which he had spent so much of his life. But the painting showed the same combination of stern features and kind eyes that had attracted her fifty years before.

The letter was addressed to Frank Huddleston, so it had to be a mistake. But the name was similar to that of her husband and his namesake, her grandson. "I could give you back to the postman. No, I shan't do that." She put the letter aside for after dinner. She would need something to occupy her then.

Dear Frank,

    I don't know if this will reach you, but I thought you'd want to know what I figured out talking to James Spalding. You wrote three years of letters to him from France! I reckon there must be fifty! James showed me one from just before you were injured—you'll want to see that.

    When are you coming back? The days go slowly without you here to keep me company. James is very good to me, and we gab as much as his teaching schedule allows, but you're my Special Friend.

    Tomorrow, I go to the Jefferson Clinic to talk to Connie—Dr. Constantine—the fellow I told you about. I wish you were here to go with me. I'd feel so much more steady if you were here to see me through.

    With fond regard,

    Jersey

Mrs. Huddleston held the letter between two fingers as if it might burst into flame at any second. Frank had to be Francis, her grandson. It was beyond belief, but fifteen years ago she had watched Francis and his friend, James Spalding, chase squirrels in the park like a couple of puppies. It had to be Francis this Jersey person addressed, but if Francis wasn't dead, where had he been for the last year? Why did this woman write to him here? What was her relationship with her grandson?

"Mrs. Huddleston, your coffee."

Her husband would not have approved of the coffee, having grown up Quaker, but her standards had relaxed somewhat since his passing. "Thank you, Betty." The young woman set down the tray and turned to go.

"Betty, I must…." She did not know what to do.

"Do you need something, Mrs. Huddleston?"

That lawyer. He would know what to do. "I need you to take a note into town." She looked at the clock on the mantelpiece. "In the morning. Would you do that first thing?"

"Yes, ma'am."

She moved with increasing speed toward her husband's study. "I'll have it ready when you return for the tray."

When Betty returned, she picked up the letter. "Mr. Ronald Matheson, Esquire. You know that you could use the telephone to call him, ma'am."

"Don't be impertinent, Betty."

The next morning, Mrs. Huddleston wrote a letter to the Germantown Friends School requesting information about her grandson. In the afternoon, Mrs. Huddleston got out knitting she didn't care for but needed to keep her hands busy. After missing a stitch and failing to notice it for two entire rows, she threw the yarn aside in disgust. She tried reading a new novel by Willa Cather, but much as she loved Cather, reading proved like planning next year's garden: impossible for her to contemplate in the dark and rainy season.

She got up to stare out the window at the brown and dripping trees that bordered the lawn. *I must ask the gardener to rake again when the rain has gone.* There was a knock on the front door. She waited for Betty to show the visitor into the parlor. Could it be Francis, come to retrieve his letter? She snapped open the drapes to admit more light into the room. The visitor proved to be Mr. Matheson, the lawyer for whom she had sent.

"Mrs. Huddleston. It is so very good to find you well."

Mr. Matheson was a pug-nosed gentleman of indeterminate years who wore black suits of an old-fashioned cut. She knew him to be capable, but his habit was to conceal his purpose under a thick layer of cosmetic language. "Mr. Matheson. I'm certain you're well too. Please come in." She led the way to her husband's study. "I want to talk to you about my grandson."

"Yes, ma'am. Your grandson. I'm very sorry, but I thought he was... gone to his reward."

"Oh, for Heaven's sake. You may speak plainly. I called you here because I received a communication from a young lady—or I assume her to be so—who appears to be a friend of my grandson's. The letter was addressed to him here and is quite recent. I have, therefore, reason to believe that my grandson may be alive and that he may have been on his way to Plainfield when the letter was written. But he is not here."

"That is very good news, ma'am. I am so very pleased for you." Mr. Matheson spoke with an energy that belied his stationary form.

"Mr. Matheson, do you think that you could refrain from using the word *very* again for the remainder of our conversation?"

"I'm sorry?" Mr. Matheson's eyes widened.

"Never mind. I worry, and it has made me irritable."

"Yes, ma'am. Your note was not specific as to how I might help you."

"I need your assistance. As I said, my grandson may have been on his way here when the letter was written, but he is not here. I want him found."

"I see." Mr. Matheson's face lost all expression. "Have you considered the financial implication, should the boy be found?"

"How could you possibly believe that I—" She stopped, mindful that she had asked the man to speak directly. "I suppose you are only doing your duty as you understand it, Mr. Matheson. Please listen carefully. My *only* concern is to see my grandson restored to his family—restored to me. If that should mean that his inheritance is restored to him, that is only right and proper. I do not wish to speak of financial considerations again."

Mr. Matheson's face regained some feeling, although she wasn't certain what feeling it expressed. "Yes, ma'am. You are very clear. Your desire is that I should make inquiries as to the location of your grandson."

"Yes." She tapped the arm of her chair to punctuate her words. "Immediately."

"Very well. There remains only one other small consideration. Your husband, when he was alive of course, was in the habit of paying my firm a retainer so as to ensure that there would be no impediment to a rapid and thorough response whenever he desired our assistance. Since he died, I'm afraid—"

"Too many words, Mr. Matheson."

Mr. Matheson stopped and waited.

Mrs. Huddleston tapped again. "We shall resume my husband's practice."

"Very good, Mrs. Huddleston. I shall begin inquiries immediately. I need a description of your grandson, a picture if you have one. Might I be permitted to see the letter?"

"Mr. Matheson, you are transformed. I will give you a photograph taken at his college, although it is outdated now." Mrs. Huddleston removed the letter from her husband's desk drawer, but paused before handing it to the lawyer. "I need not tell you to preserve this carefully."

"No, ma'am." Mr. Matheson was reading before the words left his mouth. When he finished, he glanced around the room and pulled at his tie.

"Mr. Matheson. Do you recall my first instruction?"

"Very well, ma'am." He sighed. "I cannot help but wonder the reason for the young lady's imminent visit to the doctor."

"You are thinking she may be with child."

He nodded, reluctantly. "It would explain the boy's distance from your family, if he were involved in a relationship of which he thought you would not approve. The letter is peculiar. Why, for instance, would your grandson be pleased to learn that he had written letters to Mr. Spalding? How could this be news to him?"

"I don't know, Mr. Matheson. I don't know what to think. I only know that I want my grandson back—no matter what his situation."

Mr. Matheson rose and bowed formally. "I regret, ma'am, that your husband's business did not bring me here more often."

DR. JONES raised a sausage-like finger. "The doctor who is certain is certain to be wrong. That's what I say. In my profession, we are often faced with difficult decisions. For instance, do we save the mother or the unborn child? The practitioner who hasn't faced that dilemma hasn't been in practice long. Sure, the family must decide, but what if the treatment that might save the mother is certain to kill the child? Perhaps the husband wants to save the mother and the mother wants to save the child. Have I any right to weigh in?"

The doctor paused his rumination to sip his coffee, the delicate cup looking like a piece from a child's tea set in his giant paw.

Frank's first surprise of the evening had waited in the dining room. The small infirmary in which he had been housed had a tile floor, Shaker furniture, and tin ceiling. It was a tidy extension to the doctor's well-equipped, if sparsely decorated, surgery. But the dining room into which the doctor led him looked like the common room of a college dormitory. Books were stacked on the table, on the chairs, and on the floor. A double folio ledger lay open at one end of the table. Arrayed into groups around the ledger were piles of small objects: buttons, safety pins, jacks, coins, and tiny bones. Each item had a numbered label attached to it, which Frank assumed must correspond to an entry in the ledger.

The doctor ignored the collection and guided Frank to the other end of the table, took position at a polished sideboard, and asked Frank if he wanted wine or coffee.

The second surprise was Agrippa. She wore her usual black dress and white apron, so Frank was not surprised when she carried in a platter of fried chicken and dishes of roasted potatoes and rutabaga, but then she filled a plate for herself, folded her apron over a chair, and settled herself across from the doctor.

The doctor, having refilled his cup, continued his soliloquy. "People do the damnedest things, but when you tease out the story, there's usually a reason. It may be a bad one, but there will be one you can comprehend if you know the circumstances." The doctor cocked his head slightly and peered at Frank from under lowered lids. "For instance, why would a well-spoken young man with a recent haircut jump a freight train? For the first time, judging from the result. He doesn't speak like one, but he has the calluses of a farmer or ditch digger. His clothes might tell you something, only he doesn't have any. It's a fine mystery."

Frank thought of dissembling, but he owed the man. "I'll make you a deal, Doctor Jones. I will tell you why I jumped the train, if you will explain what those things are and why you're collecting them."

"Ha! A fair price for my curiosity," said the doctor. "I thought I'd have to wile it out of you."

Frank laughed. "Now that I come to it, I don't know where to start." He raised his hands. "Don't say at the beginning. That's the problem. I don't know the beginning, so I'll have to start with the first thing I remember clearly: some cows in a barn and a one-legged man perched on a milking stool. I wanted to know how he had lost his leg."

"SO JERSEY and I went to Philadelphia to look for letters. We had some success discovering where I lived and so forth. The people at the school were very good to us. But I couldn't remember a single person introduced to me. Even my childhood friend, James Spalding, meant nothing to me. It was… discouraging."

"You were close?" Agrippa held out a hand, fingers crossed. "Like so. You and this friend?"

Frank's neck clicked when he twisted in the direction of the thickly accented voice. He'd all but forgotten Agrippa was there.

"I'm told we were. He was crushed when I didn't know him."

Agrippa shook her head. "Is terrible thing."

The doctor leaned his great head back and blew out his cheeks. "Seeing old friends and acquaintances has not helped? Have you tried hypnosis?"

"No," Frank said, picturing the doctor as an Eastern mystic in tent-sized flowing robe and turban.

"I see you are skeptical. I believe it has been tried recently to help soldiers recover from traumatic events. Some of my colleagues argue one must relive the trauma to be rid of it. Trauma is associated with memory loss."

"Trauma?"

"You drove an ambulance near the front. You may have witnessed much."

"You hit head?" said Agrippa.

"I don't know, exactly. All they told my grandparents is that I was found in a lane by some soldiers and taken to an aid station. I don't remember anything at all. It's odd, *je parle le Français un peu*, but I don't remember learning French. I can drive a Tin Lizzy, but I don't remember learning that either."

"Part of the ambulance training, I expect."

"Certainly, but why do I remember how to do things but not people or events?"

The doctor grunted. "We know very little about how the mind works."

"I'm still curious about that project." Frank nodded toward the end of the table.

Jones ran his eyes over the collection. "It is my attempt to make sense of the incomprehensible."

"What do you mean?"

"I have been in medical practice for many years, mostly in New York City. You might say this small community is my retirement home." Jones smiled at Agrippa. Her returning look was a veil lifting.

Frank shifted his gaze to his coffee cup, unwilling to intrude.

The doctor chuckled, then heaved himself to his feet. "The objects that you see arranged—sorted, classified, labeled, recorded in the ledger— are items that I have removed from patients or that my colleagues have removed from patients. They have come mostly from the digestive tract or respiratory system, although those bullets were taken from every conceivable part of the body. The ones on the left, starting with that pile of buttons, were fatal. The ones on the right were removed from the living. All are classified by outcome, type, and the location from which they were extracted. The ledger contains the name of each patient, pertinent details, and measurements."

Frank's attention was drawn to a bright button imprinted with the words, *Honor Roll*. It lay in a pile on the left side of the collection.

"I have tried for many years without success to measure any difference between the items on the left and the items on the right." Pointing at the ledger, Jones continued. "Please satisfy your curiosity. You need not be embarrassed."

Frank read descriptions, names, dates, and outcomes until he could take in no more.

"You have not said how you came to be on that train or what happened to your friend, Jersey," Jones prompted.

"The head of school, Mr. Underwood, found an address for me. My father's parents. They were in Plainfield, but I lost the address. It was in my coat when it was stolen from me on the train. I had no money and Jersey… chose to stay in Philadelphia, so I jumped the freight."

The doctor's eyes glinted from under gray eyebrows. "Did you and your friend have a falling out?" Frank had not realized he was so transparent.

"He wanted to stay at the school. There was a girl—I don't know. He just wanted to stay. Why do you want to know about Jersey?"

"You talk of him warmly." Agrippa opened a hand, palm up. "Then, poof, you are alone. Then you fall off train."

"I was thrown off the train," Frank said sharply.

"Of course, of course." The doctor's eyelids were half-closed.

"You think I tried to kill myself."

"Actually, I don't. But the idea crossed my mind. The sheriff's too, I suspect."

"Why would I try to kill myself?"

The doctor put his thumbs in the pockets of his vest and moved his belly gently as one would rock a baby. "There is the world as we would have it and there is the world as we find it."

Frank said nothing.

The doctor sighed. "What do you hope to find in Plainfield?"

"A memory."

"And if you should not?"

"A new beginning."

"What about your friend?"

"He has his own life to live." The doctor's skeptical look reflected his own unhappiness at the thought of leaving Jersey behind. He busied himself with a further examination of Dr. Jones's collection. It was time he found his own way to accommodate his losses.

IT NEARED lunchtime when Frank heard a distant bell. He was attempting to read one of the doctor's medical books, a random selection from one of the stacks that littered the room. He set it aside when he heard footsteps approach. He'd curled up on a settee in the doctor's sitting room, wearing a tentlike pair of pajamas tied around his waist with twine. Their arrangement and drape had caused Agrippa to have another fit when he modeled them, but he'd followed Agrippa to the sitting room and stretched his legs on the settee with an exaggerated sigh, nonetheless.

"He here, Mr. Sheriff. You want coffee?" Agrippa showed Sheriff Bloom into the room.

"Thank you, ma'am. I'd take a cup."

"How are you, Sheriff?"

"A little surprised, Mr. Huddleston, I got to say."

"How so?"

The sheriff appraised Frank's makeshift attire with a grin. "It seems there's more to you than meets the eye."

"You'd not tease a man in his infirmity? Tell me what you mean."

"I had a visit this morning from this lawyer fellow, Matheson, works for a law firm out of Plainfield. Seems there's someone looking for you, Frank, or should I say, Francis Huddleston. That is your name, isn't it?"

"So they tell me."

"Thought so. Seems the prodigal has returned."

"Wait! From Plainfield?"

The sheriff nodded. "Your grandmother is very eager to see you."

Frank's heart began to pound. Here was his chance to reclaim his past. He tried to picture his grandmother. Was her hair gray or white? Was she tall like Mrs. Underwood or plump like Mrs. Rohn?

CHAPTER 18

IT TURNED out the Huddleston family home was only ten miles from Dr. Jones's place. Had he felt up to it, Frank could have walked there. But the sheriff, whether seeing a political opportunity or pleased to have a front-row seat at the family drama, offered Frank a ride. He also lent Frank a suit of clothes until such time as he could acquire his own. To Frank's surprised thanks, he responded by suggesting, enigmatically, "There'll be something in it for me—one way or another.

"That's it there," said the sheriff, pointing at a rambling house. The colonial main section had a portico supported by fluted columns, but the house appeared to have grown additions like extra sons, none matching the original. Gravel crunched as the sheriff turned his car onto a circular driveway of raked gravel.

"This is it." The sheriff winked. "You'll not forget who helped you?"

Frank rubbed his head. "God willing."

The double doors of the mansion burst open to emit a young woman in a servant's plain dress. "You must be Master Francis! She's fit to be tied. Come right away." She had led him into the parlor.

"Francis!" An old woman ran to him, arms wide. Her hands went to her mouth when she saw Frank's arm in a sling.

Frank stepped backward, involuntarily.

"What's wrong, Francis? What happened to your arm?" she said.

Frank tried to control his breathing. "I'm sorry, ma'am. I don't wish to hurt you. It's just that I don't remember you. I've had amnesia since the war."

Frank watched his grandmother absorb the news of his amnesia. The softness of her face and hands belied the formal restraint of her coiffure and widow's black. He thought she looked like a stage actress at her retirement party—still capable of reaching the back rows, but fearful she was no longer wanted. When she spoke it was with disconcerting directness. "I would have preferred that you remember me." Mrs. Huddleston reached for Frank's hand and held it with both of hers. "An old lady's vanity is a tattered thing. But you are home now, and that is the important thing."

THE HOUSE to which his grandmother introduced Frank was inhabited by a ghost. There was no translucent wraith in the study, nor were there knocking sounds from the walls. The ghost that inhabited this house was the man who had built it—his grandfather, Francis Xavier Huddleston. He was present in the selection of books in the study: seafaring, American and Far Eastern history, Chinese culture and art, volumes of John Fox and the early Quakers. Oriental watercolors decorated the walls of the room. The man's extensive travels and eclectic taste was apparent in the furnishings. Philadelphia school tables and chairs held pride of place in the dining room. His grandfather's plantation desk had enough slots and drawers to hold every book and piece of paper in the Clark home.

Perhaps it was the way his grandmother introduced each item with the particulars of its acquisition by his grandfather: the ship, the port, the year of the voyage. She explained that the family business was shipping and that her grandfather had been one of the first to specialize in the clipper ships that made possible rapid trips to the Far East and West Coast. Her husband, in turn, had introduced steamships. There was much of Grandfather the Ghost in the rambling mansion, but the gray-haired lady before him remained elusive.

"Why didn't you write to me in Michigan? I would have come directly."

His grandmother's blue eyes glistened. "I didn't know where you were. I learned from the AFAU that you had been severely injured, but they had no record of what happened to you afterward. Their secretary died in the same influenza outbreak that took Joe and Adele. The man who wrote to me had just returned from France. He thought you must have died with your parents. Adele didn't want anything to do with her parents, didn't invite them to the wedding, so I never knew exactly where they lived. I couldn't imagine you would go there. When I didn't hear from you, I believed that you were gone. I am so ashamed." She pressed fists into her lap. "I lost faith."

They finished a tour of the house and settled in the study. "I was dead, in a way," said Frank. There was a book on the table between them, a feather marking the place where the reader had given up. *What does she read? Religious tracts like Eddy Clark?* Frank was unable to see the author's name. He would find out later, when he wasn't so tired and sore.

"I could not imagine that you would not write. When you didn't...." Mrs. Huddleston's knuckles were white. "We were close when you were a child. My vanity kept me from scouring the earth for you. I should have realized there was another explanation."

"You weren't thinking clearly then, ma'am." The young woman who'd met them at the door stood in the doorway with a tea tray.

"Perhaps not. It's no excuse."

Betty banged the tray onto the table next to Mrs. Huddleston. "It was despair, if you want to know the truth. She was half off her rocker with grief, and she gave in to the Devil's despair."

"That's quite enough, Betty. I will serve."

FRANK THRASHED in the canopied bed that dominated the bedroom. Betty told him the room had been his father's, but the furnishings reflected nothing of a young man, nothing of the dynamic lecturer who had lured his mother to Philadelphia, nothing of the teacher. The bureau and dresser were polished and smelled of beeswax. Before going to bed, he searched their drawers, hoping to find some memento of his father, but they were empty. The blankets smelled of cedar and must have come straight from storage in a chest. It was a pleasantly appointed guest room, and he was a guest.

Before retiring for the night, his grandmother had given him Jersey's letter. She apologized for reading it and asked about Jersey. He was in such turmoil, he hardly knew what to say. He told her only that Jersey was a friend from Michigan, then pled exhaustion and retired. His arm ached, and he was tired, but the true reason for his reticence was that he didn't dare read Jersey's letter in his grandmother's presence, least his feelings show in his face.

He'd been right to worry. He missed Jersey terribly and wanted nothing more than to see him, but Jersey's letter woke the beast he would have rather left slumbering—or locked in a private asylum. What did Jersey mean by "my Special Friend"? Whatever Jersey meant, it surely was not the stuff of his dream. He woke in the strange bedroom sweating and ashamed, his mind full of images: Jersey's generous lips and stubbled chin, Jersey's slender back under his hand. He sat up, afraid to relax for fear the dream would return if he slept. Was this the identity he'd hoped to recover? Or was this perversion God's punishment for his participation in the war? He could never allow the kind old lady who inhabited this home to discover the impostor who had replaced her grandson. It would have been better had she continued to think him dead.

He swung his legs off the bed and reached for his clothes. There was no past for him here, and no future either.

JERSEY MADE his way from the train station to the Willow Wood factory. The first snow of the season melted on the cut gravel road. Tiny flakes fell ruler-straight in still air. His eyes watered from the cold.

After paying for his ticket to Mt. Sterling, he'd only had enough money left for a few days of lodging. He'd have to find work soon or return to his parents' farm. Christmas was coming. Maybe he'd go home for a few days.

A stand of white pine beside the road reminded him of the tree his father would cut and the perpetual argument over candles that his father and mother resumed every Christmas Eve as if it were yesterday they'd last decorated a tree instead of last year. His mother insisted it was not a Christmas tree without candles. His father argued that it would be a fine Christmas, indeed, if they burned down the house. His mother would win. The tree would have candles, which they would light on Christmas Eve, filling the house with the scents of pine and beeswax. After dinner, his mother would read a story she'd picked out for the occasion from the *Taperville Current* or the *Saturday Evening Post*. The December her cousin died after a fall from his horse, she'd selected a passage from the Bible, but most years it was something sappy, full of miscreants redeemed and hope restored.

He would go home and show them his new leg.

Jersey's thoughts were interrupted by the sight of a doe browsing in the trees beside the road. She must have heard his crutches on the gravel for she lifted her head and froze, nostrils wide, tasting the air. When he continued moving in her direction, she raised her white tail and bounded off. It was only then he realized two yearlings grazed nearby. They followed their mother in graceful leaps, tails flashing in warning.

A policeman he'd stopped in town had told him it was two miles to the Willow Wood factory. He was to pass a creek and bear right at the fork that followed. He reached a bridge and figured he'd found the creek. The bridge was made of rough-cut planks and required attention, lest he catch a crutch in a gap. Safely across, he saw the fork ahead. In the distance, a small cluster of buildings shared the same red as his father's barn. The slanting rays of the winter sun reminded Jersey how quickly dark would come this time of year. He would have to find a place to stay for the night after visiting the factory.

After Gould told him the cost of the Willow Wood leg, he'd been up and down like a polo player on a green horse. He'd cut circles in James's carpet for a week, and finally decided to follow the salesman's suggestion and instruct Gould to send a complete set of his measurements and a cast of his stump to the factory. After the storm and his mortifying display of weakness, he fired off a note saying that he would visit for a fitting. He told no one the cost of the leg.

There were three red buildings, each with white-painted window frames that gave them a well-tended, cheerful air. Chimneys on the smaller buildings sent faint plumes of smoke to merge into the gray sky. They must have been running a furnace or smelter in the larger building, because a dark cloud roiled upward like the plume from a passing locomotive. A quarter mile away, he caught the flat sound of shouting on the dead air. *What in heck is going on over there?* The answer came when orange flames appeared above the roof of the larger building. It was on fire.

BY THE time Jersey reached the Willow Wood property the main building was fully engulfed. Writhing fingers of smoke and flame darkened the tops of the cheerful window frames. While Jersey watched, men in leather aprons and coveralls ran from every doorway and even climbed from the windows of the burning building like ants streaming from a disturbed anthill. With surprising speed and organization, they reformed into a bucket brigade fed by a water pump at the side of one of the smaller buildings, but it was apparent that their best efforts could do little to douse the inferno. If they were lucky, they might prevent the other buildings from igniting from the rain of hot sparks landing on their roofs.

Jersey was not the only one to come to this conclusion. After a series of terse orders barked by a dark-haired man in a white shirt and waistcoat standing a few yards ahead of Jersey, the workers split into two lines and laid ladders up the sides of the smaller buildings. Soon buckets were making the perilous climb from hand to hand to the rooftops. Drawn to see the man who was directing the brigades, Jersey swung himself forward until he was as near as the buffeting heat allowed. He stood shoulder to shoulder with the man for nearly an hour until the outcome was no longer in doubt, Jersey's companion yelling hoarse instructions whenever the efforts of the exhausted men threatened to devolve into bedlam. By morning, the building where the fire started would be little more than a foundation supporting a blackened tangle of charred beams. The other buildings would be saved.

"That's it," said the dark-haired man.

"Your men are to be commended, sir."

The man turned toward Jersey, placing his legs carefully. "Thank you." Blue eyes glinted from a deeply lined face. After a quick assessment, during which he seemed to take in Jersey's crutches, the cut of his coat, the wear on Jersey's collar, and countless other details Jersey could only imagine, the man sighed and broke into a rueful grin. "I'm afraid your timing has proved unfortunate this day." He extended a hand. "I'm Roger Ambrose. I don't believe we've met."

"Jersey Rohn. Pleased t' meet you, sir." Jersey found himself coming to attention as though he addressed a superior officer. He grasped the firm, calloused hand. "Don't worry about me, sir. I've waited near a year for a new leg, I guess another six months ain't gonna kill me."

"Pleased to meet you, Mr. Rohn. May I ask if we have your measurements?"

If they ain't burnt to ashes in that inferno. "I sent them ahead, sir. Some days ago—with a casting."

"Good. They'll be in the office. I'll make you a promise, Mr. Rohn. You come back in a month and we'll have your leg ready."

"I… I dunno what to say, Mr. Ambrose," Jersey said, impressed beyond words. "You're insured, I take it."

"Insured?" Mr. Ambrose pursed his lips as he tracked the movements of his employees. "We'll not wait for that. I must attend to my business, Mr. Rohn, but mark your calendar one month from today." He glanced back at Jersey and nodded before striding stiffly in the direction of one of the remaining buildings. "One month, Mr. Rohn, you may depend on it."

Jersey returned Ambrose's nod before beginning the slow journey back the way he had come. *In one month, I will be lucky to have two pennies to rub together. How will I ever pay for the leg?* There was no point in asking to work off the cost. The charred ruin of the Willow Wood factory was no place for a one-legged man.

FINDING A place to stay for the night proved harder than Jersey had anticipated. His arms were trembling with the strain of holding up his body after the long walk back from the Willow Wood Company. He found himself wishing for his old crutches. They might bruise, but they didn't require the same level of exertion as his new ones. After refusals at two boarding houses, he reluctantly passed the welcoming lights of the town's lone hotel, knowing that a single night there would cost more than he could afford. Stopping to belt his greatcoat more tightly, the reality of his situation flooded his consciousness like a cold bath. *Maybe the waiting room at the station?* He could think of nowhere else to go.

Go home or find a job, that was his choice, but how was he supposed to look for a job if he couldn't even find a place to stay? He leaned against a hitching post and took in the empty, cobblestoned street. In the town center, he'd passed few businesses—an automobile mechanic's shop, a hardware store, a grocer, the hotel, a few restaurants. None seemed likely to welcome a cripple, even if they had work. Why had he been in such a hell-fired rush to leave Philadelphia? There he'd had Mrs. Underwood to fuss over him and James to visit when he couldn't stand it anymore. He caught a whiff of something roasting and his stomach grumbled. When had he last eaten anyway? Pushing as fast as his trembling arms would let him, he arrived at the train station in time to watch the stationmaster close the door and bend to lock it with an oversized skeleton key.

"Are there no more trains tonight?" he called.

The stationmaster straightened from his task. "Sorry, sir. Last one came through thirty minutes ago." Looking Jersey up and down, he frowned and rattled his keys as though to ward off an evil spirit.

Jersey rubbed a hand across his brow and tried a smile. "Just my luck. When's the next one to Columbus?"

The stationmaster stepped backward, watching Jersey with narrowed eyes. "The local'll be through at six a.m., if she don't bust her seams."

"Not likely," Jersey said absently, wondering what a ticket to Columbus cost.

"Of course not. Don't know why I said that." The stationmaster continued to back away until Jersey thought he would trip on the curb. Turning suddenly, the man called over his shoulder, "Must be getting home to the missus. Ticket office opens at 5:45."

Jersey watched the man rush down the gaslit street. Large, crystalline flakes began to drift down to wet the pavement. He was done. The crutches trembled in his grip. The thought of making his way through the wet streets looking for another place, only to be refused again, was too much. He found a dry spot under the covered opening between the office and the waiting room and lowered himself to the platform, wishing for the furnace heat of Frank's body. His last thought before drifting off was an irritating picture of Frank, in a frock coat and embroidered waistcoat, leaning against the mantelpiece of an enormous fireplace with a wineglass in his hand.

MRS. HUDDLESTON crumpled the note and threw it on the floor. "Absurd!" As if a few dollars mattered. She stalked across her husband's study. How could she have lost Francis again? His note apologized for taking the housekeeping money from the kitchen and said that he would return it as soon as he could. He must have seen where it was kept when Betty retrieved the money to pay the grocer's boy the previous afternoon.

She would engage Mr. Matheson again. Matheson would find Francis, and she would not let him out of her sight until they'd knocked down whatever impediment was between them. At least she had a good idea where he would go. His obvious discomfort and refusal to speak about her confirmed Jersey's importance. He would go to Jersey, and Jersey was in Philadelphia, so that was where she would send Matheson.

FRANK STEPPED off the Number 23 trolley at Germantown and Coulter and hunched his shoulders against the cold. He was not entirely sure of his purpose in returning to the school. He told himself that he must say good-bye to Jersey, that he must put his friend out of reach of this perversion. First, however, he must visit Spalding to find out what he could—no matter how painful that would be. What to do after that, he did not know. He had driven an ambulance before. Underwood had mentioned a group of Friends at Swarthmore who were planning to go to Russia to help victims of famine and destruction in the wake of the Bolshevik Revolution. He could start fresh in some place where no one expected anything from him.

At the Underwoods' door, he paused to rehearse again what he would say. He was still watching snowflakes settle onto the cobblestone walk when the door opened and Anne Underwood burst out. "Mr. Huddleston! What happened to your arm? Do you want to come in?"

"Miss Underwood." He shook himself, grunting at the lance of pain from his arm. "Yes, if you don't mind. I must speak to Jersey. Is he in?"

"You've just missed him. He cleared out this morning. Mother's very upset. She thinks he's not fit to travel, but I think he got tired of Mother ordering him around. I think a person should be able to decide whether they want a second helping—"

"Where did he go?" Frank kicked a loose cobblestone.

"How should I know? He left a note for you. It's on the kitchen table. Are you going to come in? Because if you're not, I'm going for a walk in the park and maybe you would like to—"

"I'm sorry, but I really must think. Yes, I'm coming in. Where is the note?"

The note was brief. He held it close to his chest as he read, with Anne all but standing on tiptoes to try and see what it said.

> *Dear Frank,*
>
> *I'm sorry to leave before you get back, but I feel like a jack-in-the-box waiting for somebody to press the catch. I reckon it's time I either climb out of my box and get myself a new leg or find a hole to bed down in for good. The leg I want is in Ohio, so I'm heading west.*
>
> *Don't forget to talk to James. He's seems a fine fellow and was pretty disappointed when you left without seeing him. Your letters are good reading, especially the last.*
>
> *I'll send a note to the Underwoods when my leg's squared away. Hope to see you soon.*
>
> *Your Special Friend,*
>
> *Jersey*

If only he'd gotten to Philadelphia a day sooner... he'd have what? Gone with Jersey? Maybe it was just as well, so why did he feel like kicking down a wall?

"What does it say? Mother was steamed when he cleared out without speaking to her. His other note didn't say anything."

"His other note?"

Anne bounced on her toes. "Thank you for your hospitality and all that."

"Did he say where he was going?"

Anne stopped bouncing and stamped in frustration. "You're not listening, Mr. Huddleston. He didn't say anything!"

Frank looked at the young woman in front of him. "I would have thought he'd tell you at least, Anne."

"He hardly ever spoke to me! Since you left, he spent all his time with Mr. Spalding!"

Why did the thought of Jersey and Spalding together make Frank's gut churn even more than the idea of Jersey with Anne? Frank forced himself to smile. "Would you do me a favor, Anne? Could you find Mr. Spalding's address?"

JAMES DOZED with his students' papers spread over his lap and on the floor beside him. A knock at the door startled him. Who could be visiting at this hour? He'd have heard Jersey coming up the stairs. He rose, groggy, and watched a stack of papers slide off his lap and scatter onto the floor.

"Who is it?" he called.

"Frank Huddleston. I need to speak to you, Mr. Spalding."

He nearly tripped getting to the door. "It's James. Come in. I take it you prefer Frank now."

"I don't remember Francis. My grandparents called me Frank, so I'm used to it."

"You were with them in Michigan. What happened to your arm? Would you like some water?" James squatted to gather up the papers from his floor.

"No, I don't want to trouble you. I only need some information. Jersey has gone somewhere to get a prosthesis. I need to know where. His note only said Ohio."

James fell back onto his butt. He put his palms on the floor behind him and leaned back to look up at Frank. "You're quite a pair. I would have liked to say goodbye to *him* too."

"I'm sorry, I know you wanted to talk before I left. It's just that I don't know how to be the person you knew. I don't think I am that person anymore."

"You don't think much of me, do you?"

"What do you—"

"You think I'll judge you, that I can't understand how you feel. Maybe I can't. I can tell you how much it hurts to be addressed so... so *politely*." He was ashamed to hear his voice rising in frustration. "We were best friends. I know I've lost that. We've both lost that. But it seems to me you might at least consider me a worthy candidate to get to know again."

"I've been thoughtless, haven't I?" Frank said.

James saw tears in Frank's eyes. It only made him want to kick the great oaf. *How's that for Christian charity?* "Jersey told me you were looking for letters. I have three years of them. Let me get them." He went to his desk and found the worn leather portfolio. "You wrote regularly. You're welcome to read them all, of course, but I think this one might interest you particularly." He unfolded the last of the letters. It was dated August 21, 1918.

Dear James,

We have found a temporary billet near Reims, where we have renewed acquaintance with some of the merchants from whom we bought supplies the last time we were here. I don't think we will stay for long, as the Front is finally moving, and we shall have to follow. The Germans are rumored to be retreating before a new British onslaught, and our American boys have arrived in numbers, which means enthusiastic officers—and lots of work for Les Section Sanitaire. *Every bus returns full of the wounded. We are all exhausted and cross because we were due for a break in August. Now we shall have to content ourselves with a few hours of leave during lulls in the fighting.*

Last night I got a pass, walked into the village, and saw something appalling. A few days ago, a unit of Negro troops moved into the area in order to help rebuild the railroad which passes through the former lines near here. (The railroads are critical for supply and evacuation of the wounded.) This morning we could hear trains huffing past the barn where we are billeted, so we knew they had finished their job. They must have been given leave. When I got into the village, I saw clusters of Negroes in the square and shops.

Unfortunately, our American troops have brought with them American attitudes and prejudices. The white soldiers, particularly the regular army troops—many of whom come from the South—are none too happy to have Negroes (they use another term, which I shall not repeat) sharing their shops and watering holes. The French are, for the most part, content to serve the Negroes so long as they have money to spend. Much as I would like to credit the French for their enlightenment, I think it a purely economic issue for them. They are desperate to feed themselves and to rebuild. A Negro's money is as good as any other's. In any case, I chanced upon a group of drunken white soldiers beating a Negro outside a brothel. I knew it would be dangerous to interfere, but I edged close to hear what was happening.

The man was caught in the brothel. I hesitate to defend any man's right to visit a brothel, but the man had done nothing his white counterparts hadn't. (Is laying with a prostitute more a crime than machine-gunning the enemy? My moral compass is as battered as the landscape and fluctuates wildly with my state of mind.) In any case, the Negro's only crime was in having the wrong color skin. For a horrible moment, I thought I must watch them kill him. They stopped short. When they left, a pair of Negro soldiers materialized to pick up their fallen comrade and carry him off. I tried to help, but they told me in no uncertain terms I was not wanted.

All day, I have wrestled with myself. Would I have intervened if the soldiers had been beating a white man? What about raping a woman? What if she were a whore? Would God have me judge a man before stopping violence against him? I think not. We Friends like to talk about our Inner Light. Mine fades in the sulfurous atmosphere of the Front. I am ashamed I did nothing except observe. I plan to do better, should God present me with a chance at redemption.

Your Friend,

Francis

"You always jumped in whether your opinion was welcome or not. If you were certain what was right, heaven help anyone who disagreed. If you've lost a little of that certainty, it will make you an easier companion, maybe a better Friend too." James tapped his knuckles on the desk. "Inner Light! You had an arc lamp! You cannot shine that kind of light on anyone else. They'll only curse you for it. I once told you to go to the Methodists."

Frank shifted restlessly. "We disagreed?"

"Like lemon and milk."

"What about?"

"Everything. The war was the only thing that mattered. After the Germans invaded, you were so eager to get to Europe, you were ready to row your own boat. I thought we'd be helping the war effort one way or the other and suggested we wait until they stopped fighting. You'd have thought I'd started heel-clicking and German lessons."

"You were a conscientious objector?" Frank leaned forward.

"Of course. Most Friends were. So were you. You drove an ambulance. I worked on a farm." James couldn't help cracking a smile. "It was the most tedious six months of my life. I envied you terribly. Anyway, I fully expect you saw some Negro being abused by the crackers, jumped in, and got your head bashed. It would have been just like you—fine and dumb at the same time." He nodded toward Frank's cast. "Who'd you rile up this time?"

Frank's shoulders drooped. "All I did was say hello to them, and they stole my clothes and threw me off the train. Broke my arm when I landed."

James took in Frank's filthy, ill-fitting clothes, cast, and forlorn expression and couldn't help himself. He started to laugh.

"THANKS, JAMES. I don't really know what I'd have done if you hadn't agreed to help with the tickets. Jersey needs someone to look out for him."

"What are friends for?" said James.

If Frank noticed the irony in James's voice, he made no sign. Instead, he laid his head back on the upholstered seat. "I'm so tired," he mumbled, his eyelids fluttering closed.

James stared at his former friend and new acquaintance, taking in his pale cheeks and cinder-speckled plaster cast. *Jersey is not the only one who needs looking after.* What would it have been like if he and Francis had traveled together as they'd planned, prior to the war? Would they have stayed as close as they'd been in school? Or would age have hardened their differences?

They'd traveled by train once before on a day trip to the state capitol during the summer break of their sophomore year. Francis had wanted to buy food on the way, just for the adventure of it, but James's mother had packed a lunch of cold chicken, boiled eggs, and apple pie, insisting that trains were unreliable and you never knew when you might find yourself wanting a good meal. They'd played games all the way to Harrisburg, trading lines of verse that mentioned things they saw through the grimy window of the train, and laughing together at the forced rhymes and improbable imagery. *What was that one that involved a cow, a milk bucket, and a casket?* They'd laughed until a proper gentleman trying to read the morning paper in a seat across the aisle had risen with a loud harrumph and taken a seat at the other end of the car. James reached out to shake Francis's shoulder and ask him, but stopped himself at the last moment, the memory gone stale.

It was replaced by a picture of Francis with his cardboard suitcase, a great grin on his face, as he prepared to board the train that would take him to New York, the first stage of his journey to France. He'd clasped James's hand in both of his own, tears in his eyes, and asked him to pray for a *bon voyage.* At that moment, James had wished he could break free of his rigid interpretation of the testimony of peace and go as well. Their disagreement on whether driving an ambulance furthered the war effort put more distance between them than the roiling sea. It was the first time James had stood up for his faith in the face of Francis's certainty. Had he gone with Francis, he might have prevented the incident that robbed them of their shared past. Then again, he might be moldering in a French quagmire instead of staring out at the stubbled fields and plump haystacks of Lancaster County.

CHAPTER 19

"WHAT IS thy business with him, Mr. Matheson?" Having shown him into the parlor, Mrs. Underwood offered neither a chair nor refreshment, but merely looked him up and down—he the corpse and she the undertaker.

Matheson strove for a reassuring expression. "My business is private, ma'am. However, you may be certain that my client, Mrs. Huddleston, has the best interest of the boy at heart."

"Thy client is a relation?"

"Yes, ma'am, his grandmother."

"We were under the impression that he went to New Jersey to find his grandparents."

"That's right, ma'am." What to say that would reassure? "Mrs. Huddleston and the boy were reunited briefly, but the boy left before Mrs. Huddleston could… make her purpose clear."

Mrs. Underwood pursed her lips. "Is thee aware of the boy's condition?"

"Indeed, ma'am. I believe Mrs. Huddleston would not take it amiss if I were to tell you that she regrets—nay, that is too strong—she fears, that she may have inadvertently frightened the boy in some way. She does not intend the boy harm, quite the contrary. Her sole purpose is to see him well situated."

"I believe thee spend too much time in court, Mr. Matheson. Thy face reflects a habit of equivocation." Mrs. Underwood pointed at a chair. "However, I think thee mean no harm."

He had no notion how to respond, so he merely sat on the edge of the straight-backed chair.

"I will tell thee what I know. Unfortunately, it is all too little."

"Then you have seen the boy?"

Mrs. Underwood examined him for briefly before sighing. "I have not. However, my daughter told us that she spoke to him two days ago. He came looking for his friend, Mr. Rohn. I was not at home at the time, but Anne said that he had injured his arm. Have thee any knowledge of that, Mr. Matheson?"

"My client did not mention that. It explains your caution. Would Mr. Rohn be any relation to Jersey Rohn?"

"Of course. As I said, Frank came looking for Jersey. But Jersey left earlier in the day."

"Apparently, I have been confused. Am I to understand that Jersey Rohn and Mr. Rohn are one in the same? How curious. I—my client too—was under the impression that Jersey was a woman. Why then did he—"

"I don't know how thee got that impression, Mr. Matheson," said Mrs. Underwood. "But it is none of my concern. Jersey is Frank's friend from Michigan. He is a veteran who also returned from France recently."

"A veteran!" Matheson allowed some of his satisfaction to creep into his voice. "I begin to comprehend. Would you supply me with a description of Mr. Rohn? It might assist me in finding them."

"In for a penny, in for a pound," said Mrs. Underwood. "Would thee care for a drink of water, Mr. Matheson?"

FRANK SHIVERED in the bone-cold crypt. He could not see the ghosts, but their hands touched his neck, brushed his face, clung sour on his lips. Desiccated voices hissed incomprehensible prayers into his ears. Ahead of him, a casket waited. He looked into the emptiness and giggled. It was no home for him. The dead don't shiver. Was there a word for a group of ghosts? How about a gasp?

"Wake up, Frank! We're arriving in Mt. Sterling."

Frank tried to pull his greatcoat more tightly around himself, stymied by the cast on his arm. "We just left Pittsburgh."

"Hardly, chum. You've slept through."

Frank looked out into the night. He could make out little beyond an occasional fleeting square of yellow window. "I hope there's someplace warm to stay in this godforsaken place. Why'd Jersey pick this company of all companies to get his leg from?"

James laughed. "He said it was beautiful."

"Mt. Sterling?"

"The leg, numbskull. Very shapely, I take it."

Frank continued to stare out the window. "He's pretty enough without attaching any new parts." When James didn't laugh, Frank's face heated. He'd meant it as a joke, hadn't he?

The train slowed as it approached the station. "We'd better get ready," said James.

Frank got his bag and monkey-walked down the swaying aisle, until the train jerked to a halt. A light coating of snow slicked the platform.

"What now, O Captain! My Captain?" said James.

Frank peered down the poorly lit platform toward the tiny station house. The building consisted of a waiting room and an office, separated by a covered walkway leading to the street. Neither part showed any sign of habitation. "Let's get out of the wind."

They walked toward the opening between the buildings. The conductor called out something and waved at the engineer, who answered with two short blasts of the locomotive's whistle. The locomotive took up the slack with a swift series of clanks. The great drive wheels spun on slick rails. Frank watched as the engine regained traction and began its rhythmic drive, sending a plume of smoke and steam into the night.

"Wait! Wait!" A thin figure in an old army greatcoat and flat cap hopped and scrambled past Frank onto the platform. Before the man reached the train, he slipped on the wet surface and landed flat on his back with his cap askew.

"Christ almighty!" He began a string of obscenities audible even over the departing train.

James looked at Frank, his expression shifting between disapproval and amusement. "I'm not sure if we should pick it up or muzzle it."

Frank laughed. "Make a waste of the trip. We could write to his mother."

The figure in the greatcoat stilled. "Frank? James?"

"At your service," Frank said. "Will you keep a civil tongue if we pick you up?"

"How did—"

"Come on," said James, "a civil tongue or I'll sit on you."

"What'd I ever do to you?"

"You left without saying goodbye."

"Sorry." Jersey rolled onto his belly. Before he could untangle his crutches, Frank leaned over, grabbed him by the collar, and lifted him to his feet.

"Between the two of you, you almost make a civil person," said James.

"We'll take you on, one-armed or one-legged," Frank said. Replacing Jersey's cap, he had to laugh. Jersey's face was smudged with black, and his hair flecked with ash and cinders. "Did you work your passage shoveling coal?"

"Oh God, my leg!" Jersey groaned.

Frank tried to look at Jersey's stump, but it was hidden under Jersey's greatcoat. "You okay?"

"Hunky-dory, but my beautiful leg is ashes. You're not gonna believe what happened! I hiked out that way"—he thrust out a crutch—"all the way to the Willow Wood factory. Got there just in time to watch the whole place go up. I couldn't even join the bucket brigade. Had to stand there like a department store dummy and watch it burn clear down to the foundation. Well, they saved the office and wood shed."

"But you got here yesterday, didn't you? I didn't get to Germantown until after you left, and James and I didn't leave until this morning."

"That's why I was trying to catch that d—darn train." Jersey stuck his tongue out at James. "Y' know, there wasn't a single rooming house would take me last night? I mean, I know I need a wash an' all, but they was right unfriendly. Seemed t' think I weren't good for it. Now Mr. Ambrose—he owns the factory, lost both his legs and walks around... well... like he owns the place—he probably would've taken me in, but I didn't have the heart to ask him. We stood shoulder to shoulder and watched his place go up. I asked him if he had insurance and what did he say? Insurance be damned, I'll have the place rebuilt in a month. I don't think he was kidding neither. Only I ain't got the money to wait around for a month, even if I could find a room. That's why I was trying to catch that blasted train. Didn't fancy sleeping out another night. Figured there'd be any number of places in Columbus where I might find work. Only I nodded off waiting for it."

James looked at Frank. "Do you think they might think more highly of one of us?"

"I don't know about you—" said Frank.

"What happened to your arm anyway?" said Jersey.

"I've got my own money problems."

"What's that got—"

"Keep your britches on, Jersey. I'm telling you. I thought I'd take the train to Plainfield, right? But I didn't have enough for the fare, so I hopped a freight."

"How'd you get the fare to come here?" Jersey said. "What'd you come for anyway? You think I can't take care—"

"Do you want to hear about the arm or not?" said James.

"Sure I do."

"So I hopped a freight and got myself thrown off it—in my drawers."

"Who threw you off? Why, I'd like to—"

"Will you shut up, for Heaven's sake, and let him tell his story!" said James.

"Who asked you?" said Frank and Jersey in unison.

JERSEY THOUGHT the house must have begun its existence as a rough shelter for farmers, located outside a small village. Mature now, near the center of a town grown up around it, it had acquired fresh white paint and prim black shutters. The yard was tidy, if barren (due to the time of year), and surrounded by a rail fence. A somewhat ambiguous sign was tacked to the gate: "Rooms for Let. Spirits Prohibited."

"Fantômes comme nous pas les bienvenus!" Jersey said, for the pleasing sound of it, and just a little, to impress Frank. Something about Frank and James together made Jersey feel like a competitor.

"You get any thinner, you'll be invisible as a ghost," said James.

"Today, they'll have to make an exception," replied Frank, marching toward the front door. "I'm famished."

"Wait up, Frank," called James. "If they see Jersey, we'll never get in." He motioned for Jersey to wait outside the gate. "Stay here until we've concluded negotiations." He grabbed Jersey's shoulders and turned him so his good leg was in profile. "Hopefully, she won't recognize you until she's taken our money."

"I'm a respectable person." Jersey pulled at his collar. "Just because I happened to witness a conflagration—"

"Shush! She's coming." James hurried up the path to join Frank.

The front door opened. Jersey watched Frank and James exchange words with a bulky shadow inside the foyer. He couldn't hear what was said, but James fished his purse out of his vest pocket and handed something to the stout figure. Frank whistled. Jersey started up the path. This time the shrill words were clearly audible.

"Oh no you don't! I told that filthy bum he wasn't welcome. You can't bring him in my clean—"

Jersey faltered. James raised his voice over the protest. "He is no bum, ma'am, but a hero of the Great War, with medals for valor on his chest—from two armies."

"From opposing sides, I'll bet" came the sharp retort.

"Hey, the French was on our side!" Jersey protested.

"He needs only a bath and brush to be as respectable as you or me, ma'am," Frank said.

The woman bristled. "You could use sprucing up yourself, if you don't mind me saying so."

"Why, that's just why we came here, ma'am," James said. "Nothing like a proper establishment like that one, I said to my friends, to help us get shipshape for our business in the morning."

"What business?" The woman still barred the door, but she craned her neck to scowl at Jersey.

"That would be a private matter, ma'am."

"I'm sure Mr. Ambrose wouldn't mind us mentioning his name," Jersey said.

"Mr. Ambrose? You have business with Mr. Ambrose?"

"Wasn't I shoulder to shoulder with him yesterday afternoon?" Jersey kept his voice earnest as he set the hook. "Such a tragedy that was too. What happened to his place, I mean."

"What happened to his place?" The woman was halfway out the door now.

"Why, it was just terrible. People running everywhere. Yelling. Women screaming." James's glare suggested Jersey had gone a little too far. "Well, the one woman."

"What happened?" said the woman at the door.

Jersey ran a hand across his forehead and frowned at his filthy digits. "We gotta go, gentlemen, if we're gonna find a place to get cleaned up. If you'll be so kind as to return my friend's money, ma'am, we'll be going."

"Oh no, you mustn't. There's no bath upstairs, only the commode, but we've a tub to set out in the kitchen for your baths. If you gentlemen would take your bags upstairs, I'll start heating the water, then you can tell me the news."

"Why, that sounds fine, ma'am. We'll be delighted to oblige," said James. "Come on, Frank!"

"Why didn't you do that the first time you were here?" Frank whispered as they followed James and the proprietress into the house.

"Didn't know I was covered in soot, did I? Didn't realize I needed to plan a campaign just to get a goddamned room."

AFTER THEY got their things squared away, Frank followed James down to the kitchen where Mrs. Kettle, the proprietress, fed lumps of coal into the stove. Jersey sat on a three-legged stool, well on his way to making a great friend of the unfortunately named lady. Several large pots of water were heating on the stove. A wooden tub resembling the bottom half of an oversized beer barrel had been dragged to the center of the room.

"There you are, boys. I've set out towels. You can use the pump and bucket to fill it partway, and then add these to make it comfortable. When you're done, I'll make some sandwiches and Jersey can tell me all about the fire at the Willow Wood factory."

"Nothing would suit me better, Lois," Jersey said.

"It's Lois, now?" Frank said, after Mrs. Kettle left. "That was quick."

"There'll be cookies and milk by the time she gets the details out of me," said Jersey, with a smirk.

When the tub was full, James and Frank flipped a coin to see who would go first—the tacit understanding being that Jersey, as the dirtiest, would go last. James won, so Frank and Jersey sat at the kitchen table while James washed.

James carefully removed and folded each item of clothing until, finally, he stood ready to remove his drawers. Then he turned his back to them and removed his last covering, revealing a pale back and hairless buttocks. Frank glanced at Jersey and saw him staring at James's rear. When Jersey realized Frank had noticed, he blushed and lowered his head. James climbed into the tub and sighed softly.

Frank waited uncomfortably for James to finish his bath.

Jersey was uncharacteristically quiet, sitting on his hands like a miscreant outside the principal's office. "Guess I better leave you some hot water," said James, climbing out of the tub. Jersey's eyes remained fixed on the table in front of him. "You'll want another pot."

James took his time drying off, carefully rubbing every inch of his pale skin. He lifted first one leg, then the other, revealing the joined hemispheres of his scrotum, one side larger than the other. Frank forced his gaze away and got a smirk from Jersey, the boy's eyes bright. With that look came understanding. In an instant, Frank was relieved of a terrible solitude and laid bare.

James finished dressing, saying he would complete his toilet upstairs, and it was the next man's turn. Frank undressed quickly, tossing his shirt and pants onto the table.

"I could join Lois in the parlor, if it'd make you more comfortable," said Jersey, stretching his arms above his head.

"No need to trouble yourself." Frank unbuttoned his trousers and struggled out of them. "I expect you weren't so obvious in the army." He stepped out of his underclothes and straightened, feeling himself on a stage.

"No. I wasn't the only one looking, neither."

Frank turned to the tub. He heard a slow intake of breath behind him. "I always thought you was pretty." Jersey's voice was low and rough.

"No, that's not right. I dunno the right word. Maybe there ain't one that's right for men. Lordy, it gives me goose bumps, looking at you." The room contracted and seemed to rush toward a point near the center of Frank's body. He climbed hastily into the water.

Jersey chuckled. "Don't rush now."

Once in the safety of the tub, the kitchen resumed its normal dimensions. "I didn't know you could be this way."

"Me either. Kind of a revelation."

"Have you ever—" Frank stopped, unable to voice his question.

Jersey sat rigidly at the table. "If you're trying to ask if I ever felt so heated about a body, the answer is no, but I've always enjoyed the sight of a healthy male specimen." He paused. "Well, Andy, but he wasn't… so I didn't think on it much."

Frank scrubbed one-handed, holding his cast over the side of the tub. "What about women?"

"I like 'em well enough, but I don't itch to touch 'em."

"Have you ever—"

"Never wanted to."

Frank stopped moving. "I don't *know* if I ever—"

"Do you want to now?" Jersey pushed himself up suddenly, knocking over his chair with a clatter that startled them both. He picked it up and hopped his way over to the tub. "Give me that sponge. You'll get your cast wet."

Frank handed over the sponge and held his arm out of the water, while Jersey sponged his back and sides.

"Maybe. I don't know," said Frank, his voice rough.

"Get out. I wanna get clean."

Frank jerked into motion and climbed out of the tub. "I'll get you another pot."

"Much obliged."

Frank rubbed himself vigorously with a towel and tried to keep his eyes to himself. Jersey's tousled head disappeared briefly under the graying water. Popping up, he shook his head, spraying water like a dog.

"Hey!" said Frank.

"You didn't even look at me."

"I was afraid I'd get—"

"Even prettier."

Frank cheeks grew hot. The heat spread downward, and the room contracted again.

"You gonna get me hot water or get me in it?" Jersey grinned.

Frank dressed quickly and painfully.

"Ain't nothing to be embarrassed about. Horses get 'em all the time." Jersey said, splashing vigorously as he washed.

"You're weren't the one exposed to all and sundry." Frank took a boiling pot off the stove and carried over to the tub. "Watch out," he said, as he poured it in.

"Hold up a sec." Jersey dropped his head under the water again and came up scrubbing his face. He ran his hands through his hair and kneaded. "Now."

Mixing cold water from the tap with water from the stove, Frank prepared another kettle. When he was satisfied it wouldn't scald, he poured the hot water over Jersey's head and back. He wanted badly to run his hands through the dark curls. Jersey raised himself in the tub until his face was level with Frank's. Huge pupils nearly eclipsed the sea green of Jersey's irises. Jersey's lips parted to reveal a row of gleaming white teeth. Without conscious thought, Frank leaned in and pressed his lips to Jersey's. He stood motionless, the room contracting again to that small oval of contact until the door opened and James walked in.

JAMES SKIDDED to a stop, his shoes slipping on the wet floor. Frank was on the other side of the tub, facing Jersey, who stood in the tub with back to the door. Jersey's head tilted up. James followed a drop of water as it dripped from a wet ringlet and ran down Jersey's slender back to vanish into the deep crevice between his buttocks.

They're kissing.

Frank peered past Jersey's dark head and met James's openmouthed stare. He stumbled backward. Jersey turned and sank back into the tub, but not before James saw his prominent erection. "I'm sorry," said James, automatically. He backed out of the room and shut the door firmly behind him.

What does it mean? You know what it means. There are men who have sex with other men. He'd read in the paper of Oscar Wilde's trial and conviction for buggery. It was a sin. He remembered how Jersey's head had tilted upward. He didn't know they kissed. He had imagined, on those few occasions when he'd thought of such things, a clumsy jerk in an alley—money presented and inspected in advance—not kissing. Had James discovered two of his students, the solution would have been easy: separation, followed by expulsion on a vague charge of unsuitable behavior. But this was not some student. This was Francis. *What am I to say? What is my duty?*

Mrs. Kettle peered around the parlor door. "Are they nearly done? You'll be wanting your sandwiches soon, I expect. Nothing like a good bath to invigorate the system."

James put up his hands as if to stop her from advancing. "I'm sure they will finish quickly now."

JERSEY STOOD again, now flaccid. "Christ! What now?"

Frank closed his eyes. "I must talk to him. Get dressed."

Jersey climbed out of the tub. "What about Mrs. Kettle?"

"Tell her a story."

Frank slipped out the kitchen door and rushed upstairs after James. "Mrs. Kettle will have supper soon," he said, stepping into the room. "She will be offended if you don't try her cooking."

James wouldn't look at him. "What were you thinking?"

"It didn't mean anything. We just…." Frank concentrated on picking a piece of lint from his cast. "We were just larking about."

James shook his head. "Don't speak of it. You only make it worse."

MRS. KETTLE finished serving and retired to the kitchen. "I'll be in the kitchen if you need anything. I'm sure you men have things to discuss before your meeting with Mr. Ambrose."

James put down his fork and patted his mouth with his napkin before placing it on the table. "I must return to Philadelphia, Frank. I will lend you train fare to Philadelphia or to Michigan. After that, I must disassociate myself with you."

Frank tasted bile and pushed his plate away, the food uneaten. What could he say? James was right to judge them. His attraction to Jersey was unnatural and anyone who learned of it would condemn them. He rubbed his arms and tried to catch Jersey's eye, but Jersey busied himself by wiping the egg yolk from his plate with a piece of bread.

"What about your leg, Jersey?" Frank asked. "What will you do now?"

Jersey squared his shoulders and looked up, a wide, hopeful smile transforming his face. "I thought to go home for Christmas. Mr. Ambrose's gotta restore his shop before he can make any new legs. I ain't got the coin to wait on it." For an instant, the beguiling storyteller from the Clark's barn replaced the gaunt, worn Jersey Frank had seen since their arrival in Philadelphia. "I'd like you to come," he said.

Any compunction Frank had about spending time with Jersey went straight out the window. Jersey wanted him, uncertain past, faulty memory and all. He would follow Jersey because he felt connected when he was with Jersey. Jersey's languid drawl amid the cacophony made sense of the world. "I'm going to Taperville."

James's expression hardened. "You've always done exactly what you want regardless of what anyone thinks. I don't know why I expected that to change. There was a time I would have followed you anywhere, Francis."

"You didn't follow me to Europe."

"I have a part in this," Jersey said. "It isn't all about Frank."

"Fair enough, Jersey." James thrust his neck forward. "What were *you* thinking?"

"Don't reckon I was thinking much of anything. What was you thinking last time you kissed a sweetheart?"

James's expression froze.

Jersey continued ruthlessly. "Oh, I see. You ain't tried it yet."

"Jersey," Frank said.

Jersey smiled. "Write us a letter when you done it. We can compare notes."

James's jaw worked and his lips grew white. "It is pointless to speak with either of you. I will pray for you." He pulled his purse from his vest pocket and all but threw money at Frank before stalking out.

"That was brilliant, Jersey. I told him it didn't mean anything. You're going to drive away the one person in the world who might—"

"Christ! The pair of you get my dander up. You go on like it were life or death. All we done was kiss."

"Quietly, Jersey! Do you want Mrs. Kettle hearing?"

"Aren't you in a lather! Can't you hear her bang those pots and pans?"

In fact, Frank could hear her. She seemed to be keeping time with herself as she sang some sort of martial hymn.

CHAPTER 20

MRS. HUDDLESTON sat stiffly in her chair in the study and listened as Betty made the call on the telephone in the hall. She knew Betty would be standing one hip thrust to the side, a foot tapping impatiently. The girl would not be taught proper decorum.

"Hello, this is Miss Betty Watkins calling for Mrs. Huddleston. No, I'm not trying to speak to Mrs. Huddleston, I'm calling *for* her. Well, I would have told you if you hadn't interrupted me. Mrs. Huddleston wishes to speak to Mr. Matheson. No, not now. She would like Mr. Matheson to visit her at her home as soon as he is available. He's available now? Bully for him. I'll tell her he's on his way. What? Very well. I will ask. Mrs. Huddleston? Mrs. Huddleston!"

"Yes, Betty? There's no need to yell at me. I can hear you perfectly well from here." Mrs. Huddleston remained seated in the study.

"Mr. Matheson would like to speak to you on the telephone."

"I asked for Mr. Matheson to come to see me."

Mrs. Huddleston heard the tapping sound from the hall increase in volume and tempo. "Mrs. Huddleston would like Mr. Matheson to come to the house."

The tapping stopped momentarily. "Gladys says that Mr. Matheson would like to speak to you now. He has just returned from a trip and has news to share."

"Who is Gladys?"

"Gladys is Mr. Matheson's secretary. She answers the telephone for him at his office."

Mrs. Huddleston sighed. "Please tell Gladys that I will come to the telephone and speak to Mr. Matheson."

"She's coming to the telephone, Gladys. Get Mr. Matheson. That's right."

Mrs. Huddleston rose from her seat and entered the hall. "I don't know why we acquired this device. It's so much simpler to send for people."

Betty retracted her hip and curtsied impertinently. "Here she comes. Get him now." She passed the heavy black earpiece to Mrs. Huddleston.

Mrs. Huddleston aligned herself in front of the cone as if she were on the bridge of a ship, relaying commands through the voice tube to the engine room. "Hello! Mr. Matheson, are you there?"

"Yes, Mrs. Huddleston, I am here."

"I'm cross with you, Mr. Matheson. I asked you to visit me when you had news."

"Yes, ma'am. However, I just arrived from Philadelphia, and I thought you might wish to hear the news right away."

"Very well. What is your news? Have you found my grandson?"

"No, I have not found Mr. Huddleston, but I have discovered something that I thought you might want to hear."

"I understand that you have something to tell me. Now that you have forced me to come to the telephone, you might as well tell me what it is."

"I have discovered that Jersey Rohn is not a woman," said Matheson, with satisfaction. "Are you still there, Mrs. Huddleston?"

"I am relieved, Mr. Matheson. I assume that Jersey is also not a cow? Perhaps you would consent to tell me who or what he is."

"Yes, ma'am. Jersey Rohn is a soldier, or rather a veteran, who appears to have traveled from Michigan to Philadelphia with your grandson and stayed in that city while Mr. Huddleston came here. Unfortunately, Mr. Rohn left Philadelphia on December 20, one day before Mr. Huddleston arrived. Mr. Huddleston departed Philadelphia with Mr. Spalding—presumably the James Spalding Mr. Rohn referred to in his letter—the next morning. I have confirmed that all three boarded westbound trains. I suspect that Mr. Rohn may have intended to return to Michigan, and that Mr. Huddleston and Mr. Spalding are following."

"In that case, why did you return here?" Mrs. Huddleston fairly barked her reply.

Mr. Matheson's voice faded as though he had moved away from his instrument. "Forgive me, ma'am. I returned here because I do not yet know where in Michigan Mr. Rohn's or Mr. Huddleston's homes are located."

"I see, so you have called me to the telephone to tell me you don't know where my grandson is or where he is going."

"Technically, I suppose that is accurate. However, I thought you would want to know that Mr. Rohn—or rather that Jersey is not—"

"I'm no longer concerned with this Jersey person. I have retained your services to find my grandson. I trust the next time you drag me to the telephone, you will have a more newsworthy dispatch. Good day, Mr. Matheson."

Mrs. Huddleston replaced the earpiece on the hook and rubbed her neck. She'd been unfair to Mr. Matheson, especially so near to Christmas. It was something of a relief to find that this Jersey person was male. He was of no significance.

THE RETURN to Taperville had Frank questioning his decision to accompany Jersey, even if his doubts had as much to do with the long, uncomfortable ride in the bed of an onion-scented farm wagon as they did with Jersey's behavior. Before they left Mt. Sterling, Jersey sent a telegram warning his father of their arrival and asking that he meet them at the Grange Hall. While they were on the train to Kalamazoo, the temperature dropped, and it started to snow. Tiny crystals blew into the coach and stung their faces every time someone opened the door to the vestibule.

Jersey suggested, on lowering himself to the platform in Kalamazoo, that they visit the Farmers' Market to see if they could find someone heading toward Taperville. A young farmer leaning against the side of a wagon admitted that he might be headed in the right direction. Jersey asked him if he'd mind passengers.

"Hop in," said the farmer. He pulled a heavy rug from the box under his seat and tossed it into the back. "Looks like you'll be needing this 'fore long." The rug proved infested with fleas, which were attracted to their body heat.

Frank shoved it aside in disgust. He had splashed water into the gap between the cast and his arm while washing at the boarding house. When his arm wasn't aching, it itched. He wanted to pool his warmth with Jersey, but Jersey had woken with a whimper and shrunk from Frank's touch when Frank roused him at the station. He'd been pensive and withdrawn since. Frank was reduced to unsuccessfully tugging at his coat to try and seal it around his cast—and scratching.

"Y'all from around here?" asked the farmer.

"Grew up just south of Taperville," Jersey answered. "Frank's from Philadelphia."

Frank had nearly concluded that the farmer had a decidedly limited supply of curiosity, when the young man grunted. "What brings you out here, Frank?"

At least the pace of the conversation, which seemed timed to the slow metronome-like clop of the horse's walk, gave Frank ample time to consider his reply. "I'm visiting for Christmas. My grandparents live in the area."

As they curved down the side of a hill, the farmer leaned on the brake lever until the road flattened out beside a streambed. "Who are they? Maybe I know 'em."

"The Clarks, Charlie and Eddy."

"Nope, never heard of 'em."

THEIR TALKATIVE driver let them off at the Grange Hall. Frank was eager to warm up before the last leg of the journey. If they were lucky, Mr. Rohn would be along to pick them up before nightfall. The Grange Hall was decorated for Christmas with a holly wreath on the door and evergreen boughs to either side. Frank tossed their bags onto the porch and was about to go in when Jersey called out to him from the steps. "Hold up, Frank. Let me go in first."

Frank pushed the door open and held it, tentatively. "Are you all right?" he asked. Jersey never accepted help without a sharp comment or dark look.

"Dandy," Jersey said, as he pushed past. Frank made to follow.

"Wait!" called Jersey from inside.

"Jersey, what's going on? I'm freezing."

"Come on in now. Hop to it!"

Frank stepped inside. "What in Heaven's name has gotten into you?"

"Stop."

"Are you mad!" Frank paused to stamp the snow off his feet.

Jersey lurched into him and wrapped him in a bear hug. Raising his grinning mouth to Frank's, he kissed him hard on the lips. Something warm and insistent thrust past Frank's teeth to slide across his tongue. The sensation was so exotic he forgot his surroundings and concentrated on the living thing in his mouth until it withdrew like an eel to its nest.

"There," said Jersey, with some satisfaction. "I've wanted to do that all day. Look up." Above the door hung a bundle of mistletoe. Jersey reached up and plucked a berry. "For good luck," he said.

Frank's heart raced and his lips felt swollen. "You've lost your mind."

"No need to get your horses in a lather, nobody could see us. But someone might be upstairs in the office, so we gotta keep our voices down. Didn't you like it?"

Frank pushed Jersey back and glanced around the meeting hall. The place was decorated for a dance, with streamers arching from beam to beam. A tree stood in one corner, boughs freighted with ornaments and tinsel. "What do you mean you wanted to do that? You hardly looked at me all day."

Jersey managed to appear offended. "I had some thinking to do. Neither my mama nor Eddy wanna hear about queer goings on from some gossiping biddy in church. Farmer Clean Cut would've been delighted to tell anyone who'd listen if we'd sat a little too close. I know this town, and one thing I know for sure, we gotta be careful."

"That explains why you were so bound and determined to kiss me."

Jersey grinned. "That was special. I knew there'd be mistletoe here. They got a dance every year about this time. I never did kiss anyone under the mistletoe before."

JERSEY'S FATHER arrived after dark, his wagon lit by a lantern on the floorboard between his feet. He looked like a gargoyle with the light shining from below. Frank wondered what his reception would be at the Rohn house. He needn't have worried about Mr. Rohn. Jersey's father lifted the lantern high as Frank tossed their bags into the back, and the light revealed a grin to melt the heart of a troll. It wasn't hard to see where Jersey'd gotten his smile.

"It's good to have you home, son. You too, Frank. Sit with me, both of you, and tell me about your trip."

Frank sat on one side, Mr. Rohn on the other, with Jersey in between. Jersey's arms rested on his father's or Frank's shoulders except when they flew off to gesture or pound his knee. It was pleasant to sit and listen without the need to interject, except when Jersey invited him to expand on a point or round out a description. His mind went back to the autumn, when he'd listened to Jersey's monologues in the Clark's barn. This was even better, because this was shared history, his and Jersey's. Tension drained from his shoulders and he drifted until he caught himself tilting off the side of the wagon and jerked upright.

When they reached the house, Jersey was still full of anecdotes about the people they'd met. He seemed content to repeat everything for his mother, but Frank was ready for bed. He made himself sit through supper, and he gave an abbreviated account of his trip to New Jersey before finally pleading for rest. Laughter burst from the kitchen as he undressed in the little room, and he wondered whether his presence for the holiday would augment or diminish the family harmony.

He woke to a cold hand on his back and moaned in protest.

"Sorry!" Jersey said. "Go back to sleep, dear."

He might have done, had it not been for that last word.

GENERAL ROHN and Colonel Huddleston spent the early part of Christmas Eve executing guerrilla raids on enemy supply lines. Mrs. Rohn brandished a rolling pin and various sharp knives and threatened to remove "additional body parts," should she catch them. Their last raid resulted in the capture of a pie from the kitchen, despite the best efforts of its well-armed defender.

Frank learned that the Rohn family celebrated Christmas Eve in the German manner, which meant that the tree was put up by Mr. and Mrs. Rohn in secrecy. He and Jersey (as the children of the house) were not allowed to see it until it was finished. Mr. Rohn banished them to their room with the threat of corporal punishment, or worse—starvation— should they emerge prior to the tone of a little silver bell. When they heard the bell, they rushed into the parlor to find the prickly branches decorated with candles, ornaments, apples, candies, and cookies. To Frank's dismay, Jersey plucked a reindeer-shaped cookie from the tree and bit the head off.

"Jersey! Can't we enjoy it for a few ticks before you destroy it?"

"Where's the fun in that!" Jersey said, crumbs dribbling from his mouth.

"I've been consorting with a barbarian!" Frank said. "I'm switching sides." He bowed to Mrs. Rohn. "I lay my knife and fork at your feet."

Presents in red-and-white-striped paper were spread under the tree, a green ribbon carefully tied around each package. Frank was ashamed that he had arrived with nothing but the clothes on his back—and he could not even claim ownership of those.

If Mr. and Mrs. Rohn resented the one-sided gift giving, he could not see it. Frank received a pocketknife from Mr. Rohn. Mrs. Rohn gave him an embroidered handkerchief. He had to fight for composure when he opened the slender box in which she'd folded it and saw his monogram on top. He wondered when she'd made it. She could not have known he would visit for Christmas until they received the telegram from Mt. Sterling.

After dinner, Mrs. Rohn read a story she'd picked from the *Saturday Evening Post*. Listening to her read, her voice taking on the cadence and pitch of each character, Frank understood that Jersey's love of a good story had grown, not of a seed blown in on a random breeze, but of one planted. They ended the evening singing "O Tannenbaum," Jersey and his mother singing harmony, while he and Mr. Rohn carried the melody.

As they prepared for bed, he marveled that Jersey could rush around like a giddy child, even as they danced at the edge of a precipice.

JERSEY WATCHED Frank undress, fold his pants, and place them on a chair like a traveling salesman with his mind on the next day's visits.

He blew into Frank's ear. "Anybody home?"

"I'm here," Frank said, jerking away.

"No more'n half, I reckon."

The smells of roast goose, evergreen, and candles made Jersey light-headed and fey. He knew he'd been frolicking like a demented faun. He'd been trying to sustain the illusion of a normal Christmas. There would be time to say good-bye later, after New Year's. All day he'd goaded Frank to let loose. It was like teasing a mermaid to the surface. He capered and made faces until Frank laughed and played along. A few minutes later, Frank would sink back into the gloom.

"What do you want?"

"All of you *here*—with me." He pulled Frank over to the bed and dropped his crutches to the floor.

Frank sat heavily. "I have to go back to New Jersey. It was wrong to run away from my grandmother. I just wasn't ready to—"

"So you'll run away from *me* now?"

"Your family's here. Mine's in New Jersey—what's left of it. The past may be closed to me, but my grandmother is there, and she's a damn sight friendlier than Eddy."

"I know, dear. My family's here and I love them, but my life isn't. Don't you see? I've been saying good-bye all day. This house, everything...." He waved, trying to encompass it all—the smells of his mother's roast goose and his father's pipe tobacco, the way he felt when he rode Flash, the star he'd made when he was six for the top of the Christmas tree, which his mother had preserved as though he'd used silver instead of tin foil. "It's what my parents have made together. If I stay, I'll be giving up my life for theirs. They don't want that."

"What are you saying?"

Jersey touched Frank's hand. "I want to be with you. I've known that since you left to go to Plainfield and I felt empty without you. But I didn't think it was possible that you—"

"That's your prick talking."

Jersey felt his face grow hot. "No it isn't. I wanted to be with you even before I cottoned on to you. I was scared to let on."

"I've got nothing to lose, Jersey. I don't really have anyone but you. Charlie's all right, I guess, but he'll always side with Eddy. And Eddy? She wants someone else for a grandson. But your parents love you. What would they think if they understood what we are? If they knew how I dream about you, they'd round up a lynch mob."

"No, they wouldn't. My father'd no more hurt you than burn down his barn and plow under his carrots. But there are things he doesn't need to know."

"And your mother? How will your mama feel when she figures out she'll have no grandchildren? Have you thought about that?"

Jersey used a crutch to poke at the balsa wood airplane he'd hung from the window frame when he moved downstairs. It was the only thing he'd asked his father to bring down from his old room when he'd come home from the hospital. "My parents don't touch each other much around me. You know what I mean. Like most kids, I prefer it that way. But this isn't a large house, Frank. I see how they look at one another. Sometimes, when I wake up in the night, I hear them."

He felt himself flush, but he kept talking because he was running downhill and he had to keep his feet. "I've waited. Ever since my short and curlies came in, I've waited to see if I could feel for someone what he feels for her. Now I do, only you're a man. I've gotta live with that, just like I've gotta live with this." He touched his stump. "Maybe I'd like to have kids. Maybe my mother would like to have grandkids, but kids need a mother and father who love one another. I've had that. I couldn't bring a child into the world and not give him that."

Unable to sit, Jersey pivoted on his leg. "You and I—it's fine so long as they think we're friends."

Frank watched him intently. "If they knew.... I can't risk losing you, Jersey. If we act on our feelings, we risk everything. What if James tells someone?"

"James will come around. He's got to. He's no more ready to give you up than I am." Jersey placed his arm around Frank's neck. "I'm scared, too, but it's the same as running across that field outside Chateau-Thierry with all those men around me. I couldn't stop because they were counting on me. I won't stop now either, so long as you're running beside me."

JERSEY WATCHED his father's buckboard jingle down the lane until it reached the place where the lane cut through a rise and all he could see was his mother's hat floating between the fence rails. He and Frank stood a little apart in the late afternoon sun. Frank's shadow seemed to lean toward his. It was New Year's Eve, and his parents were going into town to attend the dance at the Grange Hall. His mother had asked if they wanted to come. She'd even offered to pay the entrance fee. In answer, he'd joked about his sore butt from their last wagon ride and rattled his crutches. She asked Frank if he felt any more sociable, but Frank said he'd not be much of a friend if he left Jersey alone on New Year's.

They watched the wagon roll out of sight.

"What do we do now?" asked Frank.

"I've got a cribbage board."

"Hmm." A crow alighted on a fence post down the lane and protested the sorry state of the world.

"You like Gin Rummy?" Jersey said.

"I'm indifferent to it." Another crow landed on the other side of the lane.

"Let's go inside," he said. "I reckon we'll think of something."

"Very likely." Frank did not move. The crows exchanged epithets and imprecations.

Jersey planted a crutch and hopped around it. "Come on, Frank. You ain't the fire and brimstone type and neither am I. James told me about your *Inner Light*. Truth be told, it don't sound no different than my mama telling me to listen to my heart."

"It isn't my heart that bothers me."

"Which part is it, then?" Jersey stopped circling and crowded Frank until he smelled the coffee on his breath and felt the heat off his face. "You got parts sticking out all over."

"Was I made this way? Or did something happen to me in France?"

"Like what? The devil come up and whisper in your ear? What happened is you lost your memory and got a chance to start over—fresh. Some mornings, I'd take that as a gift, even if it meant I didn't get to wake up with your good morning poking me in the ass."

"Jersey!" Frank's eyes widened.

"If there is a hell, we're bound to be there together."

Frank stared, jaw working. Finally, he let out a whoop and kicked out one of Jersey's crutches. "We might as well get a head start." He caught Jersey before he fell and threw him over his shoulder. "You're going to regret this."

"Goddammit, Frank! You know I don't like being hauled around like a sack of feed."

CHAPTER 21

FRANK TOSSED him on the bed, and they kissed. At first, Jersey felt content to explore Frank's mouth with his tongue. He thrust a little, then let Frank taste him in turn. It didn't take much of that before he wanted more. He wanted to feel Frank's skin against his own. He wanted to feel the muscles of Frank's chest and to find out whether Frank's nipples were as sensitive as his own.

"Take off your clothes," he ordered.

He thought Frank would refuse for a second, so he tossed his own coat in the corner and began to unbutton his shirt, watching the desire build in Frank's eyes.

Frank stopped him. "Let me," he said, his voice rough. He pushed Jersey onto the bed and knelt in front of him. He ran his hands over Jersey's shirt as if to smooth it, then worked his way down the buttons, touching and smoothing between each button. By the time he reached Jersey's belt buckle, Jersey was frantic.

"Let me help you," he said, reaching for Frank's coat.

Frank had his own ideas and shrugged off Jersey's touch. "Be patient." He unhooked Jersey's braces and unfastened Jersey's trousers, his fingers brushing Jersey's belly through his shirt. Jersey shuddered. "Lean back," Frank demanded.

He pulled off Jersey's trousers and put them aside. Then he ran his fingers over Jersey's foot and massaged lightly before pulling Jersey's sock off. To Jersey's shock, Frank leaned down and took Jersey's big toe into his mouth. Jersey arched his back and made an embarrassing squeak.

After a moment of bliss, which completely emptied Jersey's head of coherent thought, Frank released Jersey's toe and stood.

Jersey gulped and found his voice. "Please, Frank, take off yours."

Frank grinned. "In good time." He removed Jersey's shirt and put it aside. Jersey's erection, hard since they'd started kissing, pushed up and out against the soft cotton of his undergarment.

Frank cocked an eyebrow. "Seems not all of you is small. Come here, I want to kiss you." He lifted Jersey and pressed their mouths together, rubbing his hands up and down Jersey's back. Jersey could feel the evidence of Frank's own arousal poking him in the hip.

"Undress me."

Jersey yanked Frank's jacket off his shoulders and tossed it on the chair. He slid Frank's braces off his shoulders and tore at his shirt, desperate to reach skin. He put his nose to Frank's chest and breathed in the mingled scents of soap and sweat. Uncovering a nipple, he flicked his tongue over the raised nub. Frank gasped.

"I got you," Jersey hummed, delighted. After exploring both nipples, he unfastened the waistband of Frank's trousers and unbuttoned his fly. "Take them off." This time, Frank complied. It still wasn't enough. "I want to feel your skin. Take off everything."

"Demanding hussy, aren't you?"

"Just get them off."

"Okay, little man," Frank said.

"Not where it counts."

"Not where it counts." When Frank stepped out of his drawers, his cock sprang free to salute Jersey.

Jersey couldn't take his eyes off Frank. Frank took him in his arms. They kissed again, and he felt a hitch in Frank's breathing when their cocks brushed. Jersey tried moving his hips a little.

"Oh, Lord that's—"

Jersey thrust harder, and Frank lost the power of speech.

Jersey grinned. Frank thrust his tongue into Jersey's mouth. Jersey's knee let go and they fell onto the bed.

It was Jersey's notion to play the woman. After they'd kissed and rubbed until they were both frantic for release, Jersey turned Frank onto his back and licked salty skin until Frank's cock jumped at every flick of his tongue. Frank emitted a continuous half moan, half hum. Jersey realized he wanted to feel Frank inside him. Had he stopped to think about what he was doing, he might have felt doubt or even revulsion, but he was too aroused to care. He slid up to kiss Frank briefly, then whispered in his ear. "Frank, I want you to fuck me."

FRANK STARED in shock. He'd never actually heard anyone use the word except in cursing. Hearing it from Jersey was more erotic than he could have imagined. He nearly shot his seed then and there.

"Are you sure?" he stammered.

"Yes, but we have to switch places. I wanna see your face while you do it."

"Put your leg on my shoulder," said Frank. He lifted Jersey's leg. "Are you sure," he asked again.

"Do it. I wanna feel you in me." Jersey thrust his hips up. He grabbed Frank's prick and guided it toward his hole. He gasped when its tip touched the sensitive skin around his anus.

Frank was painfully aroused. His body thrust forward of its own accord against the tight pucker. "I can't, I'll hurt you."

"Yes, you can, I want it… there, now push. Oh, God. Wait!"

Frank froze and started to pull away.

"No! Don't move! Just give me a second." Jersey panted for a moment, then the impossibly tight opening relaxed a fraction. "Okay, now push. Slowly!" Jersey closed his eyes and groaned.

"Are you okay?"

"Keep going," Jersey hissed.

Frank pushed slowly but steadily until his whole length was inside. The grimace on Jersey's face both horrified and excited him. He felt the ring of muscle around his cock loosen more.

"Okay, now move."

He pulled out a little, then tentatively pressed his hips forward. Jersey's eyes took on a glassy sheen.

"More!"

Frank pulled back and thrust again, harder.

Jersey groaned. "Yes."

Frank thrust again, hard. The heat and pressure surrounding his cock felt exquisite. His hips moved of their own accord, and his balls slapped against Jersey's body with each stroke. Jersey moved as well, arching his back and thrusting his hips to meet Frank's. "More, more," Jersey chanted.

Frank's fear of hurting Jersey brought him back from the brink, but he was close again. "Jersey, I'm...."

"Harder!" Jersey had lost some of his erection during Frank's initial invasion, but his member was full and bouncing heavily in time with their movements. Jersey looked at him with dark eyes and pleaded, "Touch me. Please, Frank!"

Frank grasped the head of Jersey's cock and pulled the foreskin in time with his thrusts. It took only a few strokes before he felt Jersey tense. The ring of muscle around Frank's shaft spasmed. Jersey cried out and shot a ropy strand of fluid onto his chest.

Frank continued to thrust while Jersey pumped four more times onto his belly. The sight and smell of the thick streams brought Frank to blissful release.

JERSEY LAY on his stomach in the bed. His arse burned, but he was languid as a cat in a window. *We need something better'n spit. Vaseline?* Papa had a tin in the tack room. Frank rested on his side, a hand at Jersey's waist, his breath warm on Jersey's shoulder.

"That tickles," Jersey said. He swallowed. "Does it feel like that for a woman? I mean, when you were inside—"

"How would I know?"

"You never visited *une maison close*?"

"If that means what I think it does," Frank sighed heavily, "how would I know?"

"You might've told James about it."

Frank rolled onto his back and closed his eyes. "I haven't read all the letters yet. Even if I did, I know it wasn't anything like this."

Frank rolled off the bed. "Where're you going?" Jersey asked.

"I need to wash."

Frank returned with a towel, which he used to wipe the sticky mess off Jersey's chest. Jersey stretched his arms above his head. "Fine pair you sling around."

Frank frowned. "What?"

"Between your legs when you show me your backside." Frank's cheeks bloomed to ripe apples. Jersey looked up at him. "Tell me what you see," he whispered.

Frank put a knee on either side of Jersey's leg and leaned over, his eyes dark. "You're so beautiful I can hardly believe it—so lean. Like a living anatomy lesson. Your skin hides nothing. I see every muscle and sinew of you."

WHAT HAVE I done? As Frank's languor passed and he listened to the soft sound of Jersey's breathing, he thought about how he'd used his friend, and the shame of it grew in his mind until he lay rigid with disgust. He'd meant… he didn't know what exactly he'd meant to do when he'd carried Jersey into the house and thrown him onto the bed. Kiss him certainly. Press his nose into the hollow below Jersey's collarbone and breathe in the scent of him. Even tell him that he loved him. But not use him! Not make a woman of him. No matter how Jersey felt, surely it was a sin to use a man like a woman. He pressed his arms to his sides as tears ran down his cheeks. Even as he thought of what he'd done, his prick thickened with a new rush of blood.

He had to leave, return to New Jersey, and take up the reins of the life Grandmother Huddleston offered. He had to leave this temptation behind. Could he leave Jersey—even if it was the right thing to do? Had he the strength of character? His thoughts flew round and round until he woke to the bleaching light of dawn, his arms clutching the living flesh beside him.

CHAPTER 22

1965

THE DOCTOR stretched his leg out. "The nurses tell me you aren't sleeping, sergeant."

The sergeant turned onto his side in the hospital bed, his back to the doctor. "None of your business."

"That depends. I can't rightly determine that until you tell me *why* you're not sleeping. Is your leg hurting?"

"Some."

"Why aren't you taking your pain medication?"

The sergeant mumbled into his pillow. "I take it."

The doctor chuckled. "Actually, you put the pills in your mouth, then you take them out and hide them in your mashed potatoes after the nurse has left."

The boy twisted back to face the doctor. "Fuck."

"If you prefer to tell me why you deserve pain instead of why you aren't sleeping, I'm flexible."

"You don't know what it's like. Fancy doctor like you, I bet you never served."

"Actually, as I recall, I got a gold chevron, a wound chevron, a Distinguished Service Cross, and a *Croix de Guerre*." He crossed them off on his fingers.

"What in Hell is a *Croix de Guerre*?"

"It's French. They were touchingly grateful."

"Jesus, what war did you fight in, World War II?"

"Actually, the one before that. I was seventeen at the time."

"You fought in the First World War? That's impossible. My grandpa fought—"

"Exactly. I could be your grandfather," said the doctor. "Now that we've established my imminent senility, let's get back to your hero status."

"I'm no hero."

The doctor glanced at the folder in his hands. "I've seen your service record. It's impressive."

The boy turned his head away. "Shows how fucking much you know."

"Okay, so why don't you tell me what really happened when you got wounded."

"Why should I?"

"Because you're stuck with me until you do, or until you start taking your pain medication and sleeping like a good boy."

"I'm not a boy." It came out in a sergeant's growl.

"My apologies, Sergeant. It slipped out."

"Don't they teach shrinks to treat their patients with respect?"

The doctor smiled. "I'm a slow learner. You think I don't respect you?"

"Always the fucking questions."

CHAPTER 23

1920

"GERALD ALBRECHT Rohn, Junior. You mean to tell me you traveled half across the country, spent your last penny, visited your doctor friend in Philadelphia, even visited a factory that makes prosthetic limbs, and you still—" She gasped for breath. "You still came back here with no notion at all of where or when you're going to get yourself a proper leg?"

Jersey and his mother sat side by side on the porch swing wrapped in heavy winter coats. Watching his mother get up to speed in the cold was like watching a covered pot come to boil: she started with little puffs and worked up to longer bursts, until she made continuous steam.

"The factory burned to the ground, Mama. What was I supposed to do?"

"How are you going to find a job?"

"I can write folks, can't I? That don't take two legs."

"How do you think you're going to get anyone to hire you when you talk like that, I don't know. Your father has better grammar than you do."

"My grammar is fine—when I want it to be."

"Why it pleases you to sound like an ignorant sharecropper, I don't know."

Jersey smiled and watched crows line up on the fence like nuns at a baseball game. Suddenly, they swept off in a cyclone of dark wings, shrieking havoc. A black bowler hat bobbed into view, propped up by a rare sight: a frock-coated gentleman on a gaited riding horse. He rode with one hand on his hat to keep it from blowing off in the wind. "Is that a Tennessee Walker? Nice horse."

"I wonder what *he* wants? I'll get your father." His mother went into the house.

Jersey continued to rock the porch swing with his toe, as he watched the gentleman cross the yard.

Still on his horse, the man tipped his hat. "Good day, sir. You must be Jersey Rohn. I'm pleased to make your acquaintance."

"You got the better of me, sir."

"My apologies. My name is Matheson. I've come to find Mr. Huddleston. Is he here, by any chance?"

Jersey's father and Frank came out onto the porch. "Good day, sir. I'm Gerald Rohn. What brings you to our farm?"

Mr. Matheson smiled. "I was just telling your son, Mr. Rohn, I've come to find Mr. Huddleston. I expect he's the young man at your side, is he not? You've led me on quite a chase, Mr. Huddleston, but all's well that ends well. Mrs. Huddleston will be pleased to know you're well."

"Mrs. Huddleston?" Frank said. "You've come from my grandmother? How did you find me?"

"Well! That's a tale worth telling in full, but perhaps now is not the time to do so. To make short of it, you are a fine-looking specimen of a man, if I may say so, Mr. Huddleston, but you are not particularly unique in description." He leaned over to examine Jersey and nodded. "Young Mr. Rohn on the other hand, being minus an appendage"—he pointed— "and being possessed of green eyes." He raised his finger. "Those are features which will lodge in a person's mind. I found young ladies to be particularly useful in tracking young Mr. Rohn."

Frank frowned.

Jersey's father removed his pipe from a pocket and knocked it against his palm a few times. "It's a mite cold for talking on the porch. If you'll get down off that fine horse, Frank and Jersey will take good care of it. You'll take coffee?"

Jersey glanced at Frank, who shrugged and took the reins of Mr. Matheson's horse. Mr. Matheson dismounted, nodded again at Frank, and followed Jersey's father into the house.

"Were we just dismissed?" asked Frank as he led the horse toward the barn. Jersey trailed behind.

"Papa likes you, Frank. If that fellow ain't a lawyer, I'll eat my hat. Papa doesn't trust lawyers. He probably just wants to figure out what the man wants."

Frank's brow knotted. "Kind of him to look out for me."

Horse brushed and supplied with a feedbag of oats, they returned to the house. Mr. Matheson and Jersey's father had taken the two best chairs by the fire. His mother had a straight-backed chair from the dining table next to her husband's.

Mr. Matheson held a steaming cup and saucer below his chin. Jersey watched him draw a long breath through his nose.

"Hello, Mr. Huddleston. I was just explaining to Mr. and Mrs. Rohn how eager Mrs. Huddleston is to see you again. She expressed to me most vigorously how very much she regrets that you did not feel sufficiently at home in her house to stay longer. She has charged me with the task of persuading you to return for an extended stay."

"It was wrong of me to leave the way I did. I'll pay her back as soon—"

"It's water under the bridge," Matheson interjected quickly. "Water under the bridge. Her primary concern is to see you happy."

"What would her *secondary* concern be?" Jersey asked.

Matheson smiled at Jersey. "You look out for your friend."

"Jersey and Frank are close," said Jersey's mother.

Matheson raised his cup to his lips, but stopped, the cup suspended. "Yet, unless I am mistaken, you are unlikely to have served together."

Frank got more chairs from the dining room. "You're correct, Mr. Matheson. I was a conscientious objector and served in an ambulance unit."

Matheson nodded. "Honorable service just the same."

"Why did you come here, Mr. Matheson?" Jersey said. He used the tip of one of his crutches to pull a chair closer, then sat down firmly.

"As I said, Mrs. Huddleston is anxious that Mr. Huddleston return to Plainfield."

"I am not the grandson she remembers." Frank remained standing, his hands on the back of his chair.

"You are, nevertheless, her grandson." Matheson paused for a beat, studying Frank with an openly interested gaze. "There is also the matter of the inheritance."

"She said nothing of an inheritance when I was there."

"It is a delicate thing." Matheson extended his round face toward Frank. "If I do say so, you did not give her much time to raise the matter. In any case, as the only living male issue, you are heir to your grandfather's estate. In point of fact, Mr. Huddleston, you are a wealthy man."

Jersey's mother gasped.

His father began filling his pipe, his fingers moving automatically, his eyes on Frank.

"I don't want her money," Frank said.

Jersey could see that Frank was considering throwing Matheson out on his ear, even if his saddlebags were stuffed with money. "Frank...."

"Nevertheless, the money is yours," continued Matheson. "There is also the matter of your grandfather's business interests. They are extensive, and they require sound management. Your grandmother is a capable woman, but she feels her years. She believes a more vigorous hand is needed."

"I know nothing about business."

Matheson leaned forward. "Precisely, Mr. Huddleston. Your grandmother is acutely aware that her time on earth is drawing to a close. If you are to learn while she can help, you must begin soon."

Frank sighed. "Have you known my family very long, Mr. Matheson?"

"My firm has had the honor of your family's patronage for many years."

"Did I know of any of this before—before I was injured?"

"I assume you refer to the injury you sustained in France."

Frank glanced at his cast and nodded.

"I don't know what you may have discussed with your grandparents. However, your father still lived when you left. Your grandfather was vigorous until a few months before he died in '17. I doubt your inheritance was much on anyone's mind."

"I see." Frank raised a hand to the top of his head. "I can't fully take it in."

"If I may suggest, things may seem less overwhelming in the morning." Matheson rose and offered his hand for Frank to shake. "Now, Mr. and Mrs. Rohn. I wonder if I might be so bold as to trouble you for a place to sleep tonight."

"It would be an honor, Mr. Matheson," said Jersey's mother. Matheson's stock had apparently risen. "You can have the boys' room. They can sleep on the—"

"Oh dear, no. There is no need to displace them. I shall be content to sleep on the couch by the fire."

TWO HOURS later, Mrs. Rohn left the master bedroom to get a glass of water. She was surprised to find Frank and Mr. Matheson at the dining room table. Frank wore trousers and a shirt, but Matheson was in a long nightshirt, his pale white calves exposed above black socks. Matheson scraped a gold fountain pen across an open notebook, while Frank leaned over his shoulder.

"Frank?" she asked. "I thought you'd gone to bed. Is there something wrong?"

"No, Mrs. Rohn." Frank smiled. "All's well. Mr. Matheson is going to help me pay a debt."

"There," said Matheson, putting down his pen. "That should do it. I'll write to them again after I return to Plainfield. We'll see it done."

"Thank you, Mr. Matheson, I'm sorry to have bothered you so late." Frank's teeth gleamed in the firelight.

FRANK SWALLOWED and brushed a dark lock from Jersey's forehead. "I have to go back to New Jersey. My grandmother…." Frank had followed Jersey into the barn for privacy while Matheson prepared for departure to the train station in Kalamazoo.

Jersey fed Flash a carrot. "I know. Papa and I were talking—if I pack my trunk before we go, we can send for it when we get there. That'll be easier than trying—"

"I mean to go alone, Jersey."

Jersey dropped the remains of the carrot and rounded on Frank. "What are you talking about? I told you I wanna stay with you. Help you remember—"

"I'm not strong enough. The way I've used you. It's wrong, Jersey. I can't keep—"

"What do you mean 'used me'? I'm no dolly! It was my idea to—" He wiggled his arse.

Frank made a harsh sound. "Maybe so, but that doesn't make it right for me to treat you like a woman."

"Who's a woman now? God! Look at you!" Jersey pushed away from Flash's stall and batted at loose straw with a crutch. "You think I wouldn't like to do it the other way? Roger you? I bet you'd like it too."

"It's a sin to use a man like a woman."

"I thought we agreed we didn't believe—"

"I didn't *know* I'd feel this way."

Jersey stared. "Well if *I* don't feel like a damn woman, I don't see why you should worry about—"

"You have to make a life for yourself. Find a job. You said it yourself."

"I can do that just as well in New Jersey—better. Come on, Frank, we got to keep running even though they're shooting at us." Jersey reached up and ran a thumb over the skin of Frank's cheek. "Otherwise, who are we?"

Frank leaned into the touch. "You'd make me a hero when I'm really just a—"

"You're as much a hero as me."

"No, I'm not," said Frank, pulling away.

"God damn you."

FRANK'S SECOND arrival at his grandmother's house in New Jersey hardly fit the Edwardian fantasy of the returning heir that Jersey had teased him about before their parting argument. But this visit was far more comfortable than the last time. He was met at the train station by his grandmother in her Packard touring car, driven, to his surprise, by her sharp-tongued helpmate, Betty.

The young woman was decked out in long black leather gloves and an automobile racer's leather helmet she must have liberated from a slow-moving suitor. Frank would have been scandalized if he hadn't been laughing so hard. She'd be wearing bloomers next.

Mrs. Huddleston, in widow's black, sat stiffly in the back seat.

"Mr. Huddleston! Over here!" Betty called, waving gayly, if indecorously.

Frank made his good-byes to his train-board companion, Mr. Matheson. Snatching up his borrowed carpetbag, he trotted over to the car.

"Grandmother! Thank you for meeting me. Hello, Betty. How are you?"

"Welcome home, Frank," said Mrs. Huddleston. "It's about time you were back where you belong." She craned her neck at the small cluster of people standing on the station platform.

Frank caught sight of Matheson's rapidly retreating back. Mrs. Huddleston frowned. "Wherever is that man going? I want to speak to him!"

"I'm forgetting my charge. Mr. Matheson sends his regrets, but he must run to catch his grandson's first baseball game."

"Baseball. His grandson!" Mrs. Huddleston's lined face broke into a smile. "I had no idea. I suppose I must forgive him. Betty! Are we to sit here until they mount a plaque on the running board and dedicate a new park? Let's go home."

PLEASANT AS he found her companionship, Frank couldn't help feeling that his interactions with his grandmother were colored by an odd urgency, almost as though she were courting him. He speculated that she must fear he would disappear again in the middle of the night were she to frighten or fail to amuse him. Perhaps it was his newfound prosperity and status, but it embarrassed him that she should think him unreliable. Striving to reassure her, he found himself forcing a bonhomie that had him more convinced than ever that he was a fraud. In truth, he missed Jersey terribly and missed the intimacy they'd established.

He reached the breaking point after an exhausting dinner two weeks into his new life. He'd consented, at his grandmother's request, to meet a group of his grandfather's business associates. He got into trouble soon after the guests arrived. Like a junior associate at his first appearance in court, he froze, unable to think of a single thing to say to the sober pair of businessmen to whom she'd introduced him. Worse, as he fumbled for words, he realized he'd already forgotten their names. After apologizing profusely, he left them staring as he rushed blindly up the stairs. Picking a door at random, he slipped into his grandmother's sewing room.

He closed the door with a sigh, loosened his starched collar, and actually prayed—thinking himself as poor a religious as he was a shipping magnate—that no one would find him for ten minutes. Ten minutes, and then he would return to the world of men's men, firm handshakes, and appraising eyes, the world in which Grandfather the Ghost had excelled, as he'd apparently excelled in all things.

His grandmother's knitting lay in a basket on the table. She didn't seem to enjoy knitting, often muttering crossly to herself as she unraveled a row to fix a missed stitch. Nevertheless, the yarn and needles were her constant companions during the long evenings of their strange courtship. Without thinking, he picked up the half-finished sweater and knit a row. When he realized what he had done, he stared in shock at the alien hands in his lap.

"You'll get yourself a reputation as an oddball, you will, if you keep up this kind of thing, Mr. Frank," said Betty from the doorway. "You make quite a pair, what with the old lady talking to her dead husband when she thinks nobody's listening and you sneaking off to do her knitting."

"I didn't realize I knew how to knit."

"Imagine that! But I'm forgetting my orders. Her ladyship wants you in the dining room."

"Right." He forced a smile. "Must show the flag." He rose and started for the door.

"Wait," Betty said. "You go out looking like that and they'll be spreading rumors the old lady found you at an orphanage. Let me." She reached up, reattached his collar, and adjusted his necktie, her cool fingers lightly brushing his neck.

"Thanks," he said, feeling a flush warm his cheeks. "I'm really not used to this sort of thing."

"You'll do all right once you get your bearings. I heard the old lady say so just the other day. You need to relax and stop trying so hard."

"Oh." He tried to regain his balance. "Don't you think she'd be angry if she knew you were eavesdropping?"

"Not really. Was me she was talking to at the time." She slipped out the door with a saucy grin.

Frank wondered how far Betty's libertine spirit would take her. If he were to flirt with her, it might put off embarrassing questions. He felt himself flush again.

JERSEY WOKE with his morning wood bent painfully against his pajama bottoms. In his dream, Frank had been exploring the sparse trail of hair that led downward from Jersey's belly button. Likely the sound of his father's boots hitting the floor had woken him. In the dream, a knock on the bedroom door had caused him and Frank to erupt into a panic-stricken rush to find their missing clothes.

Tempted to stay and finish the job Frank had started, Jersey was dissuaded by the sound of his mother murmuring to his father in the kitchen. He sighed and reached for his bathrobe. Today, he promised himself, he would write to at least three prospective employers before treating himself and Flash to a ride. If only he had some idea of what he might do besides clerking in some office. The idea left him listless.

How were Frank and his grandmother faring? Maybe when Frank was settled into his new home, he'd permit a visit. Even though he was still angry at his friend, Jersey knew he would walk there, leg or no leg, if he thought Frank would have him. He'd have to do something about his missing pin soon, but the idea of strapping on some ugly, bargain-priced, government-issue appliance made him want to tear the recruiting posters from the post office walls.

"HOW MANY did you put in the mailbox today?"

Jersey suspected his mother already knew the answer to her question. He searched the room as if he might find an excuse propped on the mantelpiece next to the photograph of Grandpapa Rohn.

"I couldn't find anything that seemed—"

"Are you planning to sit on the porch for the rest of your life?"

"No, Mama, but there wasn't anything in the paper—"

His mother shook the paper. "You circled four advertisements last night."

"I know, Mama, but this morning they didn't look so good."

She sat down next to him on the sofa. "Tell me what's wrong with them."

"They're not what I want!" He hadn't known he was angry, but his hands curled into fists.

His mother looked at him expectantly. "What do you want?"

"I want to go to New Jersey to see Frank."

Her face lost expression. Jersey doubted that was what she expected to hear. Well it wasn't what he'd expected to say. She placed her hand on his. "I know you miss him, but you need to concentrate on yourself now. Frank has his own life to live with his grandmother and his family business."

"It's just that…." He stared at his mother's face, hopelessly.

THE GLARE off the snow-covered yard made Charlie's eyes water. The winter sun threw spears of ice. It felt like the sun was freezing a hole in the center of his chest. *Why the frozen glare, Old Man Winter? I'm just a tired old man splitting logs for the fire. I get enough hard looks from Eddy.*

He set the wedge in the crack he'd made with his ax and lifted the heavy mallet to drive it home. The tool sagged in his hands, and he tried to remember what had gotten him so fired up to go outside into the cold and blinding sun.

It wasn't as though they needed more firewood. He'd stacked logs almost to the gables along the side of the house and had a smaller supply drying on the porch. He'd had some fool idea about seeing the world on February 29, 1920—leap day in a leap year—but the notion seemed silly now and the mallet seemed twice as heavy as usual. The house had been close with Eddy blaming him for Frank's sudden departure—as though he'd been the one telling a grown man whom he could and couldn't see.

Every so often, when they were lingering over coffee, he'd make a joke and the corners of her mouth would soften, and he'd see in Eddy the woman he'd married forty-one, no, forty-two years ago, but those moments had been rare this winter.

The last day of the coldest month. *A funny day to leap into something new.* The sun widened the hole until his whole chest was burning. He blinked and dropped the mallet, scarcely noticing when the handle landed on his boot. *I don't recall a sun so bright in winter.* The weight of it bore him down until his backside was in the snow without his meaning to sit. *Eddy will nag me for getting my trousers wet.* He closed his eyes against the unrelenting glare.

EDDY GLANCED out the kitchen window into the yard where Charlie was working. *What is that old fool doing, lying in the snow like that? He'll catch cold!*

"IT'S Charlie." Frank held out the telegram to his grandmother. She took the flimsy from his hand. He felt lost, standing in the doorway in his dressing gown.

> TO FRANCIS HUDDLESTON PLAINFIELD NEW JERSEY
>
> CHARLIE DEAD STOP FUNERAL MAR 5 STOP COME NOW STOP EDITH CLARK

"I'm so sorry, Frank," she said.

"Will there be any reply?" asked the telegraph boy.

When Frank stood motionless in the doorway, the draft rushing past him, his grandmother asked Betty to get a nickel from the grocery money.

When Betty returned with the coin, she handed it to the boy. "No, not now."

"Thank you, ma'am," said the boy. He jogged down the steps to the bicycle he'd left leaning at the bottom.

"I liked him." Frank looked at his grandmother helplessly.

She put her hand on his arm. "Betty will pack your bag."

THE LITTLE church on the outskirts of Taperville was unusually full, with latecomers standing in the back. The coffin was finally closed in preparation for its trip to the cemetery. For reasons she kept to herself, Eddy had insisted on an open coffin for the afternoon viewing, which had lasted for three long hours.

Frank's attention was drawn time and again to the gaunt, rouged face of the corpse, which would have suited a wax museum. He did not see Charlie there. His was the gruesome curiosity of the bystander at a fatal accident. He pressed to see the gore, even as it sickened him. Eddy insisted on staying in the church for the whole time to exchange greetings with the friends and family members who came for a last look at Charlie. The doors and windows of the church were firmly shut against the cold. Packed rows of heavily dressed mourners heated the church to the point where Frank could feel rivulets of sweat running from his chest to his belly under his suit and waistcoat.

Eddy's insistence at stage-managing every detail of the entire funeral, from the precisely arranged bouquets of flowers to the order of procession, felt a little unseemly, as though Charlie had been a man far above his actual station. He doubted Charlie would have liked this ostentatious send-off. A wake at his home would have been more his style, attended by the local men whose barns he'd helped repair after tornados or fires, men who'd done the same for him. Prohibition and his wife's troop of starched and hatted church women nixed that idea. At least the crowded church would have pleased him.

Reserved for family, Frank's seat in the front row banished him from the company of anyone he'd ever met before, apart from his grandmother. Charlie had brothers far more prolific than he, for cousins abounded, many sharing Frank's own fair skin and blond hair. He'd had no idea it had come from Charlie's side of the family. Charlie's hair was fully white as long as Frank knew him.

Frank glanced at his grandmother. Eddy's gray hair was invisible, pinned up under her black hat and obscured by a veil. He'd always pictured the Clarks in the isolation of their farm or perhaps attending a church function in town. Had Charlie's marriage resulted in alienation from his family? What had Charlie sacrificed to marry Eddy?

"Stop staring at me, Frank, and pay attention to the minister."

"I'm sorry, Grandmother."

The oppressive heat and airless church had him out of sorts. The minister was winding down. His words, none of which penetrated Frank's thoughts, would be followed by another reading by one of the church deacons and a selection of hymns. A group of Elders would carry the coffin down the aisle to the waiting hearse.

He wished he could help with that, but Eddy had vetoed the idea, saying it was inappropriate. She wanted him by her side. The hearse would lead a mixed procession of horse-drawn conveyances and automobiles to the family cemetery in the woods above the Clark farm. He hadn't known it existed until Eddy told him. He was happy, at least, that Charlie would rest near the farm he'd loved.

What would happen to the farm now that Charlie could no longer work it? He imagined that Eddy would sell it and move into town, but he hadn't had an opportunity to ask her. She'd been entirely occupied with the minutia of coffin, flower, passage, and hymn selection since he'd arrived. Had she family who would want her? It was difficult to imagine. He was being unkind again. Perhaps her dry-eyed obsession with the details of the funeral was a tribute to her husband of over forty years, but he would have found it easier to sympathize with tears, especially if they'd unlocked his own.

THE CLARK family cemetery was a square of white, striped by the shadows of barren oak trees. Tufts of brown grass poked up from under the snow and gave the stone markers fringes like upended buckskins. A trio of bareheaded gravediggers stood under the trees, waiting to fill the grave after the mourners left. One of them must have ridden, because a horse was tied nearby. His grandmother's boot slid on the packed snow of the lane and she tightened her grip on his arm.

"I told you to have Robert's boys clear the lane."

"I asked them. You can see they dragged a snowplow through. If they'd gone any deeper we'd be in mud to our ankles."

"It'll be mud anyway, on the way back."

"Very likely." Frank watched the progress of the men as they lifted the coffin from the back of the hearse and carried it to the fresh grave.

"It looks like they're nearly ready. Where's the minister?" Eddy asked. "Come on, Frank. Must you move so slowly?"

"I think they'll wait for us, Grandmother."

They took up position next to the minister and waited while the long line of conveyances disgorged their passengers.

"Are you ready, Mrs. Clark?" murmured the minister.

Eddy nodded briskly. "You may proceed."

The minister raised his head and caught the attention of the people clustered around the grave. "Thank you for coming to this committal service for Charles Clark. The passing of a loved one is always a great loss and a sad occasion. But for one who knows the Lord, as Charlie does, it is a joyous occasion because he is now in His glorious presence."

As the minister spoke, Frank examined faces in the crowd. How many people had come to his parents' funeral in Philadelphia? Had their passing been lost among the thousands caused by the pandemic? Where had he been at the time? Had he even been aware of their passing? He sniffed. His face was wet and his nose was running. The minister stopped speaking, and Frank felt the weight of Eddy's hand on his arm. Was something expected of him? He could not seem to bring his thoughts into order. The sweat that had soaked his underclothes in the hot church was now clammy on his skin and his muscles convulsed in a shiver. Eddy tugged his arm and said something indistinct. People drifted away from the grave, some stepping over to express their sympathy, but he was rooted in place.

Where were his parents buried? He didn't even know. Why hadn't he thought to ask when he was in Philadelphia? What was wrong with him that he hadn't thought to ask? The minister moved into his field of vision and said something, but he couldn't make sense of it. Eddy pulled at his arm again, then the weight of her hand fell away.

"Frank! You're shivering. It's time to go home."

He felt an arm around his shoulders and leaned into the familiar embrace.

"Jersey, you've come."

Jersey pressed something worn and soft into his hand. "Wipe your face." A warm hand pushed the handkerchief gently to his face.

"I didn't know they were sick. They died, and I didn't even know they were sick."

"Who was sick, Frank? Charlie went quickly, didn't he? They said it was his heart."

"My parents. They were sick and I didn't know it."

"Come on, Frank. I'll walk you back to the car. It's time you were someplace warm."

Jersey turned him toward the lane and shoved until he had to take a step or fall over. Once moving, his legs regained their function.

JERSEY MANEUVERED Frank toward the waiting car. Mrs. Clark sat stiffly in the back of the Model T. A blond young man with a startling resemblance to Frank was in the driver's seat. *Must be kin.*

"What are you doing here, boy?" Mrs. Clark's voice was dry and sharp.

"I came to pay my respects to Charlie. I'm sorry for your loss, Mrs. Clark."

"He was no kin to you."

"No, but I liked him, ma'am."

"Leave my grandson alone. He doesn't need any help from you."

Jersey nearly dropped his arm from Frank's shoulders, but caught himself and tightened his grip. "I think that's for him to say."

"Come on, Frank, get in. I'm cold," said Mrs. Clark.

Frank raised his head and seemed to take in the scene around him for the first time since Jersey had caught sight of him shivering at the graveside. "You've no call to be rude to Jersey, Grandmother. I'm glad he came. Charlie liked him."

"You've no need of him now you're well. I'm sure you'll do your duty without his help."

Frank looked at his grandmother as if he were seeing her for the first time. "My duty?"

"The farm, Frank! It's been in your family since your great, great grandfather cleared it. It's time you took it over."

Jersey knew that Frank could do it. Frank would be good farmer. He knew the work. Judging from his last letter, he'd probably be a damn sight more comfortable growing corn than he was trading market tips with Grandfather the Ghost's cronies. Who would look askance if he hired a local boy to work around the house or keep his accounts? Jersey's parents would welcome a job that kept their son close.

Mrs. Clark pointed at the young man in the driver's seat. "One of Robert's boys can help you when you need another pair of hands. You've no need of a cripple."

She was right, of course. Frank had no need of him. The tow-headed young man in the driver's seat turned to eye Jersey curiously, revealing pink cheeks and striking blue eyes. He *was* Frank's kin, probably a cousin. Somehow, Jersey had always assumed that Frank's good looks came from his father's side of the family.

"Jersey's no cripple. I don't like it when you call him that," Frank said, his voice tight. "It's disrespectful. We'll talk about the farm later."

Dropping his arm, Jersey turned to go. "It was good seeing you, Frank."

"Wait, Jersey, how'd you get here? Do you need a ride?"

"Brought Flash. He's over there." Jersey pointed toward the trees where the gravediggers waited.

"I thought that horse looked familiar."

"Yeah, he wanted to take off soon's he saw you."

Frank laughed and somehow the vibration resonated from Jersey's ears to his belly.

"I don't expect Bobby here's got it out for him. Listen, I thought I'd stop to see you while I'm in town. Would tomorrow be all right?"

Warmth spread through Jersey's gut as though he'd swallowed a mouthful of brandy. *He wants to see me.* He shifted uncomfortably, suddenly conscious of the position and weight of his prick within his trousers. How was he to get on with his life when the only thing that woke him from his lethargy was the thought of seeing Frank again? It was maddening.

"Sure, Mama and Papa would love to see you."

THE FRONT room of the Clark house was provisioned for an army. Apparently, the women of the Taperville Methodist Church were certain food played a critical role in recovery from loss. If that were so, he and Eddy would soon be skipping through the meadow of life. Unfortunately, Frank was not hungry at all, nor did his grandmother show any inclination to sample the tuna casserole, cold cuts, potato salad, chocolate cake, or oatmeal cookies laid out on the sideboard. The food was for the visitors who stopped by every so often to see how the bereaved widow was faring. Most of them brought offerings of their own. The resulting operation was a sort of rolling potluck.

Eddy cooperated by feeding everyone who appeared. During the busier moments, one might have thought she ran a soup kitchen, so many lined up for a serving.

Few visitors dared ask about Frank. Many seemed surprised he had returned for the funeral. The prevailing opinion was that he had been sent away to an institution last fall. Frank learned this disturbing news from his cousin, Bobby, who proved gregarious when fortified with a plate of roast beef and sweet, German-style potato salad. Neither Eddy nor Charlie had tried to quash the rumor of his institutionalization, Bobby told him. Bobby remarked blandly that it was sometimes easier to let people think what they would than share the truth. Frank left Bobby's fishing expedition unanswered.

Frank knew he had to talk to his grandmother about her future, but he didn't know how to raise the issue. Charlie was hardly cold in his grave, and he didn't want to be insensitive, but he felt a consuming need to resolve things.

She wanted him to stay and work the farm. The idea was not without appeal. He loved the valley, even now as the melting snow revealed mud and rotting leaves. Farming was peaceful, renewing—and a mite boring.

Or so he felt now that the greater part of his mind had returned from its long vacation.

On the other hand, the proximity of family appealed. The funeral had revealed the existence of a large family of distant kin into which he could, if he chose, lose himself. But to immerse himself here, he would have to give up his Grandmother Huddleston, and the wider world offered by his grandfather's legacy.

He had Jersey to consider as well. Hard as his grandmother tried to engage him, he was miserable in New Jersey without his friend. To live with Jersey would require a covering marriage in his grandmother's community, ruled as it was by the starched ladies of the church.

In the morning, he tried twice to raise the issue of the farm and Eddy's future. Eddy avoided the issue each time by finding a new person to greet or feed. Now it was early afternoon and Frank still hoped to visit Jersey, so he got himself a glass of lemonade—beer was forbidden in the Clark home—and cornered his grandmother in the kitchen.

"Grandmother, I need to talk to you...."

His grandmother continued to divide a pan of brownies into precise squares.

"I don't mean to press you, but it's just that I probably won't be here for very long and we must talk before I go."

"I knew you would abandon me in my time of need."

"Nobody's abandoning anyone, Grandmother. That's what I want to talk to you about. Have you thought about where you want to live?"

"Where I want to live? I've lived in this house for more than forty years. I have no intention of leaving it."

"Have you considered what it might be like to live closer to town? Nearer to the church and your friends?"

"I have not." His grandmother continued to make cuts in the pan of brownies. By now, the pieces were taller than they were wide.

"If you were to sell the farm, you could buy a nice little house, one that would be easier to care for than this old heap."

She straightened, her eyes ablaze. "Charlie and my father built this house out of wood they cut themselves, up on the ridge."

Frank cringed inwardly and tried again. "I'm sorry. I didn't mean to disparage your home. I just meant that it's a big house. They built it for a big family, didn't they?"

"I expect you'll find a girl one day and start filling it."

He could think of no response that didn't involve lying. Tasting bile, he took a gulp of lemonade. "I'm sorry, Grandmother, but I have to leave. I have to go back to New Jersey to manage Grandfather Huddleston's businesses. You'll not want for anything. I'll see to that. If you want to stay here, I expect I can hire someone to work the farm. You don't have to decide now. I'll leave you my address."

Eddy threw down her knife and marched into the bedroom. The sound of the door slamming shut echoed through the house.

FRANK ARRIVED at the Rohn farm in a rented Willys-Overland from Kalamazoo. He saw no one when he bumped into the yard, but a thin trickle of smoke rose from the chimney of the house. He shut off the engine and bounded up the steps to the porch. The door opened before he could pound on it.

"It's Frank, Jersey, come and see! I'm so sorry for your loss, Frank. Jersey told us he saw you at the funeral. How is Mrs. Clark?" Mrs. Rohn dragged him into the house.

Frank quickly found himself seated at the dining room table with a cup of coffee at hand. Mrs. Rohn was eager for details of the funeral. Jersey said little, but sent hot, questioning looks in his direction whenever Mr. and Mrs. Rohn weren't paying attention. Frank was ready to carry Jersey off like a fireman when a whispered comment from Mr. Rohn to his wife finally brought him a private moment with Jersey. Shortly after, Mr. Rohn announced that he had chores to do.

"Stay for supper, Frank." Mrs. Rohn said. Then she and Mr. Rohn disappeared into the kitchen.

"It's good to see you," Jersey said.

"I've missed you."

Jersey pushed himself upright. "Let's sit by the fire. How are things with Grandmother Huddleston?"

"Fine. She's very tolerant," Frank said, following.

Jersey glanced over his shoulder, concern furrowing his brow. "You're not running away again?"

"I'm not running away. Listen, there's something I want to ask you."

Jersey smiled. "Something you couldn't put in a letter?"

"I couldn't... how's Flash?"

"Flash is very fond of his stall and so are you."

"I came to tell you that I'm sorry. What we did surprised me, when you... when I—"

"It's okay, Frank. You don't have to say it."

"I think I do. I've been able to think of little else since I left. I think about what we did, what it meant that you opened yourself to me."

Jersey stared, eyes wide.

"You gave me a gift, and I threw it back in your face. I punished you for my shame. I don't know how you can bear to talk to me. I'm sorry."

"You were scared. I knew that."

"That didn't give me the right to—"

"Frank, stop. You've said you're sorry. I think you should go, before we hurt each other again."

"Won't you forgive me?"

Jersey blinked. "Forgive you? I never blamed—"

"Then you'll have me back?"

"I don't understand. What about your grandmother, the farm—"

Frank spoke so quickly his tongue felt uncoupled. "Come back to New Jersey with me. Stay with me. I need you."

"What about Mrs. Huddleston?"

"I told you. She is very tolerant. She wants me to stay, despite my failings."

"You haven't told her anything—"

"No."

"Won't she—"

"I don't care. I need you."

CHAPTER 24

JAMES STRUGGLED to close the door against the winter wind. When the wind finally released the heavy door, the bang echoed in the empty meeting room. He looked around at the familiar white walls and plain benches. The polished surfaces gleamed in the late afternoon light. He checked the stove to see if there was any remnant of fire to coax to life, but the grate was empty and the ashes had been removed. He collapsed onto a bench and considered making a new fire, but he could not induce himself to move.

How long had it been since he and Francis had sat together in silent communion? His boyhood friend would always be Francis to him, never Frank. If Francis had attended a meeting since his return from the dead, he had not mentioned it. Would it change anything if Francis were to meditate on his relationship with Jersey here, in this spiritual place? He kicked the bench in front of him. Meditation had not helped him. It had not cleansed the image of Jersey's naked buttocks dripping with bath water, nor the tilt of his head as he kissed Frank. It was true that James had not yet kissed a girl, but it wasn't because he hadn't wanted to. As a boy, he had delighted in the warmth and weight of Francis's arm thrown across his shoulders. There was nothing unnatural in that. Nothing at all.

James had come to the meeting house to clear his head, but all he could do was review every innocent touch from his childhood. Not only had Jersey stolen the intimacy he'd shared with Francis before the war, he'd stolen the joy of James's childhood memories. The smallest gestures had become suspect: he and Francis tickling one another on the sofa of his father's home, Francis's hand on his neck after he'd hit a home run in Fairmount Park. Everything stank of fish left in the sun. It was Jersey's fault. If Francis had been vaporized by a German shell, it would not have so thoroughly destroyed his friendship. Francis's death would have left their past untainted.

There was nothing for him in the meeting house. His inner light revealed nothing but corruption. He put his hands under the edge of a heavy bench and threw it over, grunting from the effort. It hit the floor with a satisfying crash. He moved on to the next.

"REMIND ME why I'm here?" Jersey asked again, as the houses thinned to larger estates. "This is your world, not mine."

They went by a gated park with a stone carriage house larger than the farm house in which Jersey grew up. He and Frank reclined in the back of a taxi. Frank rubbed his left arm, a habit he'd picked up since the cast had come off.

"I've come here twice without you, Jersey. The first time I didn't even last the night. I'm not making that mistake again."

Jersey pointed toward a large Victorian mansion with doors that must have been twelve feet tall. "I couldn't live in a house like that. There's no porch. Where would I go if I couldn't sleep?"

"I'd build you a porch—the best goddamn porch you ever saw, with a swing and wicker furniture and screens to keep off the mosquitoes."

"What am I gonna do here?" Jersey asked.

"You don't have to do anything." Frank must have seen something in Jersey's face, because he changed course hastily. "We'll find something. You told Mrs. Underwood you wanted to read. I'll buy you all the books you want."

Jersey put a hand on Frank's knee. "Rein it in, Frank."

The taxi turned into the drive of the Huddleston house. It was not as big as Jersey had imagined, and it was rather plain—apart from the columned entrance. "That's it? I've seen farm houses bigger'n that! Why even...." He fell silent when he caught sight of the wings that extended from the rear of the house.

They got out and followed the driver as he carried their bags to the front door. The door opened before they reached it. Mrs. Huddleston came out briskly, followed at a more leisurely pace by Betty.

Mrs. Huddleston put her hand on Frank's arm as though he were guiding her promenade. "It's so good to have you back, Frank."

Jersey noted the use of Frank rather than Francis. Frank had been working on her, it seemed.

Mrs. Huddleston examined Jersey. "You will introduce your friend?"

"Grandmother, this is Jersey Rohn." Mrs. Huddleston's eyes widened. "Jersey, this is my grandmother, Mrs. Huddleston."

"How do you do, Mrs. Huddleston?"

"Frank has told me a great deal about you, Mr. Rohn. Mr. Matheson told me your home is in Michigan. What brings you here?"

Jersey smiled and lifted a crutch. "I'm at loose ends until I get my leg squared away, Mrs. Huddleston. Frank invited me for a visit, if that's all right with you."

Mrs. Huddleston finished her appraisal. "Of course. See to their luggage, Betty."

MRS. HUDDLESTON raised a wine glass to her lips. Prohibition had decidedly not reached the Huddleston home. Jersey lifted his own glass cautiously. His father liked a mug of beer on Friday or Saturday night, but he had never offered any to Jersey. Jersey had experimented with wine in France, when he was on leave. The result of that experience had been a lasting queasiness associated with all spirits. Frank, on the other hand, didn't hesitate. His usually rosy cheeks were plumy.

"How long do you plan to stay with us, Jersey?" asked Mrs. Huddleston.

"Jersey and I are great friends, Grandmother," Frank said. "I enjoy his stories. Tell Grandmother a story, Jersey."

Farm life, the army, boxing—Jersey could conceive no subject appropriate for the elegant lady before him. He sipped his wine.

"I would be pleased to hear how you and Frank met," said Mrs. Huddleston.

He didn't want to tell that story to Mrs. Huddleston—ever. He addressed Frank. "Did I tell you about the first time I rode Flash? After I lost my leg, I mean?" Frank shook his head. "It was only a couple of days before the American Legion meeting at the Grange Hall."

"No wonder you fell off when Eddy…." Frank hastily took up his wine glass.

"Who's Eddy?" asked Mrs. Huddleston, following the arc of Frank's wine glass.

"My other grandmother, Edith Clark," said Frank. "Everybody calls her Eddy."

"I believe I would prefer you continue to call me Grandmother."

"Of course, I wouldn't… I mean, Eddy's different."

"How so?"

"I don't—"

"Flash, he's this horse of mine," Jersey said. "Why, he's almost as old as I am. I been riding him since I was eight, so we're pals, see."

Mrs. Huddleston smiled at Jersey. "Thank you, Jersey. But I believe I would like to hear more about Mrs. Clark."

Frank relaxed visibly when he saw the humor in his grandmother's expression. She might have been a schoolmarm interrogating a favorite truant.

Jersey grinned at her. "I reckon Frank'll have to explain about Eddy."

MRS. HUDDLESTON was at her husband's desk in the library when Betty knocked. "Mrs. Huddleston? They're at it again, the little ruffians! Shooting squirrels or some such in the far field. Do you want me to call the sheriff?"

"Certainly not, Betty. My husband never found it necessary to ask for help managing the neighbor's children." She placed a paper into a folder and took off her reading glasses. "I shall visit their parents on Saturday."

"Your husband would have run them off with a shotgun," Betty muttered just loudly enough she could hear.

"That will do, Betty. I am busy," said Mrs. Huddleston, replacing her spectacles.

WHAT WERE they doing? She didn't pry when Frank asked for a stool and gardening tools. Her relationship with Frank was cordial, but there was a membrane around his thoughts she had yet to pierce. She would be patient; she did not want a repeat of the disaster when Frank left in the middle of the night. So she didn't question, but showed him where she kept the key to the garden shed on its hook in the pantry, just as she had not questioned when he insisted that he and Jersey take adjoining rooms on the second floor. She was curious what gardening they might do in March, so she fetched her husband's binoculars from the study and made the climb to the third floor guest bedroom. From there she could see nearly three acres of hardwoods and meadow extending beyond the back yard.

It was like watching a silent movie. She needed only organ music to complete the illusion—a jaunty tune to fit the scene. Their lips moved, but she could hear nothing but the ticking of the radiator below the windowsill.

The pair strolled past the mowed and tended yard, now dry and brown, and continued under the trees—barren or she would not have been able to follow—until they reached the natural meadow that her husband had insisted the gardeners leave unmolested. Frank carried the stool and garden rake. He positioned the stool for Jersey, then paced and pointed. Jersey waved a crutch like a conductor's baton. Frank marked a rectangle in the dead grass, using the rake. It occurred to her that they planned a vegetable garden. Frank returned to Jersey's side and placed a hand on the younger man's neck. The music in her head swelled. She should stop intruding on their privacy.

She was about to put down the binoculars and quit her ridiculous spying when she heard the flat crack of a rifle shot. The effect on Jersey was extraordinary. He flinched, thrust out his leg as if to rise, and sent the stool over backward into the grass. He landed on his back, shaking visibly.

Frank's reaction was no less violent. He spun in the direction of the shot and yelled something so loudly that it was faintly audible from her distant vantage point, his body telegraphing anger. He sprinted across the meadow and threw the rake as if it were a spear. She did not anticipate his speed and had to lower the binoculars to track him. When she found him again, she raised the heavy binoculars in time to watch Frank grab a local boy by the lapel of his jacket. He lifted the boy from a drift of rotting leaves where he was tangled in the rake. Frank yelled, but she could not make out the words. He shook the boy, who began to cry.

She was transfixed, unable to decide whether or not to rush out into the yard. Jersey entered the field of view. He said something and put a hand on Frank's arm. Frank shrugged off his touch and continued to shake the boy, his face bright red. Then Jersey did the most extraordinary thing. He leaned in and punched Frank precisely in the jaw, losing his balance in the process. The three of them fell into the leaves together.

She put down the binoculars and rushed downstairs, cursing her aged and unreliable joints as she lowered herself down each step. She limped out into the yard, reaching the edge of the mowed and manicured part at the same time as the boys. Frank carried the neighbor boy in his arms. Jersey followed in silence.

"Grandmother!" Frank said. "Something's happened. I think we'd better call a doctor." Frank carried the boy into the kitchen and laid him on the table.

"Betty! Where are you?" she called out.

"What happened?" said Betty, coming from the dining room.

"He threw a rake at me," said the boy, rallying. "Then the gimp slugged him, 'cause he wouldn't stop shaking me. That was a swell jab."

"His leg is punctured," Frank said. "We must stop the bleeding and clean the wound."

"Please get a clean sheet from the linen closet, Betty," said Mrs. Huddleston.

"I didn't mean to hurt him," Frank said, a visible bruise forming on one side of his jaw.

"Never mind, Frank. There is a bottle of rubbing alcohol in the pantry. We'll use that to clean the wound."

"It ain't nothing," said the boy.

"You don't want it to become septic," Jersey said.

"Wash your hands," said Mrs. Huddleston, taking the alcohol from Frank. Frank went to the sink and scrubbed.

Betty returned with a sheet in her hands.

"Tear that into strips, Betty. Jersey, help the boy get his stocking off." Jersey untied the boy's boot and pulled off his knee-length stocking. The wound was in the boy's calf, where one of the splines of the rake had punctured the boy's skin. It was hard to tell if the wound was deep because of the blood welling from the hole. "Frank, my hands are too stiff. You do it."

She could have managed, but she didn't like Frank's pale complexion and open mouth. He needed something to keep his hands busy. "Clean it with the alcohol, then bind it up."

"Hey, that stings," the boy said, eyeballing Frank suspiciously.

"Betty, come with me." Mrs. Huddleston went out into the hall. "Call Sheriff Bloom. Ask him to pick up Doctor Jones and bring him here. If you cannot get the sheriff, hang up and call the doctor directly. I'll speak to the sheriff later."

"You'll not hand your grandson to the police!"

"Of course not, Betty, but we'd best explain what happened before the story has a chance to grow out of proportion."

JERSEY SURVEYED the kitchen. The neighbor boy, whose name Jersey still had not caught, was in the middle of the room, his leg propped up on a chair. A plate of cookies was positioned close at hand, and the boy looked more excited than hurt. Having examined the boy and proclaimed him in danger only of ruining his supper, Dr. Jones loomed by the back door. Frank sat opposite the boy, his hands under his chin, his elbows resting on the table. Betty hovered near the pantry. Mrs. Huddleston faced Sheriff Bloom, who leaned against the stove.

The sheriff cleared his throat. "Okay, let me get this straight. Mr. Huddleston and Mr. Rohn were in the meadow. Doing what?"

"Planning a vegetable garden," Mrs. Huddleston said, earning a surprised glance from Frank.

"Young Willy comes along, oblivious to the others in the meadow, and takes a pot shot at a squirrel, startling Mr. Rohn, who has found that gunshots make him nervous since the war."

The sheriff inspected Jersey. "They make me nervous, too, war or no war. You didn't leave the gun out there, did you?"

"It's locked in the garden shed," Betty said. "Somebody has to keep her head around here."

"Thank you, Betty," said Mrs. Huddleston.

The sheriff nodded at Betty. "Good. If I may continue? Now Frank, angered on behalf of his friend, throws his rake at Willy, knocking him down and wounding his leg. He gives him a bit of a shake. Fair so far?" There were nods around the table. "Mr. Rohn, concerned that Mr. Huddleston is hurting the boy, asks him to stop. Mr. Huddleston ignores him, so Mr. Rohn gets his attention with a jab to the chin." He chuckled. "Then you all march in here, give the boy milk and cookies, and call me. *Why* did you call me?"

"I thought to avoid any misunderstanding," said Mrs. Huddleston.

"Well, as I see it, Master Willy, you are plum lucky. A few years ago, it would have been old Mr. Huddleston after you with his shotgun. If it were my land and I caught you shooting on it, I'd beat you black and blue. Come to think of it, if I have to waste my time coming out here again because I hear you've been shooting, I *will* beat you black and blue. Understand?"

Willy flushed. "Yes, sir."

"Good. Tell your pals." The sheriff narrowed his eyes at Frank and his grandmother. "Mr. Huddleston, Mrs. Huddleston. You have a talent for wasting my time. It may come as a surprise to you, but I actually have criminals to pursue." He buttoned his coat.

"Sheriff?" said Mrs. Huddleston.

"Yes, ma'am?"

"Would you mind very much returning Master Willy to his home? We'll take care of Doctor Jones."

The sheriff sighed. "Why certainly. Didn't I just tell you I had nothing better to do? Be sure and call again, if you need me. Come along, Willy."

"What about my gun? My dad gave me that," said Willy.

"I suggest you write Mr. Huddleston a nice letter of apology for trespassing on his land and disturbing his peace. Maybe he'll feel generous."

After the sheriff and Willy left, Mrs. Huddleston turned to the doctor. "Dr. Jones, could I interest you in joining us for dinner before Frank takes you home?"

"Why certainly, ma'am. I'd love to join you. Fallen off any trains lately, Frank?"

Frank smiled for the first time since the incident in the meadow. "Got any hostages in your surgery, Doctor?"

Jersey was glad the doctor would stay for dinner. Frank had described the man's strange collection, and Jersey wanted to ask him about it. Watching the doctor check the boy had reminded Jersey of Connie's deft fingers. When Connie examined you, his dry fingers would touch and tap as precisely as a jeweler. He was so matter-of-fact, he could touch you in the most intimate places, and it was tolerable.

Jones must have noticed Jersey's interest, because he smiled. "Those are unusual crutches. Where did you get them?"

"Dr. Constantine gave them to me—in Philadelphia."

"How extraordinary! Not Rupert Constantine of the Jefferson Clinic? He was a student of mine." The doctor leaned over to look at Jersey. "Did he perform your surgery, Mr. Rohn? Might I see his work?"

"Gentlemen!" Mrs. Huddleston intervened hastily. "There will be no more examinations in my kitchen. Please, Frank, show them into the parlor while Betty and I see to dinner."

"No, it was another doc at the front. Connie was stationed at the American Hospital in Nantes, where I recovered," Jersey said, as Frank ushered them toward the dining room. "Didn't like the first guy so well, but I'd be happy to show you his work—" At a parting glare from Mrs. Huddleston, he amended, "some other time."

FRANK AND Jersey had been out for a walk and were still in long coats when Jersey spied a letter in the silver tray Betty used for new mail. Apparently, Frank saw it too, because he snatched it up, shook his head, and put it down again. He caught Jersey's eye. "It's from Mr. Underwood. I'm afraid to look."

"You don't think James said anything?" Jersey asked.

"You know him better than I do."

"He was damn good to me, but he was wound up pretty tight when we left Ohio." Jersey leaned his crutches in the corner and hopped to the table. "He already felt jilted, you not remembering him and all."

Frank blew out a long breath. "I suppose there's nothing for it." He took the letter from the tray, removed a single sheet from the envelope, and smoothed it out on the table. He read in silence for a moment, before putting his hands over his face.

"What's it say?"

"See for yourself."

Dear Francis,

James has shared disturbing news of thee. Thee must not blame him for speaking of the matter. He was distraught after his return from Ohio. He would not talk to his colleagues or explain what troubled him until recently.

Two nights ago, I was rousted from my study by determined pounding at the door. I found a policeman stamping impatiently on the steps. He informed me they had caught a vandal defacing school property. Expecting to chastise the young perpetrator of some schoolboy prank, I went with him to the Meeting House. Never in my wildest dreams would I have thought to find James in the custody of another officer. He was disheveled and subdued in spirit. The Meeting House was a shambles. He'd overturned the benches and strewn fuel for the stove about the floor.

I'm afraid I pressed him rather hard for an explanation. Even when faced with the loss of his position, he did not want to explain what had disturbed him. He finally described what he saw at the boardinghouse in Mt. Sterling. I am sure he is confused. My first inclination was to dismiss the accusation out of hand. I bounced thee on my knee, Francis! On reflection, I find myself wanting

*reassurance. I beg thee, tell me that there is nothing
unsavory in thy connection with Jersey so that I may put my
mind to rest and comfort James.*

    Yours in Christ,

    Robert Underwood.

    *P. S. I have not shared this incident with Mrs.
Underwood. It is not a fit subject for the fairer sex. I trust
thee will exercise similar discretion.*

Jersey returned the letter.

Frank folded it carefully and placed it back in the envelope. He ran his finger over the flap as though to seal it again. "What would you have me tell him?"

Jersey continued the nervous tapping he'd started with the first words of the letter. "You've got to reassure him. He *wants* you to deny it."

"I tried with James. Little good it did." Frank closed his eyes and rubbed the top of his head. "I could tell him that what James saw was real enough, but a mistake—"

Jersey kicked the leg of Frank's chair. "It weren't no mistake, but you better tell him we thought better of it."

"I hate lying." Frank sighed. "We've been so careful not to touch in public. There's enough lie in that." He sounded uncertain.

"Call it what you want. You know we got no choice." *This is not the man you once knew, James, so certain of himself and his beliefs.*

Jersey moved directly in front of Frank, close enough he could smell the coffee on Frank's breath. "Are you willing to give him up? You haven't got so many folk left from your old life. He's a well-meaning old gent, but you know what'll happen if you tell him the truth. He'll be happier if you lie."

Frank sighed. "What about James? I might convince Mr. Underwood it was a mistake. I grant he doesn't want to know the truth, but James will smell the lie."

Jersey shook his head. "I didn't think James'd start acting like a lunatic."

SOME WEEKS after Frank sent his reply to Mr. Underwood, James arrived, unannounced, for a visit. He said he'd taken the train, but it looked to Frank like he'd walked. He was self-contained and quiet, warming briefly to greet Mrs. Huddleston when she joined them in the foyer. She invited him to stay as long as he wished.

"Thank you, ma'am, but the duration of my stay depends upon Francis. It's urgent we talk."

"I'll leave you to it, then, Mr. Spalding," said Mrs. Huddleston, raising her eyebrows.

"You'll stay for dinner, at least?" said Jersey. "Heaven knows, you fed me a few times."

James flushed, but would not respond, even after the silence grew long. Jersey shook his head, the hurt clear on his face. Finally, he shoved his way out of the room. "I'll be in the library, if you want me."

"Let's take a walk, James." Frank retrieved his coat from the stand and led the way out through the kitchen. The bare branches of the trees swayed in the blustery air. Frank set off as if on a Boy Scout hike, making James hustle to keep up.

James called a halt. "Francis! Slow down!"

"Have you been here before? The meadow is particularly fine."

"We played here as boys." James formed a crooked smile. It lasted only an instant before wilting like lettuce on a hot plate. "You've no memory of it, have you? Mr. Underwood said he wrote to you. I want to hear your answer directly."

Frank's heart pounded. "What am I to say?"

"Is your relationship with Jersey honorable?"

"What do you mean?"

"Moral. Must I be explicit?"

Frank stared him down. "He is a dear friend. We care deeply for one another. Our relationship is none of your concern."

"I am thinking of your spiritual well-being!"

"What right have you?"

James recoiled as if he'd stepped on a snake. "We are—were—friends!"

The pain in James's voice was undeniable, but Frank could think of no way to relieve it. "James, I'm sorry—"

"If we are no longer to be friends, I feel I must nevertheless insist that you answer, for the boy's sake."

"The boy? Jersey is a man. He makes his own decisions."

James's face took on a red hue. He was breathing hard. "Nevertheless."

Frank found himself rubbing the top of his head and dropped his hand to his side. "I said we are friends."

"Is he your catamite?"

"Catamite! I deny it."

"Lying only compounds the sin."

"Is it a sin?" Frank spoke softly. "Is it a sin to love?"

"*That* is not love."

"Have you never loved a man?"

James turned away to stare at the house. "I love you, but not like...."

"You don't know anything about it." A button had come loose on James's shirt. His collar was frayed and stained with sweat. Frank grabbed James's arm and forced him around. "Listen to me. I want to be with him, even when he is rude. His scent is intoxicating. I lose my train of thought when he smiles. My skin jumps when he brushes against me. My member salutes him."

James winced. "Must you be crude?"

"I confess. Must I join the papists to be forgiven my sins? Or will you forgive me?"

"You believed in the testimonies once, living out your beliefs in action. What testimony is this?"

"I know only how I feel. It is the testimony of my heart."

"No more confession." James twisted his arm from Frank's hold. "It's intolerable."

Frank seized one of James's hands. "Wasn't there a time when we could talk about anything? You said we were best friends."

"I thought so. I don't know anymore. Is this truly what Jersey wants?"

"Just leave us alone."

"I asked what Jersey wants."

Frank heard himself chuckle, from a distance, as though someone else were speaking. "I know where Jersey points when Dick rises on the morning tide."

"Stop it!" James twisted away.

Frank dropped his hands. "I will not give him up."

"Then I must give *you* up." James strode toward the drive.

Frank followed. "Will you speak to Jersey? He thinks highly of you."

"I must give you both up." James all but ran across the brown and faded lawn.

Frank called after him. "I died in France. Think of it so."

JERSEY WORKED his way down the stairs as carefully as he could. The restless thrashing from Frank's bedroom had stopped, and Jersey did not want to risk banging a crutch on the steps. Frank had not been so disturbed since his days at the Clark farm, and it was entirely Jersey's fault. If he hadn't pushed, Frank would have never said those things to James, and he wouldn't have lost his only friend from before the war. It was unfair of James to blame Frank for this mess. Jersey was the one who'd ruined Frank, the one who'd pushed when Frank was vulnerable because of his injury.

He reached the bottom of the stairs and made his way through the darkened house to the library. They'd had a fire earlier in the evening. Maybe there'd still be some warmth there. If only he could get around better, he could try to find work in New York or Philadelphia. There had to be something, even for a cripple. Frank would be better off without him. Nobody could accuse him of an unsavory relationship with someone who wasn't there. He dropped into an armchair before the fireplace. He'd wait there for the dawn.

BY MORNING, Jersey's thoughts had calmed, and the idea of leaving Frank had lost its appeal. Jersey decided on a temporary escape. He lit out to seek advice from the only man he knew in the area.

Miles later, he tugged his greatcoat more tightly around himself and cursed his idiocy. *At least one of your feet ain't gonna freeze.* He should have planned better. He should have asked Mrs. Huddleston for cab fare or asked Betty for a ride in the Packard. He should have at least called the doctor to make sure he was home, but he'd been so anxious to escape from Frank's exhausting kindness. Thank goodness there wasn't much snow on the ground. Connie's crutches made the going easier, but it was darn cold.

He passed out of the neighborhood of fancy homes that surrounded the Huddleston estate and came to brown fields of plowed-under stubble. Despite the cold, he felt better.

What was it that he wanted from Frank? Hadn't Frank stood up for him? What more could he ask? Despite his confusion, Jersey was glad when the doctor's home came into view. His phantom leg hurt, and he hadn't walked so far in quite a while. After turning circles for a moment on the flagstones in front of the varnished wood building, he set his shoulders and headed around toward the side door. A handsome brass plaque read, "Henry Jones, M.D. Consulting Hours 10:00 a.m. to 3:00 p.m." He pulled open the door.

"I'M DELIGHTED to see you again, Jersey. Everyone recovered from the other week's excitement?" Dr. Jones motioned Jersey to the graceful Shaker chair positioned in front of his desk. Jersey dropped into it with relief. "You and Mr. Huddleston do have a propensity for discommodious transport, don't you?"

Jersey's hopeful mood burst like a soap bubble. *I'm too ignorant to even speak to the man.* What had he been thinking? He opened his mouth to spin some tale that would explain his presence, but remarkably, no words came out.

"You did want to see me about something, didn't you?" Jones placed two of three chins on a meaty palm and regarded Jersey solemnly. "Agrippa told me there was a young man dancing on my front stoop. However, you chose to appear in my surgery, so I assume this is to be a professional consultation. Is your leg bothering you? I wouldn't mind a look at my colleague's work."

"I'm okay, Dr. Jones. The phantom leg hurts a bit. It's fine if you want a gander, but...."

"It's not what's bothering you."

"I wanna talk. I want to ask you...." He stared at Jones helplessly, unable to remember a time when he'd had such trouble finding words. "I want to be a doctor."

"Ah," Jones beamed, "the first rays of the breaking dawn. Medicine is an admirable profession, aggravating, exhausting, and not nearly as remunerative as I would like, but admirable, certainly." He leaned forward. "What is it that you want from me?"

"I don't know, exactly."

"Should you become a doctor, you'll get used to poking around in the dark."

"I want to know if I'm being an idiot."

Jones raised an eyebrow so bushy it gave him the look of an old English sheepdog.

"I mean, am I being unrealistic?" Jersey said.

"You would have to work very hard. On the other hand, you're young—eighteen, nineteen?" The doctor peered at Jersey. "I'm guessing you went straight into the army out of high school. You've had better preparation than many college boys for the rigors of medical school. What is it that worries you? Bad grades, poor penmanship?"

Jersey wished the doctor would take him seriously. He felt fool enough without being made a joke of.

"Oh dear," said Jones. "I have offended. I'm very sorry. Perhaps I could interest you in a look at my collection? I believe Frank mentioned it to you? I could ask Agrippa to bring some coffee."

Jersey stood, relieved despite his sore arms. "I'd like to see it very much."

"WHERE IS Jersey? I need him," Frank said, looking up from the morning paper.

Betty took a folded piece of paper from the pocket of her apron. "He said to give this to you when you got up."

Frank unfolded the note. "Damn it! Where the hell—"

"Frank!" exclaimed Mrs. Huddleston, shocked. "There's no call for that. What does it say?"

"He's gone off to clear his head." Frank handed the note to his grandmother and let one of his hands drift to the top of his head. "I wish he wouldn't just take off without telling anyone."

"He told me," Betty said, folding her arms.

"There's no use moaning about it. I'm sure you'll hear from him when he's ready," said Mrs. Huddleston.

"It's cold out and he doesn't have any money. I have to go look for him."

"You'll be wanting the car, then?" Betty said.

"He said nothing about where he was going?"

Mrs. Huddleston put a hand on Frank's arm. "Let him breathe a little."

JERSEY WAS deeply engrossed in looking at Dr. Jones's collection, and was startled when the doorbell rang. He paid no attention until the doctor yelled, "Agrippa!"

"You bellow like a stuck bull," said Agrippa as she passed through the dining room on her way to the front door. Jones merely smiled. Jersey concentrated on catching his breath and getting his heart to stop racing.

"I've startled you. Still a little skittish, I take it?"

Jersey flushed. "Do you think it'll ever pass, Doctor?"

"I had a patient once, a Civil War veteran, he kept sleeping powder on his bed stand so he'd have it whenever a storm came through. Never could stand the sound of thunder. Took him right back to Vicksburg, where he… I can see I'm not helping. The truth is that we don't know very much about treating disorders of the psyche."

"I can't imagine anything I'd want to study less," said Frank, from the doorway. "How are you, Doctor?"

"Come looking for your friend, Frank?"

Frank's cheeks, already rosy from the cold weather, darkened a shade. "I thought he would get chilled."

Seeing Frank's muscular figure in the doorway, Jersey was gripped with a peculiar mix of pleasure and resignation. On the one hand, his body persisted in responding to Frank like a house plant turning its leaves to the light. On the other hand, there was Frank's damn solicitousness. He sighed and looked up into the warmth of Frank's concern. He could have worse problems.

"Hi, Frank. Take long to find me?"

"Would you like coffee?" asked Jones. "Agrippa!"

CHAPTER 25

"I HOPED you'd come visiting." Jersey slid over in the bed to make room for Frank. "We ought to oil those hinges," he said, referring to the squeaky connecting door between their rooms.

Frank climbed under the covers, but stayed on his side of the bed, tension visible in his body.

Jersey leaned over and kissed him under his ear. The result was an inarticulate groan.

"Whoa, pal. What's gotten into you?"

"I'm so ashamed. I would have hurt the boy!"

Jersey brushed the bangs back from Frank's eyes. "No, Frank, you wouldn't have. You would have remembered yourself."

"Then why did you hit me? I thought when you left this morning, it was because of what I'd done."

Jersey hooked a stray lock behind Frank's ear and tried to keep the anxiety from his voice. "I got to feeling a little impatient when you wouldn't let up on the kid. But Jeez, Frank, I'm the guy who startles like a newborn colt every time I hear a loud noise."

"You know that doesn't matter to me."

"Then why'd you get so mad at the boy? Anyway, it matters to me. You're like a goddamn mama bear, ready to take on the world for me. Most of the time, it's okay. I even sort of like it, but when you go overboard it makes me feel a little... small."

"I never meant to make you feel—"

"But you did and I'm over it."

"Will you just let me apologize!"

"So apologize. Kiss me."

MRS. HUDDLESTON lay in bed and tried to ignore the aches in her back and hands. They were familiar and as unwelcome as the rat that lived in the basement under the coal chute. She had long since reconciled to his presence too, although she would never admit it to Betty. It was a different kind of ache that kept her up this night, brought on by watching Francis and Jersey. She had seen they were close the day they arrived. It wasn't what they said to each other, even when they thought no one could hear. It was the unspoken communication: her husband had looked at her like that when he told an off-color joke at the dinner table to see if he had gone too far.

She knew Jersey suffered from some kind of nervous disorder. When he and Francis had arrived, he was thin as an Irish immigrant and had dark rings under his eyes. She'd thought him merely tired from travel and disability. He looked less like an animated skeleton now, after weeks of rest and regular meals, but he still didn't sleep. Her habit was to rise at dawn and read in the library until it was a reasonable hour to ask Betty to run her bath. She'd been a little put out the first time she found Jersey there ahead of her. She'd questioned him more keenly than she'd meant to, her first question blurted out in surprise at the sight of his disheveled form.

"What are you doing here?"

"I don't mean to be a bother. I couldn't sleep."

"Is it your habit to wander about in a state of undress?"

He'd stared at her mutely and reached for his crutches.

"Oh, for Heaven's sake. Stay where you are. Would you like a cup of tea?"

He'd rubbed his face and unleashed a smile to charm lunch from a policeman. "I reckon I would, ma'am."

She found him on other mornings after that. Perhaps it was the unusual circumstance of their dawn meetings that encouraged intimacy. She surprised herself and told him how she'd developed the habit of talking to her dead husband.

"It's difficult to be alone," he said. He took greater care with his appearance, dressing before he came down, but no early morning ablutions could wash the exhaustion from his eyes. He admitted that his dreams often woke him. This was confirmation of what she'd guessed, for she'd seen him wake from an afternoon nap with a jerk and a cry.

Then a few days ago, she'd worked too long in the conservatory. With her back aching, she'd been unable to sleep. The sound was not loud enough to have woken her, even as lightly as she slept. She thought at first that Betty might have risen to use the water closet. Then she heard voices, low and intense, and other sounds, and she realized what the squeak had been: the hinge on the door between Frank and Jersey's rooms.

Now she lay in bed and waited to see if she would hear the sounds again. What would she do if she did? What would her husband have done? He was a sailor after all. He knew about such things. She heard a muffled yell from Jersey's room. A few minutes later she heard the squeak and realized why Jersey did not always come down after waking from his dream. He might derive pleasure from their conversation—as she did—but their interactions were only one source of comfort for him. Should she try to throw him out? She was not certain that she could. The house, the shipping business, it was all her grandson's now. Should she confront them? Ask Betty to serve Bible verses with the morning coffee? She might succeed in driving them away. Then she could throw herself under a train like Anna Karenina. No, she would not be alone again. She would not drive off her grandson no matter what his affliction.

FRANK HELD the morning paper over Jersey's head.

"Come on, Frank! I just wanna see the article on the Babe. Did you hear Boston sold him to the Yankees while we were in Michigan?" He stretched for the paper. His swipe was unsuccessful, but his crutch jostled the hand in which Frank held his coffee cup.

"Damn you, Jersey, this was clean today." Frank tossed the paper on the table and went upstairs to get a new shirt. He trotted into his room and slid to a halt. His grandmother, wearing an old apron over her day dress, knelt at the connecting door between his room and Jersey's. She held the snout of a lever-type oilcan to one hinge.

"Grandmother!"

Frank was amazed to see two bright spots of rouge form on her cheeks. "Good morning, Frank."

"What are you doing?" Frank could barely get the words out.

"What does it look like I'm doing? Perhaps you are not aware that old women rarely sleep well or that sounds carry at night."

Frank was speechless.

"Oh, don't stand there looking poleaxed. Help me up."

Frank jerked into motion. "I don't know what—"

"What you and Jersey do in your rooms at night is no concern of mine. My only wish is not to know of it." When Frank drew air to speak, she thrust out a hand. "We will *not* speak of this." She thrust the oilcan into his hand. "Here, you do it."

Frank returned to the kitchen. Jersey looked up from the paper and frowned. "What happened to you? You're pale as your shirt."

"You won't believe it."

JERSEY DIDN'T believe it. It was too good to be true. Much as he'd come to respect her, the idea that Mrs. Huddleston knew about and preferred to ignore his and Frank's nighttime activities was incredible. He loved his family, and he knew they loved him, but he fully expected that discovery by his parents would result in condemnation. Combined with the inadequacy he already felt in the face of Frank's education and family fortune, the new worry exhausted him. He was a fox in a trap, waiting for the hunter to return.

FRANK HELD in one hand an accounting of his inherited properties from the law firm of Matheson, Marcus, and Stadler. In the other hand, he held the bill for the gardeners who kept the lawns trim and the flowerbeds lush. Mrs. Huddleston spent more on her flowers in one year than Jersey's father would earn in ten. It would take a lifetime to spend his inheritance. He felt the weight of accumulated wealth on his chest.

"What's too much?" Jersey was curled in one of the great armchairs in the library reading something about anatomy, judging from the lurid drawing on the page in front of him.

Frank hadn't realized he had spoken out loud. "My grandfather's business interests are more extensive than I imagined. I don't know what I'm going to do with them."

"Who says you gotta do something with them?"

"It's immoral. I could finance ten orphanages without—"

"Why don't you?" Jersey said, without look up from his book.

"Your grandfather contributed to many charities." Mrs. Huddleston came into the room. "It was his intent to do more in his later years. I doubt he imagined he'd die so young."

"Hello, Mrs. Huddleston," Jersey said, his eyes betraying a hint of caution.

"While I would prefer to maintain some semblance of propriety in public, Mr. Rohn, don't you think we might use our given names in private—if you are to be part of the family?" Mrs. Huddleston perched on a hard-backed chair below the painting of her husband's last ship.

Jersey's face cycled from astonished to pleased to dismayed.

Frank loved the way Jersey could blow from fair to stormy and back again in an instant.

"I reckon—I'm so sorry, but don't actually know your given name, Mrs. Huddleston. Frank never—"

"Abigail. My mother was an admirer of Abigail Adams."

"A fine namesake, but I'm not sure that I...." Jersey smiled tentatively. "Would you be satisfied with Grandmother?"

Mrs. Huddleston sighed. "That is what Mr. Spalding used to call me, when he and Frank came to visit. I was ancient even then."

"You don't look so old to me. My given name is Gerald, but I don't like it much. I'd be pleased if you'd call me Jersey."

"That's settled, then. Thank you, Jersey."

Jersey abruptly gathered his crutches and lurched to Mrs. Huddleston. A faint look of horror crossed her face when he lowered himself to his knee before her and took her hands. "Thank you, Grandmother." She managed a smile when he kissed her hands.

Jersey had returned to his armchair when the doorbell rang. Frank started to rise, but he stopped when his grandmother cocked her head expectantly. They shared a smile when Betty passed down the hall, muttering to herself. They heard voices from the foyer.

"Mrs. Huddleston? There's a Mr. Greenleaf here to see Mr. Rohn," yelled Betty.

It was about time. Frank watched Jersey's eyes grow wide and narrow again. Frank shrugged and tried not to smirk.

"Well?" said Mrs. Huddleston. Jersey nodded and hoisted himself to his feet.

"Show him into the library, Betty."

Jersey continued to stare while they listened to Greenleaf's slightly uneven steps recede down the hall to the library.

Frank motioned Jersey ahead.

"HOW'S THE leg, Mr. Rohn?" called Mrs. Huddleston from the back porch. Jersey looked up. She was bundled against the chilly spring air and shielded from the sun by an umbrella. He motioned to Greenleaf that he was taking a break.

"It feels good, Mrs. Huddleston."

"I'm so glad."

"I believe you are ready to walk on your own, Mr. Rohn."

"I think so too." Jersey lowered his voice. "Mr. Greenleaf, what did it cost for you to come out here, special, just for me?"

"I couldn't say. That was all taken care of by Mr. Matheson and Mr. Ambrose."

Jersey's irritation flared. "You don't know what it cost?"

Greenleaf pursed his lips. "I really couldn't say."

"I get it. Never mind." Jersey lit out rapidly for the porch. He tripped on the border of the gravel walk and fell heavily to the ground. "Goddammit! Get this blasted thing off me, Greenleaf."

"Yes, sir. I hope I've not offended."

"It isn't your fault. Get me my crutches, will you?" Jersey leaned back in the grass and gestured toward the house. Greenleaf nodded and went inside.

"Jersey." Mrs. Huddleston spoke softly. "Please think carefully before you speak to him. He cares for you. He wanted to help you."

"I know. It's just that I can't be beholden to him. I must make my own way."

"He needs you," said Mrs. Huddleston. "You know how fragile he is." Greenleaf returned with Jersey's crutches. "Mr. Greenleaf, would you very much mind waiting in the kitchen for Mr. Rohn? I wish to speak to him."

"Certainly, ma'am." Greenleaf disappeared through the back door.

Jersey examined Mrs. Huddleston and sighed. "I need him too. Only I can't be beholden to him."

"It's the money, isn't it?"

Jersey did not reply. He scanned the back of his friend's mansion and the immaculate yard that surrounded it. It might have been a golfing green.

"Men are universally stupid about money," said Mrs. Huddleston, "they confuse it with value. Accept his help. Pay him back when you're on your feet. Oh dear!" She giggled, then forced her face back to seriousness. "Pay him back when you can."

Jersey examined her lined face. "I can't even buy him breakfast."

She made a motion as if to brush away an impertinent fly. "Don't let this stand between you."

"I keep thinking I got my arms all the way 'round you, Grandmother. Then I find I've missed some part."

"Mr. Rohn! That is an entirely unsuitable figure of speech." The corners of her mouth twitched. She gave up and laughed like a tipsy woman in a music hall.

Jersey was unable to resist her. "Grandmother, you are a peach."

Later that night he woke from a new dream in which he was running down a rocky hillside faster and faster, with Frank beside him. He lost his feet and flew face first toward the ground, Frank's broad-shouldered form receding from him impossibly fast.

FRANK LAID his head on Jersey's breast. "What do *you* want?"

When Frank spoke it was like having purring cat on his chest. Jersey touched the dense hair above Frank's neck. What did he want? He thought of Connie's long fingers probing the scar tissue of his stump.

"What I want, goddammit, is to go to college and to study medicine, but I ain't never gonna have the money for it."

"Will you listen to yourself, Jersey? I've got more money than Croesus. Of course you can go to college."

"I can't accept that kind of dough from you."

"Yes, you can. You know I don't care about the money, but if it means so much to you, consider it a loan, an investment in our future."

Could he do this? If he accepted money from Frank, where would it end? Wouldn't that make him the catamite James had accused him of being? (It had taken weeks, but he'd eventually got the whole conversation from Frank, even the funny part about Dick.) It would sour their relationship. He might last longer than a bottle of milk, but the result would be the same.

"I can't have you paying for me, Frank."

Frank abruptly rolled back to his side of the bed. "I love you. Doesn't that mean anything? Aren't couples supposed to help one another?"

Jersey couldn't look at him. "We aren't a couple, not in the eyes of the world. I don't know what we are. But if I take your money, there's a name for that."

"I told you. It will be a loan, an investment. You'll pay me interest. I'll come out even richer than I am now."

Jersey tried to sort through his jumbled emotions. What was it that scared him so much about the idea? What people would think? Nobody would know who was paying the bills. He'd never really cared what other people thought, anyway. When had he started feeling so much pressure?

He rubbed the end of his stump. Why did Frank have to give him the leg? He'd been prepared to do whatever it took to get himself what he needed. It hadn't been that long since he'd come to stay with Frank. He'd been thinking about work he could do, hadn't he?

"Jersey?"

He didn't answer and tried to breathe as though he were sleeping. Frank shifted restlessly, but didn't touch him. Eventually, Jersey heard his breathing smooth out. He stared up wistfully at the crown molding.

THEY TOOK the train into New York to see a show. When Frank raised the idea, Jersey started to object because of the cost, but Frank's expression was so guileless, so excited at the prospect, Jersey's objection died in his throat. He was certain the idea was spontaneous. They took a cab from the station to the theater so Frank could pick up the tickets. They wore identical white lambswool scarves Grandmother had given them for Christmas to keep them warm in a late March cold snap.

"Wait here. I'll be right back," said Frank as he climbed out of the car.

Jersey swallowed bile and leaned back, trying to smile. "Sure thing."

Frank hesitated, looking back through the open door. "We could do something else if you want. Get a meal, walk down to the Battery."

"No, it's windy and you want this. Get the tickets."

Frank started to say something, but shrugged and turned away.

Crap. Why did he have to make this so hard? He knew he was hurting Frank, but he couldn't stop thinking about the things that James had said. Maybe it would be better for them both if he just left. Frank would get over him. Frank was better, his memory functioning normally—apart from the blank part before the war. Betty and his Grandmother would look after him.

"Can you at least try to enjoy the day?" Frank climbed back into the cab, his breath steaming. "It's cold, but the sun is out. We've time for a drive through Central Park."

"They'll start to talk, you know."

Frank put his arm around Jersey's shoulders. "Who?"

Jersey leaned back, unable to resist the comforting touch. "People."

"I don't care."

"You can't afford to ignore them."

"Can't I?" Frank grinned and rubbed the thumb and forefinger of his new goatskin gloves together.

"Goddammit, Frank. You know what I mean."

FRANK'S LOVEMAKING was frantic that night, as if he knew what Jersey was contemplating and was trying, through sheer energetic display, to convince Jersey to stay. Jersey responded with equal vigor, using the leverage of his good leg on Frank's shoulder and his arms pressed against the sheets to thrust upward. Their bodies met with meaty slaps, the hot shaft of Frank's prick filling Jersey repeatedly until he couldn't hold out any longer. He yelled Frank's name in warning. Frank responded by thrusting harder, his dilated pupils hiding the gray of his irises. Jersey's body tensed and he thrust upward, the muscles in his arse spasmed, and he shot white ribbons onto his own face and chest.

Frank groaned and Jersey felt liquid heat fill him.

Frank continued thrusting until his arms trembled. He sank down onto Jersey and caught his breath, his softening cock still embedded in Jersey's rear. Jersey's body felt liquid and warm under Frank's weight, as if he might melt into the mattress. "God, Frank. What's gotten into you?"

Frank pulled out carefully and began to lick the spunk off Jersey's face.

Jersey giggled. "Don't you want a towel?"

"Nope. You taste good."

"We're going to stick together."

"I hope so." Frank finished Jersey's face, shifted down, and used his tongue to flick the tip of one of Jersey's nipples until it stiffened.

Jersey groaned and felt his cock began to harden. "Jesus, Frank."

Frank looked up, a smirk on his face. "Do you want me to stop?"

"Please don't."

"WHAT AM I going to do?" Jersey whispered into Frank's skin. Frank snored, a faint buzz at the release of each breath. Jersey lay where he'd woken, arm and leg draped over Frank's body, his head tucked under Frank's arm. How could he leave this man who made him feel so cherished? Unable to stay still any longer, feeling his thoughts a betrayal, Jersey disentangled himself carefully and tucked the sheet and comforter over his sleeping lover.

Frank mumbled something unintelligible and rolled onto his side, but he didn't rouse.

Moving quietly, Jersey fitted his leg into place, then dressed in the tailored suit and overcoat that Frank had bought for him for the trip. Taking the room key from the dressing table, he went down into the lobby of their hotel. The ornate room amazed and confounded him. From the coffered ceiling panels and crystal chandeliers to the curling ironwork of the balustrades, to the Italian marble and gilt-work that outlined every shape of the building's decorations, it was everything that Jersey feared about Frank's new life. It was a place for generals, not corporals, however decorated they might be, certainly not the place for an immigrant farmer's son.

He lurched from the elevator (another first for this trip) into the quiet lobby, still a little unsteady on the new leg. A uniformed member of the hotel staff called out to him from his place near the great brass doors. "Good evening, Mr. Rohn, shall we call a cab for you? It's a nasty night to be going out."

Startled to be addressed by name and caught without an explanation for his late night excursion, Jersey mumbled, "No, no. I need to walk."

"Watch yourself, sir. We've cleared the steps, but that's freezing rain been coming down the last hour. Are you sure we can't call a cab?"

Jersey peered across the avenue into Central Park. The city was coated in ice. Street signs, railings, trees, everything sparkled softly in the yellow light from the street lamps. It was magical, but he knew the sidewalks would be deadly for anyone unsteady on his feet.

Ahead, he saw a wide walkway lined with lampposts leading into the park. He felt a twinge of phantom pain from his leg. As his dreams had taught him, his nose filled with the cloying stink of the battlefield. He shuddered, half expecting that if he turned, he'd see the cratered fields of France stretched behind.

"Are you all right, Mr. Rohn?"

The voice brought him back to the gilded lobby, all thoughts of a walk gone. "Yes, I'm fine. I think I need to sit down for a moment."

"The lounge is still open, sir. Right through there."

"Thank you." He moved slowly, still caught between the past and the future. The lounge was decorated in gleaming wood and brass. Near to closing on a blustery night, it was mostly empty.

He caught the eye of a waiter, then made his way to a table near the windows. The waiter brought a glass of water and raised a questioning eyebrow. Jersey glanced around the room and then at the glass, uncertain how to ask for something stronger with prohibition in effect.

The waiter nodded gravely, his gaze sliding to a table of late-night revelers. The well-dressed men and women were laughing it up with a degree of inhibition suggesting they'd discovered the magic words. "We have a punch you might enjoy, sir. Very popular this time of night."

Jersey widened his eyes at the waiter's knowing look and nodded. The punch, when it arrived, proved suitably strong. Jersey tried to keep from coughing as the unaccustomed heat burned his throat. When it was gone, he signaled to the waiter and started to reach into his pocket for his wallet.

"Sir?"

He left his wallet where it was. "I think I'll charge this one to my room, if you don't mind."

"Very good, sir."

JERSEY SHOOK Frank awake. "You'll have your secretary write it up?"

Frank blinked sleepily. "This couldn't have waited until morning?"

"No."

Frank rubbed his eyes and pushed himself up in the bed. "I will have it written up just like any other contract."

"It will be legal?"

"Yes. We will write a formal contract. You will pay me back," Frank said. "I will even charge you interest—a reasonable percentage."

"How much?" Jersey asked.

Frank rolled his eyes. "Three percent."

"That's not enough. Make it four percent."

"Whose side of the table are you on?"

Jersey ignored him, still intent on the contract provisions. "When will I have to start paying you back?"

Frank sighed. "Three months after you receive your degree."

"What if I fail? I was never a good student."

"You will not fail."

"What if I fail?"

Frank stared at Jersey as if he'd lost his mind.

"Come on, Frank. It's important. What if I fail?"

"I'll charge a penalty of ten dollars per year for every year you are late matriculating from medical school."

"That's not enough. Make it forty dollars."

"Done. Forty dollars."

"We have we an agreement?"

Frank looked at Jersey, a slow smile forming at the corners of his mouth. "Why are you dressed? Come back to bed."

Jersey glared at Frank. "Have we an agreement?"

Frank slowly lost his smile. "Yes, we have an agreement."

"Good. I want to fuck you."

Frank's eyes widened. "I thought you didn't—"

"I want to now."

"You'll go slow? I've never—"

"I won't hurt you." Jersey grinned, his mood breaking. "I want to make love to you."

Frank reached for him, his gray eyes shining. "Come here."

Dear Francis,

I was greatly relieved to receive thy reassurances regarding thy relationship with Jersey. I do understand the intimacy produced by shared experience, and I see that your wartime experience might lead to an unusually strong bond with your friend. Regretfully, I am forced to conclude that James, faced with your memory loss, and seeing the intimacy thee share with Jersey, must have allowed an ungodly jealousy to overwhelm his common sense.

Thee must not think too badly of James. He is a good man, if perhaps a little immature. On that note, did he tell thee of his determination to join the American Friends Service Committee volunteers in Russia? He left soon after his return from New Jersey. It was a bit sudden, and left us short a teacher, but I cannot judge him poorly for wanting to be of service.

I hope when he returns, thee might find it in thy heart to forgive him. Perhaps his experience in Russia will inform his understanding of thy own. I like to think thee might become friends again some day.

I must run, for I am still filling in for James. We must find a new man to take his classes soon, for I have other duties. Mind you, I am not sorry to return to the classroom. It was always my great joy.

Yours in Christ,

Robert Underwood

Jersey handed the letter back to Frank and leaned back in his chair. "That's it, then. James must not have said anything before he left."

Frank sighed. "We've been lucky, but it saddens me nevertheless that I cannot be honest with Underwood."

"He would not thank you for it."

"So you say."

"He's like Grandmother in that."

Frank uncrossed his legs and leaned forward. "You're wrong, Jersey. She doesn't deny the truth, she merely refuses to discuss it."

Jersey resisted the temptation to check that nobody could hear them. Grandmother Huddleston and Betty had gone on a shopping expedition into the city. He and Frank were alone in the house. They'd slept in and found the letter from Underwood when they'd come down looking for sustenance. "Is that so different?"

Frank collapsed back onto his chair. "I don't know. Maybe not. You know what I miss most from my past?"

"I know what *I* miss from before the war."

Frank eyed him thoughtfully. "You miss your sense of complacency."

Jersey tried to keep the hurt from his voice. "Complacency? Do you think so little of me?"

"I'm sorry, Jersey, I didn't mean to disparage you." Frank rose and came over to kneel before Jersey and took up his hand. "I'm talking about the complacency of youth. You know, that sense we all have that the future stretches before us like the open sea, with adventure just over the horizon." Frank rubbed a thumb over the palm of Jersey's hand.

Jersey allowed himself to be soothed. "Oh, right. So what do you miss? You know you can't miss something without remembering it just a little."

"Certainty." Frank rose. "Come into the study with me. I want to show you something."

Jersey placed his new leg carefully and pushed himself to his feet with the walking stick he'd taken to carrying instead of crutches.

Frank watched him without moving to help. "How's the new leg?"

"Now you ask? It's been weeks."

"I was afraid you'd bite my head off."

Jersey tried to look apologetic. "It's all right."

"The stick is enough?"

"I reckon it has to be. I ain't carrying crutches for the rest of my life."

Frank led the way into the study. "I've been thinking about Grandfather's money."

"It's your money now."

"Yes, well, that's the point. I want to show you something I've been working on." He unfolded a large sheet of graph paper on the desk.

Jersey leaned over to look. He saw a set of sketches that appeared to represent parts of a building.

"You know I went over to visit Jones the other day? I asked for help with these. They're not proper plans, but just some ideas."

"Are those baths?"

"Yes, that's right. And that's the recreation room."

"You're not building a resort hotel?"

"Not quite. It's a new hospital for veterans. A place for fellows like us who were injured in the war."

"It looks more like a spa than a hospital."

"So it does. Some injuries aren't obvious—they require new thinking, new kinds of treatments."

Jersey took in the open enthusiasm on his friend's face and tamped down his insecurity. Frank didn't think he needed... no, this was as much about Frank as about him. He took a breath. "Will it cost a lot?"

"Not more than I can manage. There's something more." Frank put a hand on Jersey's back and pulled him close. "I want your help—when you get back from medical school. Don't you see? It's the perfect excuse for you to stay. You'll be my consulting physician. We'll build it together. We'll help veterans, and no one will be able to question our association."

"You've got it all planned, haven't you?"

"You gave me the idea with your talk of becoming a doctor."

"You gotta stop threatening to build something every time I open my trap."

"I'd build you a palace if you'd let me. Speaking of your trap, come here." Frank turned him around and leaned in find his lips. The kiss included an intimate exploration of Jersey's mouth.

When they finally paused for breath, Jersey nodded in the direction of the stairs. "Do you think we could…."

Frank grinned. "Breakfast can wait."

CHAPTER 26

1965

JERSEY STRETCHED his arms above his head and yawned. "My new one told me his story today."

"And?" Frank said.

"It's an old story. Survivor's guilt. He thinks he screwed up and killed his buddies. The whole thing was all the more tightly wrapped because he had feelings—platonic, I think—for one of the boys who died."

Frank rolled onto his side and put an arm around his friend. "That's eerie."

"My story's hardly unique." Jersey lay on his back and raised his stump toward the ceiling.

"How many sessions?"

"You know I don't like it when you make a game of it."

"Yeah, it's a very serious matter—but how many sessions?"

Jersey knew that if he looked, he'd see Frank's teeth gleaming in the pool of light from his bedside lamp. "You're gonna burn in Hell." He waggled his stump, then gave it a thorough massage.

"At least we'll be there together. How many sessions?"

"He told me in the fifth session." That included the first visit, when he didn't actually speak to the boy, but Frank didn't need to know that. "We're not done just because he told me his story. It's just the start of the process."

"I know. Did you take off your leg?"

"Christ! Have I become so predictable?"

"Only to me, baby. This going to be your last one?"

"I only take off the leg when it's relevant," Jersey said.

"Uh-huh."

Jersey sighed. "Probably, at least for the Army. The party's next week. After that, I've got a week to get my papers in order."

"You think you'll miss it?"

"You weren't exactly climbing the walls when you retired."

Frank ran a finger through the matt of gray hair on Jersey's chest and across a nipple. "It wasn't the same and you know it."

"Of course I'll miss it." Jersey turned to kiss his lover. "But I'll have you to work on in my spare time."

"Some things never change."

JERSEY PACKED the personal items from his office into a cardboard box. He lifted the diplomas from Princeton and Columbia from the wall and wrapped them in newspaper before he packed them away. A paperweight of Venetian glass followed, along with a silver-plated letter opener. His papers, those he would keep for his research and writing, were already packed. He would have to get help with the Persian rug.

That left the framed contract that sat on his desk where another man might keep a picture of his wife and children. He ran a finger over the glass, tracing the faded ink, then picked it up and held it at arm's reach. It was difficult to make out the handwritten terms and conditions without his reading glasses, but the signatures were as bold as the day he and Frank had signed it. His students sometimes asked about it. Why keep the record of an old loan? Usually he evaded the question—a long story, some other time. He told one persistent colleague that the loan had paid for his first home. That neared the truth.

JOHN C. HOUSER'S father, stepmother, and mother were all psychotherapists. When old enough, he escaped to Grinnell College, which was exactly halfway between his mother's and father's homes—and half a continent away from each. After graduation, he taught English for a year in Greece, attended graduate school, and eventually began a career of creating computer systems for libraries. Now he works in a strange old building that boasts a historic collection of mantelpieces—but no fireplaces.

AUTHOR'S NOTE

THE TOWN of Taperville does not exist. It is not intended to represent any existing community in Michigan or anywhere else.

Although the Society of Friends (Quakers) did operate an ambulance service in France during the World War I, the Friends Ambulance Unit (FAU) was organized by the British Religious Society of Friends. It operated in France from 1914 to 1919, and was reorganized in 1939 to serve in various countries during World War II. Although there were a number of American ambulance services operating in France during World War I, none were organized by the American Friends. The American Friends Service Committee was, however, founded in Philadelphia in 1917 and provided humanitarian services during the Great War.

In 1947, the Quakers, as represented by the American Friends Service Committee and the British Friends Service Council, were awarded the Nobel Peace Prize for their service and efforts to promote peace. The award was accepted by Henry Cadbury, a relative of the chocolate-manufacturing Cadburys. Not surprisingly for a Quaker raised in the tradition of the testimony of simplicity, Cadbury did not own a long-tailed coat appropriate for the award ceremony. He appeared in a suit borrowed from an AFSC warehouse, which had been collected in a charity drive for the Budapest Symphony Orchestra.

Sadly, use of the plain speech among Quakers has become rare. Grammarians and readers of old literature may find the construction, "Thee is," odd. "Thou art" would be grammatically correct. However, "Thee is" was the common usage among American Quakers—including my grandmother.

The Jefferson Hospital and Clinic in Philadelphia did indeed help to organize a Red Cross hospital in France during the Great War. However, Dr. Rupert "Connie" Constantine and his patients are products of my imagination.

The Ohio Willow Wood Company exists to this day in Sterling, Ohio. It continues to manufacture prosthetic devices, although I rather doubt they are still carved from willow wood. The company was founded in 1907 by William E. Arbogast, a double amputee, to create prosthetic legs. The Roger Ambrose Jersey meets in this novel is entirely my invention. While the Ohio Willow Wood factory did burn at one point in its long history, I moved the date of the fire forward in order to suit my story.

Dr. Jones's collection of objects removed from his and other patients is modeled after a real collection at the marvelous Mütter Museum, which is located at The College of Physicians of Philadelphia.

John C. Houser
April 4, 2011

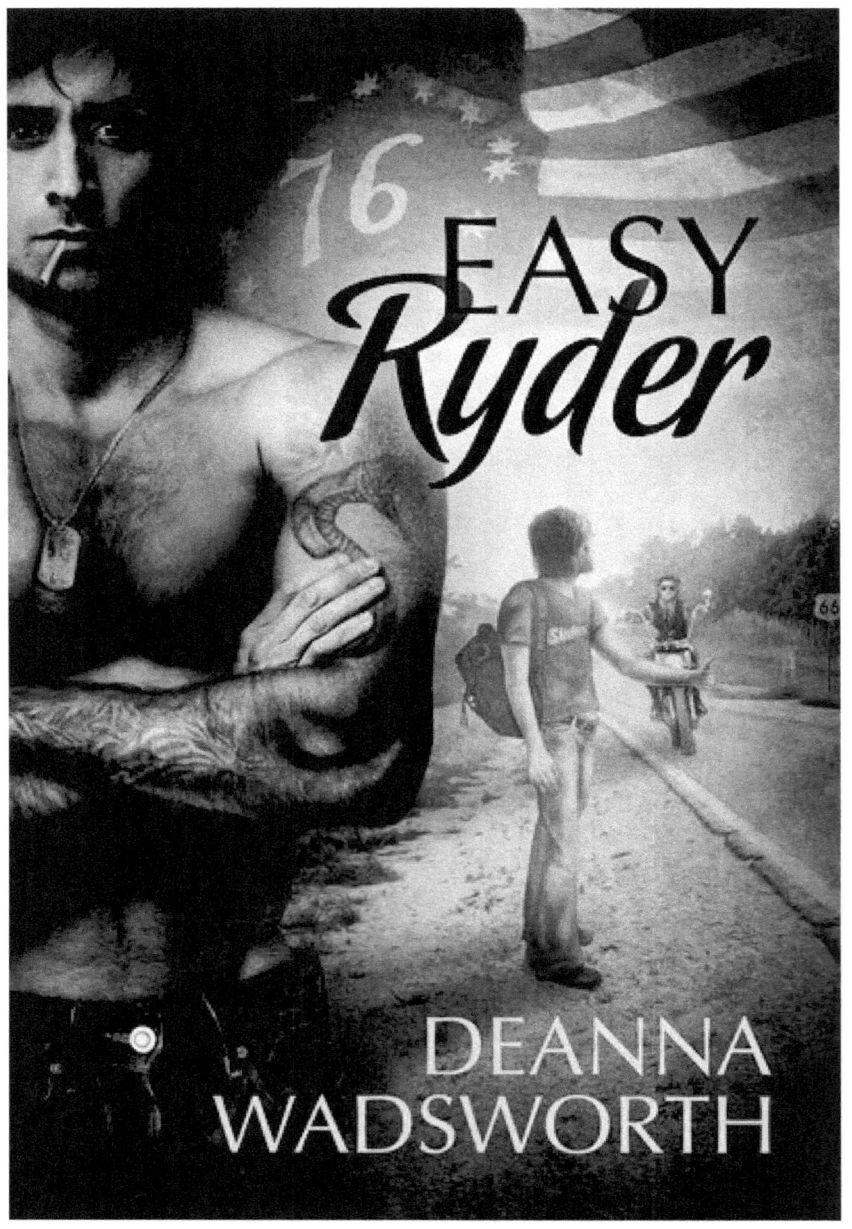

LOUISE BLAYDON

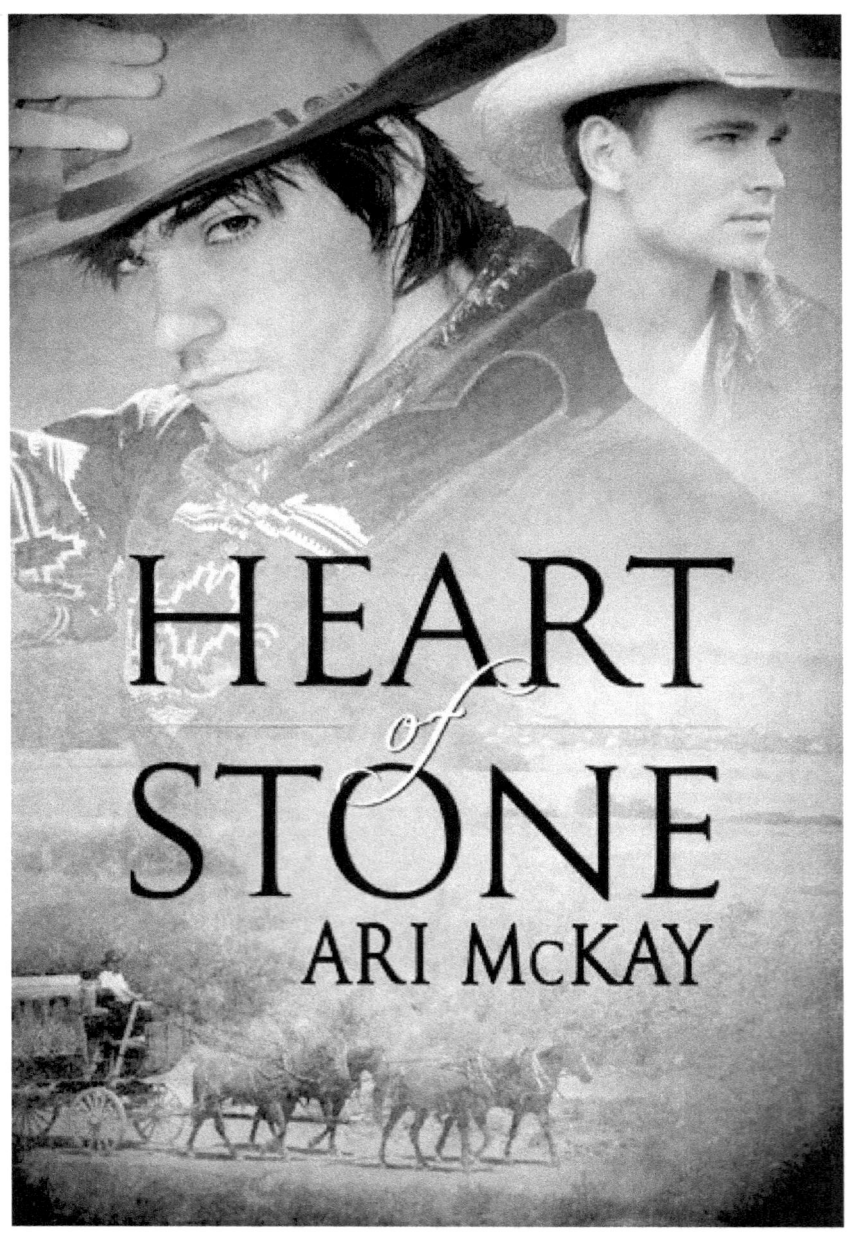

Also from DREAMSPINNER PRESS

http://www.dreamspinnerpress.com

www.ingramcontent.com/pod-product-compliance
Lightning Source LLC
Chambersburg PA
CBHW051632260626
47170CB00004B/1150